Serendipity

carly phillips

BERKLEY BOOKS, NEW YORK

THE BERKLEY PUBLISHING GROUP
Published by the Penguin Group
Penguin Group (USA) Inc.
375 Hudson Street, New York, New York 10014, USA

Penguin Group (Canada), 90 Eglinton Avenue East, Suite 700, Toronto, Ontario M4P 2Y3, Canada
(a division of Pearson Penguin Canada Inc.)
Penguin Books Ltd., 80 Strand, London WC2R 0RL, England
Penguin Group Ireland, 25 St. Stephen's Green, Dublin 2, Ireland (a division of Penguin Books Ltd.)
Penguin Group (Australia), 250 Camberwell Road, Camberwell, Victoria 3124, Australia
(a division of Pearson Australia Group Pty. Ltd.)
Penguin Books India Pvt. Ltd., 11 Community Centre, Panchsheel Park, New Delhi—110 017, India
Penguin Group (NZ), 67 Apollo Drive, Rosedale, Auckland 0632, New Zealand
(a division of Pearson New Zealand Ltd.)
Penguin Books (South Africa) (Pty.) Ltd., 24 Sturdee Avenue, Rosebank, Johannesburg 2196,
South Africa

Penguin Books Ltd., Registered Offices: 80 Strand, London WC2R 0RL, England

This is a work of fiction. Names, characters, places, and incidents either are the product of the author's imagination or are used fictitiously, and any resemblance to actual persons, living or dead, business establishments, events, or locales is entirely coincidental. The publisher does not have any control over and does not assume any responsibility for author or third-party websites or their content.

SERENDIPITY

A Berkley Book / published by arrangement with the author

PRINTING HISTORY
Berkley mass-market edition / September 2011

ISBN: 978-0-425-24383-1

BERKLEY®
Berkley Books are published by The Berkley Publishing Group,
a division of Penguin Group (USA) Inc.,
375 Hudson Street, New York, New York 10014.
BERKLEY® is a registered trademark of Penguin Group (USA) Inc.
The "B" design is a trademark of Penguin Group (USA) Inc.

PRINTED IN THE UNITED STATES OF AMERICA

10   9   8   7   6   5   4   3   2   1

*In loving memory of Buddy,
my beloved wheaten and my best boy,
who taught me about unconditional love
and was there for me in good times and bad.
You are missed, Buddy boy.
More than you'll ever know.*

Change is never easy but it's the people you surround yourself with that make it bearable. To the Plotmonkeys, Julie Leto, Leslie Kelly, and Janelle Denison (especially Janelle, who read and reread every word in this story more than a gazillion times), your friendship and support mean the world to me. And to Shannon Short, whose wisdom and insight I rely on daily . . . make that hourly. Thank you all for believing in me always. It goes both ways, it really truly does.

To Kim Witherspoon and David Forrer—the people who say agents put their own interests before those of their authors don't know you. Luckily for me, I do. Thank you for looking to the future when it would have been much easier to remain complacent. It's been an interesting journey. I hope it goes on and on! And to Leslie Gelbman and Cindy Hwang, thank you for having faith in Serendipity and in me!

One

Ethan Barron sped down Main Street in his hometown of Serendipity, New York, with one thought only. *You can't outrun your past.* He ought to know. He'd tried hard enough.

He was still trying, if buying the old Harrington estate under a corporate name counted. But he had his reasons. It was one thing to let his brothers know he'd returned. He didn't mind allowing the rest of the town time to squirm, wondering who'd purchased the town landmark from the SEC auction block. Ethan hoped the fate of the previous owner wasn't a bad omen for him. He'd like the next phase of his life in Serendipity to be better than the last.

Ten years after taking off, he was back to face his past and make amends, if such a thing was possible. So far, his younger brothers weren't interested in any family reunion he had to offer. His recklessness had destroyed their lives, and he'd compounded his mistakes by leaving town—and leaving them to social services. They weren't ready to forgive.

Understandable.

He was still working on forgiving himself.

Nash and Dare were adults now, but Ethan owed them and he intended to prove they could count on him for the duration. Hopefully then they'd come around. And he'd be waiting, no matter how tough the road or how long it took. Buying the most prominent house in town was his first step. Evidence that he'd made something of himself and proof he was putting down roots, no longer the selfish ass who'd caused more trouble than he cared to remember.

As he approached the turn to the house he'd only been living in for three weeks, he noticed a woman standing on the grass beside the long driveway. He turned and slowed to a stop, then climbed out of his Jaguar, another concession to his success.

He walked toward his visitor, taking her in at a glance. The woman had shoulder-length blond hair and, even in the heat of summer, wore a dark pair of denim jeans and a collarless but clearly expensive jacket. Hearing his approach, she turned toward him, her eyes shaded by large black sunglasses masking her face. He didn't recognize her and yet a flicker of *something* he couldn't name passed through him.

"Anything I can do for you?" he asked.

She shook her head. "No. I was just taking a walk." Her soft voice touched a memory deep inside him, but it was gone just as quickly.

"Well, this is private property." He cocked his head toward the main road, hoping she'd take the hint.

He wasn't in the mood for small talk with strangers. Although this well-put-together female definitely sparked his interest, he wasn't here for anything but family and setting the past right. No distractions. Not even sexy overdressed ones. In his experience, those kinds of women were the most dangerous.

She lifted her glasses and her golden eyes seared him straight through to his soul as she held his gaze for a long, deliberate moment. Like she was judging him.

"Yep. Still an arrogant ass," she muttered, her previously mellow voice now pissed off and angry.

Familiar.

She slipped the sunglasses back in place, squared her shoulders, and headed down the road, turning her back on him just as he'd intended.

"Wait," he called after her, the word coming out like a direct order.

"I'm not your damned yo-yo," she tossed back over her shoulder and kept walking.

But he couldn't let her go. "I said wait." He took a quick jog to catch up with her and grabbed her arm.

"What?" she snapped at him, and jerked her arm back, annoyed.

He inclined his head, unsure what had come over him. "Do I know you?" he asked, the answer niggling somewhere in the deep recesses of his mind.

"You tell me." She lifted her glasses, this time perching them on top of her head, giving him a full view of her face and features for the first time.

Soft creamy skin with a hint of freckles, golden-brown eyes, and a perfect nose. Her pulse beat hard at the base of her throat, giving life to the memory that had been hovering just out of reach. Another hot steamy day, him on his motorcycle, her in her cheerleading outfit, walking from school to the house *he* now called home.

"Well, I'll be damned," he muttered as more memories slammed into him.

He'd offered her a ride home that day. No one had been more shocked than him when she'd taken it. Instead of driving up the hill, he'd taken her behind an abandoned building in town and kissed her senseless. He'd wanted more. She'd rejected him.

He was right. He couldn't outrun his past.

"So you do remember," she said, her tone clearly challenging him.

He inclined his head. "The princess from the mansion on the hill," he mused out loud.

She placed one hand on her hip. "What does that make you as the new owner? Prince Charming?"

So word had gotten out after all. He should probably thank his housekeeper, Rosalita, for that. She'd come with the house, needed the job, and didn't like him at all. She provided him with all the gossip he didn't want to know about the town of Serendipity and its inhabitants. She talked nonstop while she worked. Of course she'd tell the prior owner's daughter who had bought their home.

"Well?" his trespasser asked, drawing him back to the present.

Ethan grinned. He liked her spunk and couldn't help but laugh. "I don't remember you being a wiseass."

She raised a delicate eyebrow. "Maybe that's because you didn't know me all that well," she said in the haughty tone he remembered.

"And whose fault was that?" He deliberately baited her, the memory of her rejection surprisingly strong after all these years.

Awareness and definite remembrance flickered in her gaze. He was struck by how those amber eyes still provided an open window to her soul. When he was younger, he'd been captivated, mesmerized by how pure and untouched she appeared compared to the girls he normally hung around with. Girls with a harder edge, willing to give it up to anyone but especially to him because he had a reputation for being bad and had no problem living up to it.

She'd been different. Special. Another reason her rejection had stung so badly.

Looks like I'm facing another unresolved piece of my past, he thought, disgusted with himself for still caring. Although to be fair, she'd only been sixteen and a good girl at that. No way would she have put out for anyone, let alone him.

She shifted on her high-heeled sandals.

Uncomfortable or restless to leave? Ethan chose the former. He'd like to think he'd gotten to her—the same way she'd gotten to him. Inside his skin just as she had way back when.

She flipped her glasses back onto her face. "Okay, I think we're finished reminiscing. You go home to your place." She gestured up the hill. "I'll go back to mine."

"And where would that be?" All he knew of her family now was that her father was in jail, and her mother lived on the other side of town, a comedown for a woman with her attitude and former wealth.

He hadn't known the princess was back here at all. Apparently Rosalita had chosen to omit that bit of information.

"I'm renting a place over Joe's on Main." She tossed her hair in a way that indicated her new digs were no big deal.

He knew better. Joe's was the local bar where guys like Ethan used to hang out. But he knew not to pity her. "Interesting," he said instead.

"What is?" She pursed her glossed lips.

Definitely not a deliberate move but seductive nonetheless, and he longed for a hot, wet taste. Wondered what might have been if she'd given in to temptation all those years ago.

But this was now and her question still hovered between them. "It's interesting how the mighty have fallen." *No pity, just truthfulness,* he thought and held her gaze, not backing down.

She raised her chin a notch. "Like I said, you don't know me at all."

"Then fill me in."

She exhaled a puff of air and paused. Probably trying to decide how much to reveal, a feeling he understood too well.

"I came back for a fresh start," she said at last. "I'll be opening an interior design business in town. What about you?"

He shrugged. Easy enough question. "I own a weapons software development company."

Her mouth opened then closed again.

"Nope, didn't end up in jail after all," he said, catching the shock that had registered on her face.

"I didn't think—"

He folded his arms across his chest. "Yeah, you did."

The first hint of a smile pulled at her lips. "Okay, so maybe I would have thought that, but you buying this house gave me a clue you'd turned things around."

A hint of admiration touched her voice, and though he appreciated the sentiment, he didn't deserve it. He'd still screwed up a lot of people's lives. But recent years had been better. He'd gone to college on the army's dime and put his affinity for computer simulation gaming to good use. After two tours of duty overseas, he'd ended up working at a military base stateside in the management information system department doing software-related work and dabbling in his own development work on the side.

On graduation, he'd taken a job with Lockheed but had chafed under their restrictions. He turned independent contractor, picked up a few contracts that enabled him to support himself, and within a few years he'd perfected a system that revolutionized the capabilities of the country's next proposed fleet of military jets. He sold his system to the government, netting him a small fortune and enabling him to buy her old house.

None of which she'd care about. "And what were you doing *here*?" he asked, moving the subject away from himself.

They both knew he meant the land, the property, and specifically, her old home.

She swallowed hard. He had no doubt the subject was a painful one. "I came to look," she admitted. "To remember."

He nodded, understanding. Her family's fall from grace couldn't be easy for her, yet she'd come back.

Maybe they had common ground after all, he thought,

finding a more than grudging respect for this woman and her strength. She was right. He hadn't known her then. Didn't know her now either, but suddenly he wouldn't mind rectifying that fact. If he had the time or energy to invest in someone who wasn't family-related.

He didn't.

"Look, I really need to get going," she said. "The heat's killing me. I only meant to take a short walk through town. Next thing I knew I ended up here."

As if on cue at the mention of the sweltering weather, he caught the bead of sweat trickling down her throat, her chest, disappearing between swells of her breasts, visible beneath the silk top she wore under her jacket.

He swallowed a groan. She was dangerous, all right. But he couldn't let her walk back in those ridiculous shoes, and she'd overheat in the damned clothes. "Come on. I'll give you a ride back to town."

She shook her head. "I appreciate it, but—"

"It's hot as hell and I'd bet my last dollar your feet are killing you. So come on." He waited a deliberate beat. "Unless you're afraid to be alone with me, princess?"

Her breath caught in her throat and a slow but knowing smile tilted her lips. "You know I'm not."

That quickly, they were back ten years and he was daring her to climb on his bike. And she had. She'd been afraid of him and he knew it, but she'd accepted the challenge and he'd never felt anything like it.

He wanted to experience that same rush again. Wanted to feel her arms wrapped around him, her body pressed against his, trusting him to keep her safe. But most of all he wanted to feel her fingernails digging into his skin—and not because they were riding a motorcycle. He remembered thinking that if the bike had gotten her that worked up, he could only imagine what she'd be like during sex. He'd wondered if she'd scream when he pounded into her and made her come. Hell, he'd been so hard for her on the ride, he'd barely been able to see straight to drive. He'd tried to ease the ache she'd caused. And of course she'd turned him down for *that*.

He couldn't deny she affected him still.

He turned toward the car before she could notice. "Come on and I'll drive you home."

"One question first."

He gritted his teeth and glanced over his shoulder. "What?"

"Do you even remember my name? Or am I still just that spoiled princess to you?"

Oh, he remembered. He just liked "princess" better. But from the determined look on her face, his answer mattered.

As if he'd forget. He'd taken a philosophy class his senior year in high school. The perky cheerleader had also been in that class, one of the few sophomores there. They'd been given an assignment to explore the meaning behind their names. For once, he hadn't cut class and he'd been there the day she'd had to discuss hers. *Her* name had everything to do with unquestioning belief and complete trust. Something that no one had ever had in him. Ironically, he couldn't remember what the hell his name meant, but he recalled hers.

"Well?" She tapped her foot impatiently.

He shook his head and let out a groan. "Get in the car . . . Faith."

Faith Harrington bit down on the inside of her cheek. So Ethan remembered her name. Damn it. She had been looking for an excuse not to take the ride. Any reason to avoid being in an enclosed space with a man who was too sexy for words. If his bad-boy persona had awed her as a teen, this new-and-improved adult version—too long jet black hair and all—took her breath away. Not that she'd let him know. Faith was finished letting any man have the upper hand.

But she'd take the ride. Her feet ached in her heels and were probably swollen from her unexpected walk. She'd avoided her childhood home since her return to town a few weeks ago, but she'd been drawn back today. For what, she didn't know. Maybe she thought she'd try to see how she'd missed the signs that the father she'd adored had been another person entirely? A Bernie Madoff in disguise. He'd bankrupted the rich and the working class alike.

He'd duped everyone he came into contact with. Including his daughter.

His betrayal had ripped a hole in Faith's heart the size of New York State—then her ex-husband had driven a Mack truck right through it, destroying everything that was left. She was free now and had been for the last six months, from her father whom she'd disowned and from Carter Moreland whom she'd divorced. She wanted nothing to do with either one. Instead, she'd returned home to figure out who in the world Faith Harrington really was.

She blinked into the afternoon sun. Ethan still waited, reminding her that apparently she was a woman who found the onetime rebel an extremely sexy, desirable man.

Uh-oh.

She lifted her chin a notch and strode past him, heading for the car. He beat her there, opening the passenger door for her to get inside. She made the mistake of glancing into his heated gaze, disarmed by the banked desire she saw there, and blinked in shock.

"Don't look so surprised," he said, misunderstanding her reaction. "I picked up some manners since you saw me last."

She couldn't help but smile. "As I recall you had good manners back then too." When he'd taken her home, he'd helped her off the back of the bike, ignoring her mother's disdainful glare.

Ethan shook his head. "I'm sure my mother would have been happy to hear that," he said wryly.

But she caught the hint of sadness in his tone and she couldn't let the moment pass. "I'm sorry about what happened to your parents. It was an awful tragedy and a senseless accident." One that had rocked the entire town.

Until today, she hadn't known what had happened to the oldest brother. She couldn't deny she was glad to see he was back and in one piece. Even if he was now the owner of her childhood home.

"Thank you." A muscle ticked in his jaw. "But they shouldn't have been on the road that night at all." He shifted uncomfortably and cleared his throat. "You getting in?" he asked, annoyance in his tone as he gestured inside.

She recognized a subject change when she heard one and slipped into the sports car. The sleek black Jag with its deep red interior suited him. Big and imposing, dark and brooding, at the same time.

He slammed her door, walked around to the driver's side, and joined her, placing his sunglasses on his face and turning on the ignition. The air conditioner hit her full force and she let out an involuntary moan of relief. She didn't know what had possessed her to walk here on a scorching ninety-degree August day.

He raised his sunglasses for a brief moment, a knowing smile lifting his sexy lips. "Hot?" he asked.

She couldn't mistake the dual implication or the amusement in his rich brown eyes.

"Very," she said, knowing her words were a distinct tease yet unable to control the banter that seemed to come too easily with him.

He shook his head, slid his glasses back onto the bridge of his nose, and pulled the car onto Main Street. He drove confidently with one hand on the wheel, the other on the stick. She couldn't tear her gaze from his big, strong hand cupping the shift.

"You can drop me off outside Cuppa Café," she said in a voice she barely recognized. She pointed to the coffee shop on Main.

"Suit yourself." He eased the car into the open spot in front of the store, idling the engine.

She turned to face him. "Thanks for the ride."

He slid an arm over the back of her seat. "My pleasure, princess."

"Not anymore," she muttered under her breath. Because what he'd said earlier, about how the mighty have fallen? He was right. In more ways than he could possibly imagine.

"I guess I'll be seeing you around." She reached for the door handle and climbed out of the car.

She headed into the coffee shop, needing space and air that didn't include Ethan's musky scent and the sensual awareness he inspired. Ten years ago, he'd tried to steal more than a kiss, making her desire things she'd had no business yearning for at sixteen. Making her want *him* in a way that surpassed anything in her previous experience. Little did he know that his kiss had meant everything to her—even as she'd known she'd been just another girl he'd tried to add to his list of conquests.

But that was then. Now she was an adult, fully aware of the meaning of her body's response to him. But she was also at a crossroads and would be better off focusing on figuring out who she was before she got involved with any man. Especially one who made her feel . . . so very much.

Two

Faith had one mantra in life that hadn't changed: The perfect latte made getting through any day easier. Today, however, she ordered it frozen, grateful the person behind the counter wasn't someone she knew or recognized. She needed to cool down not just from the warm temperature outside but from the heat inside her body too, courtesy of Ethan.

She was glad not to have to deal with one of the many variations of greeting she'd received since moving back to Serendipity: welcomed, scorned, hugged, or ridiculed, depending on how she'd known the person in her past life and whether or not her father had violated their trust in some way.

Faith picked up her frozen drink and settled into a small table in the back to wait for Kate Andrews, her best friend since kindergarten. Kate was the only person Faith had kept in touch with when she'd left for college, through her more isolated married days, till now. And Kate was the one person Faith trusted in a world that had proven unworthy.

Faith was halfway through her drink when Kate rushed in harried as usual but predictably upbeat and bubbly. "Sorry I'm late. I had a dentist appointment that ran longer than I planned."

Faith laughed. "Your appointments always run over." And Kate never learned to budget for extra time.

Kate grinned. "And you love me anyway."

"You know I do." Faith felt herself relax for the first time since her run-in with Ethan.

"Well, the feeling's mutual," Kate said, then turned, her auburn ponytail flipping around with her. "Hello?" She waved at the woman behind the counter, trying to get her attention.

"Hang on!" the woman, a different person from the one who'd waited on Faith, yelled back.

Faith recognized Elisabetta Gardelli from high school. Elisabetta, known as Lissa, was one year older and one of the local town kids who'd hated the rich girls, like Kate and Faith.

"What are you doing?" Faith asked.

"Hang on a sec." Kate waited for Lissa to look over before yelling back once more. "I'll have the usual, please!"

"Are you kidding me? You have to go up to the counter and order," Faith said.

"Coming right up!" came Lissa's surprising reply.

Kate swiveled back around in her seat, a smug look on her face. "Waiting in line is how it works in a Manhattan coffee joint. Here, you just have to know someone. And when you never leave this burg, you know *everyone*."

Faith glanced at Kate's grin. "Fine. I stand corrected."

Unlike Faith, who had gone to New York City and lived away from home, Kate had opted to stay home. Despite her family's ability to pay for her to go away to college, Kate liked it here. She'd attended a local university where she received her teaching degree and master's. Typical small-town-girl story. The only thing missing was the husband, but Kate claimed she just hadn't met the right man, and unless someone new moved to Serendipity, she was in trouble on that score.

"So, Lissa doesn't mind serving you like that?" Faith asked.

The other woman shook her head. "I guess we all grew up."

Faith took the last sip of her frozen drink. "Good to know." Maybe there was hope for Faith's relationships here, but considering how her parents had treated people even before her father's fall from grace, she doubted it.

"Coffee for Your Highness!" Lissa said, interrupting them with a good-natured laugh as she placed a tall cup in front of Kate.

Kate handed the other woman a ten-dollar bill. "Want another one, Faith?"

She shook her empty cup. "Sure. But I'll have a hot one this time."

Lissa's expression turned frosty. "Then get in line with the rest of the working people, hon. Now that you're one of us, I mean." She turned her back on Faith and sashayed her way to the counter.

Faith's stomach cramped at the latest humiliation, so sorry Kate had to witness it.

"No way will I let her get away with that crap!" Kate, face flushed red, rose from her seat.

Faith grabbed her friend by the arm, stopping her. She didn't want or need Kate fighting her battles. Besides, she knew it would take time for the people in town to realize she was nothing like her father or mother and accept Faith as one of them.

"It's okay. Lissa's not the only one with a chip on her shoulder. I'm getting used to some people snubbing me." Faith couldn't deny the mean-girl treatment at this stage of her life hurt, but she'd manage to get through it and would come out the other side. *What doesn't kill us makes us stronger and all that,* Faith thought.

Kate's green eyes sparked with anger. "I come from your side of town, and Lissa and I have made peace over the years. I mean I've tutored her daughter. She can't treat you like that!"

"She can," Faith said firmly. "Until she gets to know me the way she knows you, she's going to take perverse pleasure in how my life has turned out. And believe me, she won't be the only one. I appreciate the pit bull defense, but I can handle it."

"Well, I can't." Without giving Faith a chance to object, Kate jumped up and headed behind the counter to talk to Lissa.

Faith groaned. How could she get her friend to understand that she'd expected Lissa's kind of treatment when she'd returned to Serendipity? She'd just have to earn their respect.

Trouble was, she was still trying to respect herself. Not for being blindsided by her father. She hadn't been alone in that. But for believing in him so deeply she'd allowed him to lead her into a marriage and a life that benefited no one but Martin Harrington and her ex-husband, Carter Moreland. Instead of searching for her independence like most girls in their early twenties, Faith had looked for the same security she'd had growing up. So when her father had introduced her to the smooth-talking Carter Moreland, Esquire, the summer after her college graduation, she'd been swept into his world. A familiar world she'd accepted without stopping to think whether or not the dinner parties and charitable works Carter encouraged her to participate in fulfilled *her*.

Thanks to Faith and Carter's union, Faith's father took over the investments for Carter's co-workers, while Carter gained entry into a world far wealthier than he'd ever imagined. By the time Faith's father's crimes came to light, Carter was already firmly entrenched as legal counsel to the upper crust. Faith was merely an accessory, trapped in a situation she felt powerless to change or escape.

To add insult to injury, the same day she'd discovered the accusations against her father were true, she'd caught Carter screwing his paralegal. He hadn't even pulled up his pants long enough to look her in the eye and inform her she could accept it or leave. He'd already gotten what he needed from their marriage. It didn't take a genius to figure out this hadn't been the first time he'd cheated or that her father's disgrace had merely given Carter license to not hide his affairs.

In that one unbelievable night, Faith had lost the life she'd known and the security she thought she'd still have because her asshole husband had already buried his assets. Somehow his law firm, which had enabled them to live in a penthouse with furnishings that rivaled the house on the hill, suddenly showed a loss. The bastard had sat across the table from her, looked her in the eye, and claimed he was broke. Nothing to be had or shared, and he'd sold the penthouse to cover their debts to prove it.

Fortunately her father had informed her that Carter knew more about Martin Harrington's business dealings than Carter would want the world to know. And he had proof. So Faith had asked the lawyers to leave the room and presented her soon-to-be ex with a quid pro quo. Her silence for a fair settlement. Faith hated dirtying her hands with blackmail, but her very survival had been at stake. She'd come away with enough money to keep her in Manolo shoes if she wanted. She didn't. Faith wanted only to use enough to subsidize her new beginning. The rest she'd put aside for a rainy day. Because Faith Harrington intended to make it on her own in the only town she'd ever truly called home.

And Ethan was living not just in town but in her old house. The only solace she found in that particular irony was the fact that Ethan's life hadn't been easy either.

She still couldn't believe he was back. The only contact Faith had had with him after that incredible bike ride had been when she'd pass him in the hall at school. He'd lock that arrogant gaze on her, the corner of his sexy mouth tipping upward in a *knowing* grin. Remembering, her stomach did that crazy flip again now, reminding her she hadn't felt anything like it since.

Until today.

Kate returned, slamming her covered coffee down on the table, pushing another tall cup toward Faith.

"Successful?" Faith asked, trying to keep the sarcasm from her voice. She knew better.

"Lissa knows how I feel about her attitude. Which sucks, by the way. She's just bitter because her husband ran off with a wealthier, younger woman."

Faith opened her eyes wide. "Well, I know how being cheated on feels."

Kate cringed. "I'm sorry."

Faith waved away her apology. "How about we just change the subject?"

"Gladly," Kate said. "Are reporters still hounding you for your story?" She propped one elbow on the table.

Faith exhaled hard. Ever since her father's arrest, reporters had bombarded her with requests for an interview. They wanted any tidbit of information or understanding they could get into Martin Harrington's mind and business. Faith's story was worth a huge chunk of change, but she wasn't telling it. Her father might not have taken the high road, but Faith would.

"I changed my cell phone number and I'm unlisted here in Serendipity. That should keep them away for a while."

"Glad to hear it," Kate said vehemently.

Ready for a subject change of an entirely different sort, Faith scooted her chair closer to her friend. "By the way, I have news."

Kate loved gossip the way Faith loved lattes and she inched nearer. "Tell me."

Faith wrapped her hands around her empty cup. "The rumors are true. I took a walk past my old house and guess who I ran into?"

"Who?" Kate's eyes opened wide with curiosity. "The

girls at Babs's Beauty Salon have been speculating for weeks. They even have a pool going, but the realtor who sold the place signed a confidentiality agreement. All anyone knows is that it was bought under some big corporate name."

"Ethan," Faith whispered. And squeezed her plastic cup so hard it cracked in her hand.

"Shut up!"

Faith grinned. "You sound like your students." Kate taught middle school.

"Seriously? He's back? How's he look? What's he like? Did he remember you?"

"Gorgeous, still brooding, and yes, he remembered me." Faith's body tingled at the memory.

"Oh my God!" Kate let out an actual squeal.

"Shh!"

"Okay, sorry." Kate twirled her long ponytail around one finger, staring at Faith like she knew where her thoughts had gone.

Which of course, she did.

The bike ride.

The kiss.

Ethan's attempt to go further.

And how much Faith sometimes wished she'd let him.

She shivered, the tingling she was experiencing at the moment as fresh as it had been then, because he was every inch as spectacular.

At sixteen, Faith had shared every last detail of her time with Ethan with her best friend. At twenty-six, she did the same thing, whispering the entire scenario into Kate's eager ear.

As she spoke, Faith's stomach did that silly, excited flip that only Ethan had ever caused. Back in high school, the flip had been little and she hadn't understood the impact of what it meant. Thinking about seeing him again now, she experienced a full body slam of desire that she comprehended completely.

"The last time I heard about him was the summer after graduation," Kate recalled.

"After he, that Pickler kid, and a bunch of other idiots were arrested for joy riding," Faith said, nodding. "And then his parents died in that awful car accident the same night."

"On the way to the police station to bail him out."

Faith shuddered at the horrific memory and wrapped her arms around herself much as she had then. Because today she'd seen the pain in his eyes and knew he hadn't forgiven himself for the tragedy.

Faith had been devastated when she'd heard the news, her heart breaking for Ethan and his brothers. Her relationship with her mother might have been rocky. It still was. But she couldn't imagine losing her parents that young. The judge had taken pity on Ethan and had given him a suspended sentence and a second chance. But he'd disappeared, leaving his siblings behind.

"Do his brothers still live in town?" Faith asked.

"Both Nash and Dare are still here," Kate confirmed. "They've both done well for themselves. And considering they both went to different foster homes on different sides of town, they're still close."

"I wonder if they kept in touch with Ethan."

"No clue." Kate shrugged.

They lapsed into silence, each alone with their thoughts. "You and Ethan have unfinished business," Kate said at last.

"That's the last thing I want in my life right now." But her toes curled at the prospect.

"But maybe it's exactly what you need. A way to get you back into the dating scene. Unless Nick Mancini gets you hot and bothered?" Kate raised an eyebrow, shooting Faith an inquiring gaze.

"Why would you think that?" Faith wrinkled her nose and shook her head. "No, my high school boyfriend does not do it for me." Those sparks had died the day she'd taken a motorcycle ride with Ethan.

And they hadn't rekindled since her return.

"You said yes to dinner with him next week. Was that so you could let him down gently?" Kate rubbed her cup between her hands as she spoke.

"I said yes to dinner with an old friend. I told him up front I wasn't ready to get involved with anyone right now. It's too soon after my divorce."

"I believe you. I just don't think he'll drink the Kool-Aid as easily."

Faith laughed. "Don't worry. I'll make sure he knows how things stand."

"And does Ethan Barron's return have anything to do with your disinterest in Nick?" Kate prodded, a smile curving her lips.

Faith shook her head. "No! All Nick and I had was a high school thing. As for anyone else, it's too soon for me to be thinking about getting involved." She repeated the mantra she'd already told herself.

"Not even a dark, brooding bad boy with the last name of Barron?" Kate teased.

Faith rolled a napkin into a ball and tossed the crumpled paper at her friend. She was sure it didn't escape Kate's notice that the question went unanswered.

Faith and Kate walked toward the door.

Kate paused to wave at Lissa before turning back to Faith and pulling her aside. "Did you mean what you said about wanting people to get to know *you*?" she asked.

"Of course I meant it."

"Then can I tell you something that I mean in the nicest possible way? With complete love and admiration for my best friend in the whole world?"

Faith's stomach rolled at the prelude. "Umm, sure. What is it?"

"You could start by fitting in more."

She narrowed her gaze. "I don't understand."

Kate plucked at the sleeve of Faith's suit jacket. "Ditch the

Chanel." She fingered the chunky pearls around Faith's neck.
"And the bling. And the heels, unless we're going out at night
to somewhere nice. Not Joe's. I'm sorry," she said quickly.

"Don't be." Faith closed her eyes and shook her head.
"The clothes belonged to Faith Moreland."

"I know. Faith Harrington preferred—"

"Her cheerleading uniform?" She tried for a laugh.

Kate wasn't buying. "No. Funky jeans. Denim jackets.
Anything she could get past her mother and still like for
herself."

Faith swallowed hard. "I lost myself somewhere," she
admitted.

"But you came back to find her. You told me as much.
Otherwise I wouldn't have said anything, but I know this
isn't *you*."

Kate was right. Faith couldn't expect anyone in town to
welcome her if she was presenting herself as someone above
them. Someone who thought they were better than the average person. Someone who still lived in the house on the hill.

"Are you mad?" Kate asked.

"Not at you." Faith pulled her friend into a long hug. She
was mad at Faith, the girl she used to be, for allowing herself
to change, to become someone she didn't recognize and no
longer liked.

She'd told herself she was coming back to Serendipity to
find herself. Apparently she'd have to dig deeper than she'd
ever imagined.

Ethan sat down at his desk, one of the few pieces of
furniture he'd purchased and moved into the house right
away. That and a bed. *Shows where my priorities lie,* he
thought wryly. He liked the dark wood paneling in this
room. Besides, it was the only place in the house without
oppressive ornate wallpaper crowding him and making him
uncomfortable.

He kicked off his shoes and prepared to look over the government paperwork for upcoming contracts, but he couldn't concentrate on business. Couldn't see the papers in front of his face. Couldn't think or visualize anything except Faith Harrington.

She hadn't been dressed for summer, no visible skin or body parts for him to drool over, and yet he'd been drawn to her in so many ways he couldn't begin to count them all. Their brief shared past. The road not taken if she'd just said yes all those years ago. Her unexpected wit. The brief glimpses of a sadness he could relate to. And the sexual attraction that had only grown stronger over time.

Then there was the fact that he was sitting here in her old family home, which was now his empty house. He'd bought the place expecting to feel a strong sense of satisfaction when he'd moved in here. Bad boy made good or some such cliché. Instead, he'd discovered he owned an echoing mansion.

Reminding himself he'd come here for family, he thought about approaching his brothers again. Nash, a lawyer, had purchased a town house on the edge of town; and Dare, a cop, was living with Nash until he finished renovations on an old house he'd bought and was working on in his spare time. His brothers were close; he was the outsider.

Self-imposed and self-created, he knew. Taking a deep breath, he picked up the phone and called Nash at the office—Ethan didn't have his home number and it was unlisted. He hoped they could meet somewhere on neutral ground. Dinner, maybe.

Luckily, his brother answered the phone himself. "Nash Barron speaking."

Ethan cleared his throat. "Nash, it's Ethan."

"Not interested," his brother said, ice in his voice.

Ethan gripped the phone harder. "Just give me a chance . . ."

"You had yours ten years ago," Nash said, and hung up in his ear.

Ethan winced. No way was he calling Dare right now. Maybe tomorrow, when the rejection wasn't as fresh. He balled up a sheet of paper with old useless notes and tossed it into the trash across from the desk.

He missed.

"Make sure you pick up after yourself," his housekeeper said, poking her head into the room.

The woman had eyes everywhere.

"And Mr. Ethan, didn't I tell you to take your shoes off before you come into the house?"

If any of his other employees had spoken to him that way, Ethan would have fired them on the spot. But something about the older woman amused instead of insulted him, and he actually looked forward to their verbal sparring.

"Are you sure you work for me and not the other way around?" he asked her.

She stepped into the office, duster in hand, and began cleaning the mostly empty bookshelves.

"I tol' you. I have to work here. I need the money and you need me. But that doesn't mean I have to like you."

"So you've said." He shrugged, not surprised by her bluntness.

They'd made an agreement on day one. She'd keep his house clean and he'd pay her for her services. She intended to speak her mind, and no, he could not dock her pay when she did.

"I'll win you over yet, Rosalita."

She mumbled something in Spanish, and then, "When hell freezes over, Mr. Ethan. You a bad boy."

"Was a bad boy," he reminded her for the umpteenth time.

"When are you going to have furniture in this house?" she asked. "Just so many times I can clean the floors and dust."

"There's laundry and food shopping too," he reminded her, not wanting her to grow too complacent.

But she had a point. If he was going to make this place home, it needed to be furnished. Actually it needed to be decorated so the house reflected his taste. Not an empty shell of what the landmark used to be.

I'll be opening an interior design business in town, Faith had told him. He needed an interior designer and maybe a connection to someone who didn't hate him quite so much. It seemed that all roads took him back to Faith Harrington.

Luck?

Good fortune?

Serendipity, he thought, shaking his head.

Of course he had no idea if she'd agree to take him on as a client. But at least now he had a legitimate excuse to see her again that had nothing to do with attraction and everything to do with necessity.

Or so he needed to believe.

Three

Living over a bar wasn't conducive to a good night's sleep, and Faith woke up exhausted. Thanks to the music playing, she hadn't fallen asleep until after 1:00 A.M., but when choosing an apartment, she hadn't had many alternatives. Her only other viable choice would have been moving into her mother's house, and even the noisy bar was preferable to that. If she could get used to the constant honking of car horns and police sirens in New York City, she could readjust and learn to sleep over the sounds of Joe's Bar.

After a quick shower, she looked into her closet so she could decide what to wear for the day and found herself surrounded by silk blouses and camisoles, designer-emblazoned jeans, shorts, and skirts, along with high-heeled shoes, most with the telltale red bottoms of Christian Louboutin. She had enough of those expensive babies to make Carrie Bradshaw proud.

But not Faith Harrington.

Not anymore.

She'd grown up with wealthy parents and she hadn't

wanted for anything from basic necessities to frivolous things she just plain desired. Back in high school she'd dressed like a typical teen, wanting to fit in with her friends. In college, she'd begun to carve out her own style, finding her likes and dislikes. Then she'd met Carter. He'd been a dominating presence and she'd let him lead her, succumbing to his not-so-subtle suggestions on how she should dress and behave as the wife of a powerhouse New York City attorney. She'd been drawn back into dressing to please others. Of course it helped that she'd had her father's beaming approval as well. And since her college friends had either gone on to graduate school or work, something Carter insisted she didn't need to do, she'd lost touch with people her own age she liked and really enjoyed.

It wasn't until after her divorce, when she'd had to decide what to do with her life, that she discovered Faith Moreland had no skills, no likes or dislikes, apart from her husband's. And it had taken Kate's prodding for her to face the harder truth. Her divorce wasn't enough to change who she'd become. Neither was her desire to open her own interior design business. Faith had more work to do. Not just from the inside out but also from the outside in.

Her new business needed clients and Faith needed friends. To acquire either, she had to be approachable. Beginning with how she presented herself. It was embarrassing to admit she had a closet full of clothes she wore but didn't like. Clothes that put people off and said *I'm better than you*. Faith might still be figuring out the deeper aspects of who *she* was, but Kate was right. These clothes weren't her.

And Faith resented them just like she resented herself for getting caught up in the charade.

She still had boxes in the corner of the living room left over from the move and she pulled one out now and began placing items of clothing inside. Overly elegant gowns, day dresses she'd never have use for here, the silkier blouses she used to hate when her mom wore them, all went into a box.

As she sorted through her closet, Faith came to another painful realization. Her clothes both emulated and represented what she'd always disdained in her own mother—the useless country club lifestyle that killed time and probably brain cells. Determined to put that life behind her, Faith placed a select few things into a shopping bag that she could carry with her, and when she was finished, she headed out the door.

Consign or Design was a quaint shop on a side street behind Main with only two other stores in the strip, one a bakery, the other one empty.

Faith stepped inside and the sound of bells welcomed her as did the décor. Minimalist and simple, mint green walls surrounded her along with hardwood floor and racks of clothing for sale.

"I'll be right out," a female voice called.

"Take your time!" Faith continued to browse, noting that the farther back into the shop she walked, the more unique the clothing and the more individual the pieces on display.

"Can I help you?" A woman stepped out of the back of the store, a tiny Yorkshire terrier puppy at her heels.

Drawn by the tiny animal, Faith bent down to pet the top of the dog's head. "He's adorable!"

"Thank you."

Faith rose, glancing at the other woman for the first time. She was a redhead, not a natural one, judging by the vibrant color, and her clothes were funky and pure fun. A denim vest with distinct emblems sewn on over a white tank top and ruffled skirt.

Faith realized she was staring and cleared her throat. "I have some clothes here. I wanted to know whether you could sell these items for me. There's plenty more where these came from. I just thought I'd start with the few I could carry."

The other woman's eyes lit up. "Let's see what you've got." She took the bag and walked to the counter, laying out

Faith's pieces to view. "Ohh, look at this Chanel!" She eyed the jacket Faith had worn the day she'd run into Ethan.

"What do you think?" Faith asked hopefully. If she was going to shop for new clothes, even less expensive ones, she hoped she could defray the cost by unloading what she already owned. "Is there a market for these kinds of things?"

The woman shook her head. "Not here, honey. I'd have to put these up on the Internet. I'd get you a better price there. Around here those who can afford designer clothes wouldn't be caught dead in someone else's. Even items as gently worn as these. And my regular customers need their money for more important things like paying the rent or the mortgage."

Faith eyed the other woman warily, unsure if she was being patronized, but decided to take her words at face value. They were true, after all. "Internet is fine."

"Good. If it would make it easier for you, I can drive around back of Joe's after work and help you load things into my trunk."

Faith raised an eyebrow in surprise at the offer. "So you know who I am?" The redhead hadn't given her a clue.

"And you know me." She smiled warmly. "I'm April Mancini. I wanted to see if you realized it on your own, but it's been a long time and I had a head's up: I'd heard you were back in town."

As soon as she said her name, Faith's memory clicked in. "Nick's older sister!" April was four years older than Nick and she'd had long dark hair the last time Faith had seen her.

"That's me. Now give me a hug, will you?" April pulled Faith into an embrace that made her feel welcome by someone other than Kate for the first time since her return. Not even her own mother had been as happy to see her as Nick's sister.

Faith swallowed over the lump in her throat as she pulled back and studied the other woman. "I love your hair! The color is so rich and vibrant."

"Thank you!" April made a show of primping her style.

"I love change, so I experiment as the mood suits me. Today it's red."

"Well, I think you should keep it. It definitely flatters your coloring. So, this place is yours?" Faith gestured around Consign or Design.

April nodded. "The consign part is so I can make money while I indulge my real love of design."

"Did you design these?" Faith pointed to the more unique pieces of clothing she'd admired earlier.

The other woman smiled, pride in her gaze. "I did."

"You're talented. Where did you learn?" she asked, curious about April's background.

"Self-taught." She spoke with pride.

"Amazing," Faith said, in awe.

They had a love of design in common. Faith had always loved fashion and home decor magazines. She couldn't count the number of times she'd remodeled her childhood bedroom based on something she'd seen in a fashion or design magazine. She'd shifted furniture and bought new bedding and funky accessories to match a whim or a mood. Faith had talked her father into sending her to Parsons in Manhattan so she could major in interior design. But she'd met Carter and married him right after graduation, losing any opportunity to put her skills to work anywhere except their uptown apartment.

"So what about you?" April asked. "I know you're back and things with your family have been tough."

"An understatement," Faith said laughing. She'd learned to do that—make light of something that was really deep and painful.

"But what do you plan on doing now that you're here?" April propped a hip against the counter as she spoke.

"Like you, I'd love to open my own store front, but for me it's interior design." But financially, she figured she'd have to work from her small apartment until she built up a clientele.

"Well, talk about serendipity."

Faith was sure April wasn't talking about the town. "What do you mean?"

"There's an empty shop next door." A knowing smile lifted April's lips. "The landlords were really hoping for big bucks but they've been sitting with it empty for a long time. Maybe they'll be willing to give you a deal."

Faith knew the possibility was too good to be true. "Even with a good deal, I can't imagine being able to afford it."

"How do you know unless you ask?"

"Okay . . . Where would I find the landlord?"

April grinned. "Well, I'm one. And Nick is the other. We inherited the strip mall from Dad."

She hadn't realized their father had passed away. She and Nick had plans to catch up over dinner. "I'm sorry."

April waved away the sentiment. "It was three years ago, but thanks. Nick subdivided this into two smaller stores and agreed to let me open my business here. The other shops have had the same businesses renting for years."

"It sounds perfect. It really does. But until I get started and sign my first client, I don't have any income." And she was too smart to touch her nest egg when she could work from her apartment until she was on her feet.

April merely shrugged. "Well, we don't have any money coming in from an empty store anyway. I'm sure we can work out a deal."

Faith bit the inside of her cheek. A store in the center of town. How could she turn down the opportunity? People would see her awning and know she was in business. She wouldn't have to rely solely on word of mouth. It was serendipity, like April had said. She couldn't have hoped for anything better.

Faith nodded slowly. "If Nick says okay. You talk to him, and he and I will discuss it further when we have dinner."

"Great!"

Before April could get too excited, Faith held up a hand. "One more thing. You have to promise me that if you get an offer for the space by someone who can pay you immediately, you'll tell me. And I'll move out."

"Deal."

Faith shook April's hand.

"Now about these clothes," April said, already on to another subject. "What if instead of selling some, you let me redesign and then sell? I'd cut you in on a commission. We could make so much more." She fingered the fabric once more. "The things I could do with these." Her voice drifted off in pure pleasure.

Faith laughed. "Sounds like an offer I can't refuse. Why don't you come by later and see what you like? The rest you can take to sell."

With her life looking up for the first time in a while, Faith practically skipped out of the shop and headed home.

Ethan walked up the back stairs that led to Faith's apartment over Joe's. During the day, the place seemed perfectly safe, but at night, when the drunks were stumbling around and the lights barely shone in the parking lot, he was sure it was anything but. He knocked on her door, and when no one answered, he knocked again. Since he didn't hear anyone inside, he figured he'd missed her and headed back down to his car, disappointed. He'd just have to try again another time.

No sooner did he turn the corner onto the street when he caught sight of a cop writing him a ticket. Not just any cop but his youngest brother, Dare.

Son of a bitch.

Ethan walked up silently as Dare turned around.

"Still playing it loose with the law, I see," he said, as he snapped the ticket beneath the Jag's windshield.

Ethan let out a low groan. "I only thought I'd be gone a few minutes and there were no other spots."

"Like I said, you thought you'd play it fast and loose. Do

you think because it's a nonmoving violation it's okay?"
Dare shoved his pen back into his shirt pocket, expression
grim, lips pulled into a tight line.

"I made a mistake." Ethan paused a deliberate beat. "It
wouldn't be the first time."

"Well, at least this time you'll pay. Literally, I mean. Fifty
bucks. You're also too close to a fire hydrant."

Ethan tried like hell not to wince or react as he met his
brother's steely, unwavering—and uncaring—gaze. "I paid
last time too. I'm still paying."

Dare straightened his shoulders. "Tell it to someone who
cares. Next time watch where you park." He turned and
walked away without looking back.

Well, he'd been right not to call him for a brotherly dinner
the other night. Ethan placed a hand on the hood of his car
and breathed in deeply, reminding himself he'd come back
home to accept responsibility and earn back his brothers'
respect. He hadn't expected it to happen overnight. Sometimes he thought it might not happen at all.

"Are you okay?"

At the sound of Faith's familiar voice, he straightened
and whirled around. "Don't sneak up on me like that," he
snapped at her, wondering how much she'd overheard.

"Not sneaking. Just on my way home. So, are you?"

"What?"

"Are you okay?" Her gaze was soft and concerned.

He was embarrassed. "I'm fine."

"Really? Because if I'd had that run-in with my brother,
I wouldn't be." There she went, pushing his buttons.

"You don't have a brother," he reminded her.

She shrugged, lifting a delicate shoulder. "I wish I did.
Maybe it wouldn't be so lonely."

Present tense. Apparently the princess wasn't having any
better luck making friends back home than he was.

"What are you doing here?" she asked, gesturing around
the empty alley.

"Looking for you."

Her eyes widened in surprise. "Why?"

"I have a proposition for you."

She set her jaw. "Now wait a minute."

He laughed. "A *decent* kind of proposition."

Her cheeks flushed with embarrassment. Honest reactions. Another thing he liked about her. "What is it?" she asked, clearly intrigued.

"The officer said I have to move my car or I'd tell you now." He pulled out his keys. "Unless you want to get in and come with me to find a spot?"

She hesitated.

He let out a groan. "Come on, princess. Are we going to do this dance every time I offer you a ride?"

She rolled her eyes and headed around to the passenger side. Once they were settled, he turned on the ignition and backed the car out of the spot.

"So? Are you going to tell me what this proposition is?"

"You said you plan on opening an interior design business, right?"

She nodded.

"Well, I have a new house that needs someone to turn it into a home."

She opened her mouth, then closed it again. "You're offering me a job."

"That's right."

"To decorate *my* house."

"My house now," he felt compelled to remind her.

"But the home I grew up in. The place filled with childhood memories, good and bad," she said, more to herself than to him.

She stared out the window, but he'd intrigued her. He could tell. She wrinkled her pert nose in thought, mulling the idea around in her brain.

Finally she let out a long breath of air. "It's a great offer. A fantastic opportunity," she admitted.

"That's a start."

"But I can't possibly take it."

Surprise mingled with disappointment. He hadn't prepared himself for her to say no. "Why not?"

"For all the reasons I just said. It was my home and now it's not. I envision it one way, the way I grew up."

"I saw the place before all the furniture was liquidated," he said. "It wasn't a home. It was a mausoleum."

She turned her head and glared. "Well, it was my mausoleum and I prefer to remember it that way."

Another point he hadn't considered.

Before he could react, she took him off guard by unlocking the door and climbing out of the passenger seat, leaving him sitting alone in his car.

Rejected twice in one day.

There was an old saying: If you couldn't beat them, join them. So instead of fighting the noise, Faith headed downstairs to the bar for Karaoke Night. She knew Kate would be here with some of her friends, and Faith figured she might as well start carving out a social life. Whether the good folks of Serendipity liked it or not. April's warm welcome had given her hope and a dose of courage to come down here alone. Obviously she was early because she'd beaten Kate here, so she grabbed an empty bar stool and ordered a glass of Chardonnay.

Then, realizing her drink would have been Carter's choice, she changed it to a light beer, something she hadn't had since college, but she'd always loved the malt taste. She grinned, imagining both her parents' and Carter's reaction to her drinking from the bottle.

"I thought you weren't into Karaoke Night?" Kate slipped into the empty chair beside her.

"I changed my mind."

"I'm glad. The rest of the gang will be here soon."

Faith's stomach churned and she realized she'd misjudged herself. She wasn't ready to deal with Kate's friends, but she was already here and had no choice.

"Hey, I thought you weren't going to be here for another half hour?" Faith asked her friend.

Kate shrugged. "I heard you made an appearance." She tilted her head toward Joe, the owner of the bar since he'd taken over from his father.

"He called you?"

Kate nodded. "He considers watching out for his customers part of his job."

"So, who else is joining us?" Faith asked, preparing herself for the answer.

"Well, Lissa, for one." Kate shot Faith an apologetic glance. "And Tanya Santos and Stacey Garner. Remember them?" Kate asked.

"Stacey still lives in town?" Faith hadn't run into her since her return. She'd been a part of Faith and Kate's clique back in high school.

Kate nodded. "Like you, she went off to school. She became a dentist and came back home. She works with old Mr. Hansen."

"Good for her," Faith said. She glanced around, wondering which of the women would arrive first.

"Looking for anyone *special*?" Kate asked with a grin.

"Like who?" Faith deadpanned. She really hoped her friend would take the hint and not say his name.

"Oh, a certain bad boy named Ethan Barron."

She said it, Faith thought wryly.

She didn't want to talk about Ethan, not when she couldn't stop thinking about him. Yes, there was the fact that he was so handsome he took her breath away. And he wanted her to work for him, which had scared her on so many levels she hadn't been able to get away fast enough. Stupid on her part because she desperately needed clients, and despite the emotional minefield of decorating her old home, the opportunity could showcase her talent and potentially open many more doors.

But what she couldn't get out of her mind was how badly Ethan's brother had treated him. And how Ethan had just accepted it as his due. Despite his lack of expression and reaction, she'd sensed how badly Dare's rejection had hurt.

"Here you are!"

Faith's thoughts were interrupted and she turned to see the three women Kate had mentioned earlier had joined them.

"You never sit in the corner. I almost couldn't find you. What gives?" Lissa asked, barely sparing a glance at Faith as she spoke directly to Kate.

"Faith and I just wanted a private spot to talk until you guys got here." Kate met Lissa's gaze, practically daring her to be rude.

Faith pasted a smile on her face and treated the other women to a friendly wave.

"Faith Harrington, as I live and breathe!" A perky blonde nudged Lissa out of the way and made her way to Kate, giving her a huge hug.

Her second of the day and one she was happy to reciprocate. "Stacey Garner! It's so good to see you!"

They squealed like only old girlfriends could.

From over Stacey's shoulder, Faith caught Lissa's wary gaze.

Too bad, Faith thought. She had another ally and she wasn't going anywhere. Serendipity was her home too, and Lissa was just going to have to deal with her.

Faith discreetly studied her nemesis, from the woman's silky black hair to her wide green eyes. Lissa would be attractive if not for the perpetual frown on her face, Faith observed. Recalling that Kate mentioned she was recently divorced and betrayed, Faith decided to try and not take her attitude personally.

She turned to Stacey, whom she hadn't seen in ten years.

"You need to fill me in on what's been going on in your life!"

"I will. But first let's order drinks. I see you already started," the blonde said approvingly.

"The uptown girl's drinking Bud from a bottle. Slumming with the rest of us!" Lissa noted, a renewed sour expression on her face. "I'll have a Bud Light too!"

"We all will," Kate said, deciding for everyone, and shooting Lissa a warning glare at the same time.

"Coming right up, ladies!" Joe called back.

"So you've obviously been reintroduced to Lissa," Stacey said, diplomatically. "Do you remember Tanya?"

Faith nodded. "We were in a lot of the same classes."

"Including chorus," Tanya said. "Welcome back."

"Thanks." The dark-haired woman seemed friendly enough, Faith thought, relieved she didn't have another Lissa on her hands.

Joe placed four bottles on the bar.

Everyone grabbed theirs and Kate slid the last in front of Faith. "I figured you could use a cold one. Joe said our regular table's ready, so let's go sit."

A few minutes later, the women were settled around the table, Lissa, Tanya, Stacey, and Kate chatting like old friends, catching each other up with their day. More than anything, Faith wanted to retreat, to hide away in her small upstairs apartment, but she refused to allow herself the luxury.

Kate tried to include Faith in the conversation, but eventually Faith would lose track of the people or the stories and she'd revert to being an outsider again. Faith twisted her hands together in her lap, telling herself that each time she met with this group of women, or any other group she became reacquainted with, she'd be more comfortable. She had no choice but to believe it.

"Ladies and gentlemen!" Joe's booming voice reverberated

through the bar. "We've come to the moment you've all been waiting for."

Loud hoots and hollers followed his announcement.

"It's time for karaoke!" With his light brown hair and beach-bum T-shirt, Joe was the epitome of the comfortable host, engaging the crowd. With a flourish, he pulled down a big screen behind him. "Hit it, Lenny!"

His deejay put on a rousing version of Journey's "Don't Stop Believin'," and the words to the song flashed behind him on the screen.

"These are for anyone who wants to join in or in case our brave soloist forgets," Joe explained.

The crowd responded with a round of applause.

"So, who's up first?" Joe asked.

"I don't know why he always asks. Tradition's always the same." Tanya shook her head and sighed.

"Watch this," Kate whispered in Faith's ear.

An overweight man with a comb-over stepped onto the stage and grabbed the mike. "Anyone have a song preference?" he called out to the audience.

"Who is that?" Faith didn't recognize him.

"It's Bill Brady!" Kate pointed out.

"The quarterback?"

"Yep."

"The one who dated—"

Stacey hung her head in shame. "The one and only," she said from beneath the curtain of hair that had fallen over her face.

Faith grinned. "Wow. What happened? He was so hot in high school."

"Heredity happened."

"Is he married?" Faith asked.

"With children. And he looks like Al Bundy too." Stacey groaned. "He went away to Texas A&M, played football, got drafted, blew out his knee in practice, and never recovered. So he came home and runs his dad's hardware store."

"Give the man a round of applause," Joe said when Bill's off-key rendition was finished.

Faith dutifully clapped.

"Who's up next?" Joe asked.

Nobody responded.

"A boring crowd. Just what I need. Come on, folks." He glanced around the crowded room and his eyes settled on their table. "Ladies!" he crooned in a sexy voice.

"Oh, no," Faith muttered.

"Ladies!" Joe said again. "I know you're as talented as you are beautiful. Want to know how I know? Because I went to school with you and at least two of you were in chorus. One of you even had a solo!"

Faith placed her hands on her burning cheeks. He remembered? She and Kate used to be all rah rah, participating in clubs and activities like cheerleading, chorus, and even an afterschool singing club.

"Look at them acting shy when just last month they brought the house down!" He pointed to the three women sitting beside her.

Faith's eyes opened wide. "You did?"

Lissa shook her head and groaned. "I'd just broken up with my boyfriend. My kid was staying at his father's in New Jersey."

"She was drunk!" Stacey gleefully reminded her.

"So were you!" Lissa shot back. "And you." She pointed at Kate. "As a matter of fact, *you* dragged me up there!" This time she spoke to Tanya.

"I'm waiting!" Joe said. "We're all waiting." The patrons in the bar responded, clapping and encouraging them to sing.

Suddenly a waitress appeared at their table with shots of vodka.

"We didn't order these," Faith said.

"On the house!" Joe spoke into the microphone as if he'd heard her. "Have a few of those and we'll get back to you in a little while. Jean here wants her turn." He handed the microphone to a middle-aged woman with frizzy black hair and a housedress on. She began singing while her husband clapped and egged her on.

Faith glanced at the small glasses of vodka, sure Kate would turn down the straight shots of alcohol, but along with the others, she picked up the small glass.

"Faith?" Kate cajoled, clearly expecting her to join in.

"Yeah, *Faith*?" Lissa called her out.

A definite dare. Her tone, her stare, her expression clearly stating she thought Faith would say no. Because she was too good to sit in a bar and do shots with the locals.

Well, maybe a sixteen- or seventeen-year-old Faith Harrington would have said no, but more because she'd have been afraid she would get in trouble. But she definitely would have been curious. Without a doubt, Faith Harrington Moreland would have considered herself above this kind of behavior.

And that was the driving factor behind her choice now. Never breaking eye contact with Lissa, Faith picked up the shot glass.

"To old friends, new friends, and becoming friends." Kate held Lissa's gaze as she spoke.

Then all three women downed their shots before Faith could blink.

Faith tipped the glass and did the same, forcing herself not to cough as the fiery liquid burned its way down. Faith glanced at the stage and knew it would take more than one to give her that kind of courage.

"Another round?" she asked the waitress.

Three shots later, Faith found herself tipsy and on stage with the other women, singing "Kiss Me" by Sixpence None the Richer, from 1999, and revisiting her youth.

Apparently, the alcohol had done its job, relaxing her, spiking her energy and her mood, because she got into the song as well as the dance to go along with it. She hadn't expected to have such a good time.

Oh, kiss me beneath the milky twilight
Lead me out on the moonlit floor . . .

She sang the chorus when suddenly a sense of heat and awareness swept through her. She glanced across the room to find Ethan, leaning against a wall, arms folded across his broad chest.

Watching her every move.

Four

Faith's hips shook, her body moved in time to the music, and Ethan couldn't tear his gaze away.

He'd had no intention of leaving the house, let alone coming out to Joe's Bar. But Mike Ferraro, the brother of one of Ethan's old high school buddies, had heard Ethan had bought the house on the hill and stopped by to see for himself. Ethan and Mike's older brother, Carl, had gotten into more than their share of trouble together, and Mike had often tagged along.

Ethan had invited Mike in and they'd shared a beer and caught up. Apparently, Carl had knocked up his high school girlfriend and they'd gotten married the summer after graduation. These days, Carl was an electrician like his father, with two sons and a baby daughter. It was hard to imagine his friend settled down, but apparently Carl had discovered he liked his married life, a far cry from Ethan's tour of duty and solitary path. Mike, meanwhile, two years younger than Ethan and Carl, had cleaned up his act too, no longer getting into fights or trouble. Instead, he used his hands working construction, and like Ethan, he was still single.

When Mike suggested they head on over to Joe's, Ethan had said yes immediately. At home, the walls were closing in on him, the echo of silence mixing with the memory of his brother's disdain and Faith witnessing his humiliation. The sheer emptiness of the large house was driving him mad. To the point that even showing his face in downtown Serendipity held some sort of perverse appeal.

He hadn't expected to find Faith here. She lived above the bar, but even with her change in circumstance, he still considered her above a place like this. But not only was she here, she was on stage, singing.

Suddenly, she locked eyes with his and awareness shot through him, as hot and heavy as the beat of the music. He remembered the song from his high school days, the words washing over him as Faith mouthed the lyrics.

To him.

So kiss me.
So kiss me.

And he wanted to. Badly. An ache settled low in his stomach, making him want in ways he barely recognized.

Without warning, the music stopped and the entire bar treated the women to a round of applause. Ethan and Mike included.

"They're hot, huh?" Mike asked, tilting his head toward the women on stage. "So which one's got you so worked up?"

Ethan didn't answer. Didn't want anyone to know Faith Harrington could get past the aloof exterior he intended to project to the town.

"No answer?" Mike shrugged. "Then you won't mind if I try my luck with Faith Harrington. She's back, she's hot, and considering the way her family fortune's turned, she'll probably want someone to console her." He grinned. "And I'm just the man for the job."

The words twisted in Ethan's gut. "I mind," he muttered. No way would he let Mike near her.

His friend's laughter rumbled in Ethan's ear. "That's what I thought. I was kidding. I saw how she was looking at you. I just didn't know if you were interested too."

"I just want to convince her to do my house," Ethan said, his voice lacking conviction.

"I thought you wanted her to *do* you." Mike chuckled.

Ethan had had enough of his friend. He decided to see if he could, in fact, convince Faith to take the job. "Go get yourself a beer. I'll meet you at the bar."

"Looks like you're too late." Mike pointed toward the women who had returned to their table.

A man Ethan didn't recognize stood behind Faith's chair, his hand on her shoulder.

She looked up at him and smiled.

Ethan's shoulders stiffened. "Who the hell is that?"

"Nick Mancini. He owns the construction company I work for. He's also her ex. They used to go out back in high school, but she dumped him."

"You were the same year as them, right?" Ethan asked, remembering.

Mike nodded. "One day they were *the* couple and the next it was over."

Faith had dumped Nick, Ethan thought. That had to be a good thing. "It was ten years ago. I'm sure Mancini's over her."

Like you are? a voice in Ethan's head taunted him.

"Sorry, but word around the office is he's not. The boss wants a second shot."

Ethan raised an eyebrow. "Are you telling me construction workers gossip like a bunch of girls?"

Mike shrugged. "I'm just repeating what I heard. Thought you'd want to know you had competition."

"Unless Nick Mancini has a house he wants decorated,

I don't think I need to worry about him." From the corner of his eye, Ethan saw Faith rise, wobble on her high heels, steady herself, and make her way toward the restrooms on the other side of the bar.

Ethan took that as his cue. "See you later," he said to Mike.

He strode across the room and down a hallway where he leaned against the wall across from the bathrooms and waited. He planned to be here when Faith walked out.

Faith glanced in the bathroom mirror, wondering if she looked as tipsy as she felt. The room spun a bit, so she couldn't tell. The only thing she knew for sure was that Ethan was in the bar and he'd immediately zeroed in on her. For a brief moment, nobody else in the room existed as she sang "Kiss Me" to *him.*

Oh boy.

Then Nick had come over, being all too friendly to her, and Faith had needed an escape.

Well, she'd had her break, and she'd better get back before Kate sent out a search party. She swiped some gloss over her lips, fluffed her hair, and headed for the exit.

She stepped out the door and found the man of her fantasies waiting there. Arms crossed over his broad chest, a dark look in his intense eyes.

"Hi," she said, intending to stride past him, as if there hadn't been that charged eye contact between them when she was on stage.

"In a hurry?" he asked.

She swallowed hard. "No. I just thought you were waiting for someone."

"I was. I was waiting for you."

Okay, then. She blinked, but dizziness still assaulted her except now she wasn't sure if it was the alcohol or Ethan's unique masculine scent that had her swooning.

"Hi," she said again, grinning this time.

He shook his head and laughed.

The sound rocked her world. His smile tilted it even more.

He reached out and lifted her chin with his hand, looking into her eyes. "You're drunk."

She shook her head in denial. Big mistake. She wobbled and he reached out to steady her. His hand on her bare arm branded her skin, causing her temperature to soar and her heart to pound harder in her chest.

"Maybe a little . . . tipsy." She giggled but resisted the urge to cover her mouth in embarrassment. Faith Harrington never giggled. Until now, that is. "Make that a lot tipsy," she admitted.

A sexy smile tilted his lips. "What the hell were you ladies drinking?" he asked.

"Umm . . ." She closed her eyes, trying to remember. "I had a bottle of Bud Light before Kate arrived, one after, then Joe sent over a shot or two." She opened her eyes and shrugged. "Maybe it was three bottles."

He raised an eyebrow.

"Definitely three." At least she didn't remember there being a fourth.

"You sing well." He complimented her in a smooth voice that washed over her like a warm caress.

"Thanks. It's an easy song."

"Kiss Me." The song lyrics bounced silently between them and she couldn't tear her gaze from his mouth.

His hot gaze met hers, making her wonder if he could read her mind.

"I don't usually get into karaoke," she said. "Or shots of vodka."

"I wouldn't think so, princess, or you wouldn't be feeling the effects so strongly."

She loved how he used that word, the way it rolled off his tongue like an endearment. Not that she'd ever admit as much to him.

"You're right about that. I'm definitely feeling something." Because his hand not only still held her arm, but he ran his thumb back and forth over her skin. But she wasn't complaining. She liked his touch way too much.

"Ready to call it a night?" he asked.

"That's probably a good idea. I just need to say good night to Kate and then I'll go up to my place. Kinda convenient that I live right upstairs." She took a few steps and realized she wasn't steady on her feet. She made a mental note to buy herself a pair of flat shoes. Damn Carter and his insistence she wear high heels, anyway.

But Ethan's hand was still there, keeping her upright, and she was grateful. "Thanks," she said to him. "But I'm sure I can manage this."

"I doubt that." His low laugh rumbled in her ear. "Come on. I'll take you on up myself."

Before she could argue, he wrapped his arm around her waist, and she no longer wanted to fight him. He pulled her close, his hard body aligning with hers.

She closed her eyes for a second and inhaled deeply, taking in the scent she knew would arouse her for a long time to come. "You smell good," she murmured.

"You smell better." His gruff voice brought her out of her daydream and she realized she'd spoken out loud.

He pulled her tighter against him.

Oh man.

They reached Kate's table and she leaned over to whisper in her friend's ear. "I've had way too much to drink so I'm going upstairs before I get in trouble."

Kate glanced from Faith to Ethan, who waited beside her. "Oh, honey, I think you already found trouble," Kate said softly.

Faith giggled again. "He found me."

"Are you sure you know what you're doing?" Kate asked, concern in her voice.

Faith nodded. "I'm just going upstairs to sleep."

Kate eyed Ethan warily as she spoke, then crooked a finger telling Faith to lean in closer.

Faith complied.

"Make sure that sleep is all you do. Because when you do have sex with the man, you want to make sure you're sober enough to remember every second!" Kate whispered.

Faith felt sure she was blushing, but she was so hot and bothered she couldn't be sure. "I told you I'm not ready for anything with any man." Even one who smelled like musk and made her want . . . everything.

Kate narrowed her gaze. "Well, he sure looks primed and ready to me, so be careful."

Faith hugged her best friend tight and rose.

Ethan had his hand around her before she could wobble or fall. Something told her she wouldn't be as comfortable with this situation if she were sober, but that same voice admitted she was glad she wasn't. With a little alcohol in her, she felt freer to be the self she normally would have kept in check.

"See you later," Faith said to Kate and the rest of the women at the table.

All, including Lissa, stared at Faith and Ethan, dumb-struck. Not just because he was back in town, showing his face, but also because he had his arm around Faith's waist.

Yep, she was going to have some serious regrets come morning. She looked into Ethan's eyes and realized morning was many, many hours away.

You smell good. Ethan nearly groaned just remembering her arousal-laden words, and there was only so much a man could take. Even now, she tortured him. He walked behind Faith, up the stairs leading to her apartment, his hand on her waist to steady her. And she needed steadying. Between the high heels and the alcohol, her long legs wobbled in her ridiculous but sexy heels. Then there was the short skirt and ruffled tank hanging off one shoulder. With each delicate step up, he caught a glimpse of skin on her thigh. If the back stairs weren't dark, he could probably see more. As it was, he was left to wonder if she wore lace panties or a thong. Just the thought had him breaking into a sweat.

They reached the top step at last.

"Whew. Made it," Faith said, even her voice turning him on.

He came up beside her and waited patiently while she opened her purse and began looking for her keys. "Can I help you?"

"Nope. I've got it."

But she didn't. "Hold this?" She handed him a compact mirror. "And this." A tube of lip gloss. "This." A small wallet came next.

He juggled each in his hands.

"How much can you fit into such a tiny bag?" he asked. The workings of the female mind had always confounded him.

"You'd be surprised," she murmured. "Gotcha!" She pulled out a set of keys, holding them up in triumph.

He wanted to grab them before she dropped them over the railing, but his hands were full.

"Here. Just dump all that in here." She opened her purse and he poured her things inside.

She turned to put the key in the lock, fumbling and obviously having trouble.

"Here." He intended to take the keys from her and do it himself, but she didn't let go. Instead, he found himself grasping her delicate hand and attempting to maneuver the key into the lock. In the dark. While leaning close and inhaling a fragrant scent that smelled suspiciously like strawberries. The kind he'd like to hand-feed her while her tongue slowly licked the juice off of each of his ten fingers.

The key missed its target again.

Faith laughed softly and Ethan swore.

Her skin was soft and smooth and he couldn't concentrate. "Give me the damn thing," he said gruffly.

She let go and the keys fell to the floor. "Oops!"

He bent down and picked up the elusive metal object. "Step aside."

She did as he asked.

Free from her overpowering nearness, he shoved the key into the lock and let them into a dark room. He felt for the light switch on the wall, fumbling in the unfamiliar setting until he literally felt Faith brush past him, her body touching his, then she was gone.

Finally, blessedly, she flicked on a small lamp in what looked like the den. She then flopped into an oversized chair and sprawled there.

"See? That wasn't so hard," she said with an endearing grin.

"Speak for yourself, princess." He was hard as a rock and looking at her, head back against the cushion, arms and legs spread wide, he was getting stiffer by the second.

He really ought to leave before he ended up doing something she would definitely regret come morning. If she were sober and capable of making a coherent decision, that would be another story.

Because he wanted her badly. "I should go home."

She lifted her eyebrows. "Really? Because I thought you'd want to talk about your earlier *proposition*."

She said the words with such cute innuendo, he was unable to suppress a grin. "The one you turned down?" he reminded her.

"I did, didn't I?" She sounded almost deflated.

He nodded. "You did."

She glanced up at the ceiling. "April Mancini offered me the store next to hers to open my interior design business, but there's no way I could afford the rent without clients."

Her words opened up possibilities and his pulse kicked into overdrive. "So you need me?"

She bolted upright in the chair and immediately grabbed her head in her hands. "Oh boy." She waited a few seconds and lifted her head more slowly this time. "That's better. What was I saying? Oh yeah. I need your *business*," she corrected him.

He was shocked she could recall his last statement let alone her own train of thought. Needing his business was a good start. "So you'll take the job?"

She bit down on her lower lip. "I shouldn't. I mean, I'd be designing away everything that made the place my childhood home," she said wistfully.

He took her words like a kick in the gut. He felt her pain.

"But since everything about the house and the people in it was a lie, maybe erasing the memories would be a good thing."

He remained silent as she played devil's advocate with herself. She wasn't speaking to him. Wasn't expecting a reply. She was lost in her own mind and he let her stay there, mostly because she was talking herself into taking the job, which meant she'd be working for him.

And that meant he'd see her often. At first he'd thought she'd distract him from his goal of making a family life here with his brothers. Every hour that goal seemed further and further away. So she'd be a welcome diversion in his solitary life.

"You know, decorating that house could really put me on the map in Serendipity," she mused, kicking her feet back and forth as she spoke.

He had a feeling thanks to her family name and reputation that she was already there, but he declined to tell her so. He figured that sober, she'd know it all too well.

"It definitely could," he agreed with her.

"I used to think the sun rose and set on my father, but since he pleaded guilty, I don't know who he is anymore. And I'm not sure who I am either."

Ethan wasn't sure what to say to that. Again, since he figured she wasn't really talking to him, he remained silent, appreciating the pain she'd been through. And the insight she was giving him.

Suddenly she stood, more slowly this time. "Ironically, decorating my old house—your new house—would give me the jump start I need toward finding myself again."

He liked that his job offer would give her more than cash. That he'd actually help her in some deep and meaningful way.

"My father would be horrified to know you bought his house," she said, still lost in thought.

He cocked an eyebrow at that and tried like hell not to take offense. "Yeah, I can just imagine."

She glanced at him then, the first time he realized she really was aware of him during this semimonologue. "But I'm glad it was you."

His heart beat a little faster at the admission. She didn't say why and he wasn't sure he wanted to know.

"Anyway, it'll be a good thing to take the job and wipe all traces of the Harringtons out of that house." She swung her arm through the air, spinning as she spoke and nearly taking herself down.

He grabbed her around the waist to stop her fall and she ended up in his arms, her body aligned with his in a very tempting way. She tipped her face back and met his gaze, those soft eyes filled with wanting. The same want that had been thudding through his body all evening.

"Kiss me." She sang the words softly, never breaking eye contact, her words both a dare and a plea.

He knew he shouldn't, but not even the strongest man could resist. Especially not when she wound her arms around his neck and whispered the words one more time.

"Kiss me," she asked again.

So he did. He lowered his lips to hers and captured her mouth in the kiss he'd been dreaming about since running into her again. Definitely since she'd teased him from the stage and again later when she'd tempted him on the stairs.

Now she gave in to desire. Her lips softened and she kissed him back, starting slowly, with the gentle whisper of her mouth on his. The tempo quickly changed when she slid her tongue over his lips, then opened her mouth and let him inside.

He cupped the back of her head in his hand and tilted her head, deepening the connection between them. She appreciated the change because she moaned and pressed against him, her breasts crushing into his chest, her mouth devouring his.

Their kiss ten years ago had been all rough hunger on his part, excitement that he'd gotten the good girl to take the ride, then wanting to prove he was every bit the bad boy she'd thought. He hadn't counted on being blindsided by a kiss that felt like it meant so much more. So when she'd turned him down, he'd been selfishly pissed off.

Tonight he'd gone into this kiss fully aware of the impact she possessed. Or so he thought. But when his lips touched hers, youthful memories meant nothing compared to the reality of kissing this woman again. He could make love to her mouth all night, never come up for air, and still want more in the morning.

Her hands slid to his waist and began working his shirt up so she could run her fingers over his abdomen. "So hard and tight," she murmured, surprising him with her bold exploration.

His groin pulsed in response.

He desired her with a desperation. But he needed her to want *him*. And right now, it was the alcohol talking, making her ask for more. If Faith Harrington were sober, she'd probably still be running from him as far and as fast as she could.

The bad boy he used to be would take what she offered and not look back. But Ethan had worked too hard to get past that kid, his cockiness, arrogance, and the devastation he'd caused. He was still working on it. And he wasn't stupid. He knew he could never be this particular princess's Prince Charming.

But even if they had one night or a short fling, he was determined for it to be consensual. She would know she was with Ethan.

With regret and a hell of a lot of willpower, he grasped her wrists in his hands and pulled them apart.

"What's wrong?" She looked up at him with an aroused, willing, take-me gaze that nearly had him giving in.

"You need sleep," he said in a gruff voice he barely recognized.

And he needed a cold shower.

A few minutes later, he let himself out the door, reminding her he expected to see her at his house around ten the next morning to discuss their new business arrangement. He knew he wouldn't be getting any sleep. He wondered if she'd even remember any of this in the morning, when she'd be hurting like crazy.

As he ran down the back stairs, he knew just the way to make sure the progress he'd made tonight didn't disappear with the light of day tomorrow.

Five

Faith's head pounded and her throat was raw. With a groan, she rolled over, hand over her forehead, and gingerly sat back on the pillows. Good. The familiar pillows meant she was in her own bed like she thought. She forced her eyelids open and realized she was still dressed in the skirt and top she'd worn to Joe's last night.

Last night.

The evening came back to her in spurts, but she definitely remembered the highlights. Deciding to go to Karaoke Night instead of staying home alone. Ordering beer instead of wine. Kate and her friends showing up, and Faith drinking another beer. Joe begging them to sing. She winced at that one, recalling how that had led to her drinking a shot of vodka, then another, and then a few more.

No wonder her head felt like a freight train was barreling through her temples. What happened after karaoke? She sank into her cushiony down pillows to think and the answer came to her in a distinct vision.

Ethan.

He'd been waiting for her in the hallway. Razor stubble darkened his cheeks, giving him an even more dangerous than normal aura, which was saying something. He'd worn a black shirt that emphasized his broad chest and impressive muscles. And when he'd spoken, that husky voice had washed over her like hot chocolate over vanilla ice cream. She hadn't been nearly as smooth as she'd stumbled over herself, but he'd been there, wrapping his strong arm around her waist, supporting her.

And not only had she let him, she'd leaned against him, wanting to crawl inside his skin because he'd smelled so musky and male, so . . . *You smell good.*

Faith groaned aloud. "Please tell me I did not say that out loud."

Obviously she had because he'd replied, *You smell better.*

"Oh God." She was mortified enough, but it hadn't ended there.

He'd taken her home, helped her up the stairs and into her apartment. She'd been drunk and out of control. She remembered that now. She also remembered a long, rambling conversation she'd had with him, but no real specifics came back to her except that it had led to *a kiss.*

And boy could he kiss. She was on fire now just thinking about his lips hard on hers. She grabbed an extra pillow and buried her face into the cool, soft cushion.

How would she ever face him again? Well, she wouldn't have to unless she ran into him in town, which she doubted would happen all that often. At least she hoped not.

The doorbell rang and she glanced at the clock on the nightstand. Nine A.M. It was probably Kate, coming over to find out exactly what had happened between her and Ethan last night. Having just relived it in her head, Faith wasn't ready for an instant replay with her best friend.

But the doorbell rang again.

Faith rose gently from the bed, taking care with her poor

aching head. She could barely stand, but if she wanted the ringing to go away, she had no choice but to answer.

"I'm coming!" she called out irritably.

She opened the door, shocked to find Rosalita, her old housekeeper, on the other side.

Before Faith could greet her, the other woman stepped into the apartment, a brown bag in her hand. She brushed past Faith and headed for her small kitchen, placing the bag onto the counter.

Only when her hands were free did she turn around and hold out her arms. "Oh, Ms. Faith. It's so good to see you! I miss you so much. Not your mama or your papa, I'm sorry to say, but you!"

Rosalita had worked for Faith's parents since Faith was a little girl. She'd been the one to sit with Faith in the kitchen, give her milk and cookies after school, and meet whichever friends she brought home. She worked hard so her children could have the life and education she didn't, something Faith as an adult now understood and respected.

The woman was a welcome sight and Faith stepped forward and into her warm embrace. "It's good to see you too, Rosalita." She was glad to note her old housekeeper still smelled the same, the thought giving Faith comfort. "How did you know where to find me?"

She stepped back and looked the other woman over. Rosalita hadn't changed in all the years Faith had known her. Her dark hair was cropped short near her head and her stout, round body was just the same.

"Well, Mr. Ethan, he ask me do a special errand for him this morning. I tell him no, I work around the house and I'm not his errand boy. But then he explained it was for you and I say okay." She cupped Faith's face in her hands and kissed both cheeks. "You look good."

Faith shook her head—a big mistake—and raised an

eyebrow instead. "I doubt it. I'm sure I look like something
the cat dragged in."

"*Sí*. But you still look good to me."

Faith grinned, when suddenly Rosalita's earlier words
registered. "You work for Ethan Barron now?" she asked,
surprised.

"I tol' him I come with the house and keep my job, but
he have to pay me double to work for a bad boy. Because I
know the house so well, he say yes."

Faith understood her broken English. Despite having
been in this country for decades, Rosalita had always chosen
to speak Spanish to her children at home, watch Spanish
television channels, and stick to English only when at work.

What Faith took from the conversation was that Rosalita
didn't approve of her boss and Faith felt compelled to stick
up for him. "Ethan's not a bad boy anymore, Rosalita."

She folded her plump arms over her ample chest and let
out a harrumphing sound. "Bad man. Same difference."

"He's not that either." Although exactly what Ethan was
remained to be seen. Just thinking about him had her aching
and wound up, curious, and a lot of other things all at the
same time. "You should give him a chance," Faith said to
his new housekeeper.

Rosalita pursed her lips. "That's what he say."

"Then do it." Faith narrowed her gaze. "Why would
Ethan send you here?"

"He say you will need breakfast this morning. So here I
am." She smiled at Faith.

"Breakfast?"

"*Sí*. So let me get started." The older woman headed back
into the kitchen and began pulling out ingredients from the
bag. "I make your favorite breakfast. But first, here. Coffee."
She handed Faith a large cup from the Cuppa Café, which
Faith gratefully accepted.

She was completely overwhelmed by Ethan's gracious
gesture. "He sent you to make me breakfast? That's so

considerate of him." And caring. She couldn't believe he'd thought to take care of her, and a wave of warm appreciation washed over her.

Rosalita began her prepping in the small kitchen, making herself at home, rambling like she always used to. "Mr. Ethan also say you drink too much last night." Rosalita paused to wave a wagging finger at her. "Not good for you, Ms. Faith. Alcohol make you do bad things. I ended up with child after too much alcohol." She gestured to her belly. "You be careful. Especially if you're hanging around with that bad boy."

Faith bit down on the inside of her cheek. "I'm not hanging around with him. And he's not a—"

"Bad boy. I know. So you say. But he knew you'd need coffee and breakfast this morning, so something happened between you two, no?"

Faith blew out a long breath of air, unable to deny the other woman's words. "Yes."

"Let me make your omelet."

Unable to stand the thought of eggs just yet, Faith was about to argue, when Rosalita spoke again. "Go. Shower and get dressed. You'll feel better and I'll have breakfast ready when you're done. You need to get ready. Mr. Ethan say you two have a business meeting at ten o'clock this morning. So go get ready."

"What?" Faith asked, Rosalita's words coming as a surprise. "We don't have any business together."

"Mr. Ethan tell me you will say that too. So he said to remind you that you agree to . . . what's the word? Des . . ."

"Design?"

"Design and decorate his new house. Which should be your house, if you ask me." She let out a *tsk*ing sound followed by a shake of her head. "Your father, shame on him. I never thought he was a criminal, but he disappoint me!" she exclaimed.

"Me too, Rosalita. Me too." As for Ethan, she was beginning

to recall more of that monologue she'd had with him last night, and yes, she probably had agreed to take the job.

She pinched the bridge of her nose, knowing she'd need not just this coffee and the shower, or even the breakfast he'd so generously sent over, but a good dose of courage before heading over to the house on the hill.

An hour later, Rosalita had left after making Faith the best omelet ever, a cold glass of freshly squeezed orange juice, and another cup of hot coffee. Her head still hurt a little, but overall she felt like a new woman. New enough to call her mom.

Faith and her mother had had a strained relationship from the time Faith was a child. Faith had been her daddy's little girl, while Lanie Harrington resented the attention Martin Harrington showered on his daughter, the same attention she so desperately craved. It didn't matter how much Faith's father loved his wife—she always wanted more and had often blamed Faith for dividing Martin's time when he was home. Added to the fact that Lanie didn't know how to be a mother, their relationship had never been good.

As an adult, Faith and her mother had drifted apart, which worked fine for Faith since she was able to distance herself from her mother's constant negativity and demands. They'd rarely spoken when Faith had lived in New York, but after her father's shocking revelations, Faith had held out hope she and her mother could begin to repair their fractured relationship.

Upon returning to Serendipity, Faith reached out, assuming Lanie would welcome someone who understood the pain and loneliness she must be experiencing. What Faith discovered was that her mother's holier-than-thou attitude about the world hadn't changed despite the fact that her husband was in jail and she was now living on a fixed income enforced by her settlement with the government. Everything else in their names had been sold off, the proceeds put into a fund to repay the victims of his crimes. She held on to the warped belief that her husband was misunderstood and had never meant to hurt people. Therefore, as usual, both Lanie's and her husband's circumstances were everyone else's fault.

Lanie Harrington resided in a lovely house on the outskirts of town and, in Faith's opinion, had made out fairly well, all things considered. In her mother's opinion, she'd been robbed and life wasn't fair. She'd been ostracized by the elite women of the community and shunned by the regular people Faith was trying so hard to live among and be a part of.

Still, Faith called and her mother didn't answer, whether she was sleeping in or not taking calls, Faith had been spared until next time. She left a message and turned to getting ready to meet with Ethan, beginning with sorting through her closet for business-appropriate attire. She settled on a black tank top dress with a pair of low kitten-heeled shoes that posed no threat of repeating last night's unsteady wobbling.

A few minutes later, she stepped outside of her apartment and realized she would have to call a taxi or walk to Ethan's. She hadn't owned a car in Manhattan and she hadn't thought she'd need one here either, living smack in the heart of town. Besides, a car would be another luxury and she didn't want to afford herself too many of those until she was bringing in a steady income.

She'd have no choice but to call a cab from the one-person cab company in town, which would take at least half an hour to show up, making her late. She reached into her bag to find her cell phone when the sound of a car horn drew her attention.

She turned and saw Ethan's Jag in the parking lot, the man himself waving to her from the driver's seat. She blinked in surprise and started down the stairs, careful to maintain a steady stride and not make an ass of herself— because he was definitely watching her.

She walked up to his open window, placing a hand on the car. "What are you doing here?"

"Do you have a car?" he asked.

If he was here, she had a feeling he already knew the answer. But she shook her head in reply anyway.

"Didn't think so," he said a bit too smugly for her liking. "But the truth is I just didn't want you to find an excuse to miss our appointment." His lips twisted in a wry grin.

So he thought he'd be one step ahead of her, did he? Okay, he was. And there was nothing she could do about it. Nor did she want to. The man had offered her a much-needed career opportunity and had turned out to be her savior last night and again this morning. If she wasn't careful, he'd make himself indispensable. And that was power she could never allow any man to have over her.

"Get in the car, princess." His eyes dared her to argue as she had in the past.

She merely stood taller and walked to the passenger's side of the car, bracing herself for the impact of being alone with him. There was also the issue of walking into her old home for the first time since the world as she knew it had come crashing down around her.

"Feeling okay this beautiful morning?" he asked as he pulled out of the parking lot.

The sun shone down on the town, a bright early July morning in Serendipity. The sunlight made her wince, which was what he'd been referring to.

Her hangover. "Actually, I'm feeling good." Thanks to him. "Sending over breakfast was thoughtful." Sending over Rosalita had been an emotional boost she hadn't realized she'd needed, but obviously he'd figured that out about her.

No one had ever cared enough about her deepest needs to do something that caring. Oh, her father had given her material things, and he'd given her his time, but she knew now he'd withheld important parts of himself, making their connection a superficial one at best. And forget Carter. But Ethan, who was practically a stranger to her, had sensed what she needed.

She swallowed hard. "Thank you."

He slid a knowing glance her way, then refocused on the road. "You're welcome. I figured you'd be hurting this morning, and again, I didn't want to give you an excuse to miss our meeting."

She bit the inside of her cheek. "I might not have remembered our meeting if you hadn't sent Rosalita to remind me."

He grinned, obviously amused by her hangover. "I figured."

"Well, I'm perfectly fine now."

"Glad to hear it. We have a lot of ground to cover. This place is massive and it'll take tons of furniture to make it feel like home."

She patted her tote. "That's what I'm here for." Her bag held a sketch pad, measuring tape, and a notebook for their meeting.

She just planned to take some basic notes, dig into his feelings about the house, his likes and dislikes in color and furniture type—modern, classic, traditional, et cetera. Then she'd call Joel Carstairs. She'd met Joel, a premier interior designer, through the wife of one of Carter's partners.

Joel had helped her decorate her penthouse in Manhattan and in the process he'd become her close friend. She'd attended his designer showcases, and he'd taken her with him on buying trips and had introduced her to the best design houses to work with and order fabric and furniture from. Most important, he'd held her hand through her divorce, all the while reminding her of why he and Paul, his partner of fifteen years, didn't need a piece of paper to define their relationship. He'd also promised to help her get started in interior design in Serendipity, even if visiting a small town killed his sense of flair. She grinned at the recollection.

"What's so funny?" Ethan asked.

She hadn't realized he'd been watching her. "Nothing." He wouldn't understand unless he met Joel.

Ethan shrugged and turned the car into the long

wly taking the car up the hill and pulling the
of the four garages her father had added on after
the house from the previous owner. She noted a
motorcy.. in one stall, an SUV in another.

The mansion on the hill was a landmark, the heart of the
town. All the homes that had been built in the early 1900s
by the rich and wealthy seeking to escape the hot summers
in Manhattan had fallen into disrepair.

Not her house.

This house.

His house.

She hadn't realized he'd shut off the engine and walked
around, opening the car door and extending a hand.
"Ready?"

She placed her palm against his. Electricity crackled
between them as she stepped into the familiar garage.

"Are you okay?"

She nodded. "I was just thinking about my dad's cars.
His Aston Martin would be parked there." She pointed to
one of the empty bays. "And his Mercedes convertible here."
She patted the door of his Jaguar. "Mom's car was where
your bike is now."

"I'm sorry." Ethan slipped a supportive hand against her
back. "When I asked you to decorate, I didn't think about
the emotional impact." He paused, giving the weight of his
words more importance. "Look, if you don't want to do this,
I'll take you home right now."

"Let's get one thing straight, okay?" Faith turned to face
him. "You might have pushed me into this when I was
drunk, but I wouldn't be here now unless I wanted to be."

A flash of admiration sparkled in his eyes. "Fair enough."

"Good. So let's go inside."

No sooner had Ethan entered the house than he received
an emergency business call. He didn't want to leave Faith
alone to walk through her old home, but he had no choice.
He excused himself and uncomfortably told her to look

around—as if she didn't already know every nook and cranny in the place.

Heading into his office, he took the call only to discover that his main competitor had somehow gotten hold of the specs on his company's government bid, which meant one thing. Not only did Ethan have to revamp his strategy, but he had to deal with a spy in his midst. And if that were the case, even his latest software in development was at risk.

He muttered a curse and called Franklin Investigations, the only firm he trusted to handle the job discreetly and find out who the hell was leaking proprietary business information to his biggest competitor. It could be anyone. A loner, Ethan rarely trusted people, so he knew better than to take anyone in his company into his confidence. He'd keep the investigation to himself until the mole was ferreted out and the person fired.

Knowing there was nothing more he could do until Franklin found answers, he went in search of Faith, expecting to find her somewhere on the first floor making notes or taking measurements. Instead, he wandered room to room and came up empty on the main floor. He could use the intercom system that had been installed, but he decided to keep looking instead. In the basement, he checked the media room, wondering if she'd decided to start there first. That was a room he already had a vision for and one he wanted her to implement quickly. No Faith. Wine cellar, pool table area, and bar also turned up empty.

He jogged up the stairs and then headed to the second floor where the master and other bedrooms were located. Suddenly he had a hunch and stepped quietly on the carpeted runner that led to the one bedroom that had to be hers. Pink and green striped wallpaper on walls and a floral mix border running across the top near the ceiling had screamed *girl* to him. He hadn't paid much attention when he'd walked through with the realtor and he'd had no reason to go in there since he'd moved in.

From the doorway, Ethan silently glanced inside. Faith stood by the closets in the empty room. Without furniture, the space looked as sad and lonely as she did at this moment. Sunlight streamed through the two windows on opposite walls, highlighting the soft beige carpet and putting a spotlight on the areas that were indented from the years of heavy furniture and the occasional discoloration from use and wear.

Oblivious to his presence, Faith ran her hands up and down the wall inside a small walk-in closet. She was obviously lost in old memories. Good or bad? He had no idea, but he felt like an intruder on her private time and space, and guilt rose up inside him. He considered walking away and leaving her alone with her thoughts, but if the memories weren't all good ones, maybe she'd appreciate the interruption. Besides, he reminded himself, this was *his* house and she'd come here to do a job.

He cleared his throat. "Hey. I looked all over the house for you."

She turned, not startled or surprised to see him. He wondered if she'd sensed his presence all along. "Hi. I was just visiting. This used to be my room, but I'm sure you figured that out already."

He nodded. "I sure did. Pink room fit for a princess."

A sad smile touched her lips. "Yeah."

"What are you looking at in there?" He pointed to where she'd been rubbing the inner closet wall.

"You'll think it's silly." She ducked her head, obviously embarrassed, and started for the door. "Why don't we get started downstairs first?"

His curiosity piqued, he refused to accept the avoidance technique. "Not until you tell me what you were looking at." He wanted to know her secrets. Was curious what made her tick. Maybe then he'd understand why he was so drawn to her. Why he loved her laugh and hated when she was sad. Like now. "And I won't think it's silly."

She let out a forced sigh. "Okay, you asked for it. My mother loved wallpaper." She gestured around the room, then swung back to the open closet door.

"I noticed," he said wryly.

"I'm sure you did." She treated him to her soft, appealing laughter. "Anyway, my mother had even papered the inside of my closet with her choice of color and style. But I always wanted to be able to design my room and mark it as my own."

"So the urge to decorate has always been there?"

She nodded.

He envied her knowing what she wanted at a young age. He'd never known. Never thought beyond the next round of fun and trouble he could stir up. Until joining the army, he hadn't been thinking at all.

"So one day, out of spite, I peeled back the paper in the closet," she said, oblivious to his thoughts. "Of course being the real rebel that I am, I chose a place my mother wouldn't notice." She met his gaze and grinned.

Not just their gazes connected and he laughed, feeling as if they'd just shared a private joke.

"She never found out I'd peeled off one entire wall in here because only Rosalita would go inside to put away my clothes and she'd never tell. Anyway, with the wallpaper gone, I found markings." She ran her fingertips over the wall once more.

Soft and delicate, she stroked the wall. Watching her made him long for her hands to work their way over his skin, inch by tantalizing inch.

He cleared his throat. "What kind of markings?" he asked, trying to distract himself before his body reacted even more.

"Look."

He stepped closer and her sweet scent surrounded him, taking him back to last night, the kiss, and her hands looped around his neck while her lips devoured his. This wasn't good at all, he thought. He had to focus on their conversation, not on sex or how much he desired her.

He squinted for a better look at the small pencil and pen markings that ran up and down the wall in a straight line. "What are they?" He stepped out of her personal space, giving himself some of his own.

"Height measurements!" she said, sounding as excited over the discovery as she must have been the first time. "Didn't your mom ever stand you against the wall and mark how tall you'd gotten?" she asked.

He shook his head and shoved his hands into the back pocket of his jeans. "I never stuck around the house long enough for her to get the chance. I always had somewhere to go, friends to see . . . trouble to cause." His voice dropped at the memory of his behavior.

How many times had he wished for a do-over? The chance to fix things so his memories would be more than a guilty blur? Too bad life didn't offer many of those.

She met his gaze, seemed to read his expression, and her eyes filled with understanding. Not pity.

"My mother just wasn't interested in old discoveries or how tall her only daughter was." Faith jumped back into the conversation without missing a beat, letting him off the hook without pushing for further conversation.

Score another point for her.

"But after I found these I showed them to my father. He hadn't cared that I pulled down Mom's wallpaper. Instead, he just picked up a pen and added my height line to the rest of them." Her voice took on a wistful tone. "We used to check for growth spurts every six months or so. He never forgot."

"Sounds like you love him a lot."

She stepped back and leaned against the wall, her disappointment clear. "I do. Did. I mean I do. I love him." She nodded definitively. "I just don't understand what he did or why."

"Maybe he got caught up in something beyond his control," Ethan suggested, because she seemed to need answers.

"Nothing excuses what he did."

Before he could chime in, she continued. "Anyway, most of these lines are from kids who lived in this room long before me."

"Which ones are yours?" he felt compelled to ask.

"The ones in pen. The penciled ones came before me."

He liked thinking of her in this pink, princesslike room. It was just like he'd imagined for her. Funny that it had been her mother's taste and not hers.

"The cool thing is, my markings and the older ones are all part of the rich history of this place."

"Which is?" he asked, curious.

"Don't you know the history of the house?" she asked.

He shook his head. He didn't know anything except only someone wealthy could afford a place like this. As a kid, he'd been awed by its imposing presence. As an adult, the big house represented permanency and the only second chance he'd get in Serendipity.

The people who lived on Ethan's side of town had always seemed to be in awe of Faith's father. In buying this house, Ethan had sought that kind of acknowledgment for himself. His brothers had made it clear he'd never get it. A heavy weight settled in his chest. Even his housekeeper couldn't contain her dislike. Yet he was still determined to win them all over.

"Tell me about the house," he said, wanting his thoughts off of himself.

She smiled. "Well, according to my mother, decades ago, the wealthy in Manhattan wanted to escape the oppressive heat during the summer so they sought out summer *cottages* where they could take their families. Some cottage, huh?" she asked wryly.

"Small and quaint," he agreed with a grin.

She laughed.

And everything inside his chest eased.

"Serendipity must have seemed like the perfect getaway on a beautiful lake." Her voice took on a dreamy quality.

Ethan knew the lake on the outskirts of town, a place where kids hung out and families picnicked. Just not *his* family. His father, a traveling salesman, had rarely been home. And when he was, there was always bickering he'd try hard not to hear.

"One family moved out here, bought land, and built a large estate, then others in their social circle followed, each trying to outdo the other."

Faith's story brought him back to the present.

"This house was just the pièce de résistance." She gestured with her hands as she explained, her expression animated as she related the story, her fondness for this place obvious.

Pleasure unfolded inside him from watching her.

"Over the years, the inhabitants changed, of course. And over time Serendipity became more of a permanent place to live rather than just a summer retreat. But with changing times and owners came responsibilities. Not all owners kept up their homes and many fell into disrepair. A lot of them were knocked down to build the main part of town. Subdivision of land and things resulted in the smaller parcels and homes in the downtown area. And yet this house was always maintained, always well kept. My parents did their job for the last twenty years. Until . . ." Her voice trailed off. She was obviously unwilling to go on.

But Ethan knew exactly what she'd been about to say. Her father's fall from grace had reared its ugly head. Apparently it wasn't something she liked to discuss. Just as apparently, maybe talking would make her feel better.

"Until?" he prodded.

She shook her head. "Let's *not* get into that story."

Ethan studied her through narrowed eyes, making a decision in an instant. "Yes, let's."

Six

"Let's go there," Ethan deliberately pushed.

Faith might not want to discuss her father, but she needed to hear what Ethan had to say. He had a unique perspective on a person's wrongdoing and how it affected them. He might not like or approve of her father's actions, but what Martin Harrington felt for his daughter had nothing to do with his illegal business dealings. "The man's your *father*."

"And who is that?" Faith asked. "He's not the same man who didn't snitch about the wallpaper or who remembered to come in here and measure me because it was our little secret."

That she felt betrayed was obvious and understandable. It just wasn't everything. "He's the same person to you," Ethan insisted. "He's still the man who raised you. Who loves you. The same man *you* loved."

Faith clenched and unclenched her fists. "I used to think he walked on water. Instead, I discovered he's a liar and a thief. And the worst part of it is, he was the most important person in my life, the one I trusted, and it turns out, I didn't know him at all."

Her pain touched him deeply. But unlike most people, Ethan also understood the other side. "Maybe not, but he's your father," he said again. And the man was alive. She could have the second chance that Ethan would never experience.

"He cost people their livelihood, their houses, and their savings." Even as her voice broke, her eyes flashed angry sparks. "How can I forgive him or deal with him when he did such horrible things?" she asked.

Ethan expelled a long breath of air. He had to at least get her to consider things from a different perspective. "Look, just because I was a pain in the ass, drove my folks crazy, and basically caused their deaths doesn't mean I didn't love them. Or that I don't wish I could do things over again and be there for my brothers. Everyone makes mistakes, Faith."

Her eyes opened wide at his heartfelt admission.

She couldn't be any more shocked than him. He'd meant to encourage her to rethink her feelings. Instead, he'd just laid his soul bare, leaving him raw and exposed.

She pushed herself off the wall and stepped toward him, but he didn't want her comfort. "Ethan, you didn't cause anything."

"I'm not having this conversation," he said, his dark tone warning her off. "This is about you not me."

She held her hands up in surrender. "Okay."

She didn't sound hurt or angry. She just seemed to accept and understand. Considering he'd pushed her to talk, she just scored another point with him, making it too damned easy to like her.

He wanted to retreat.

Instead, he stepped closer and lifted her chin with his hand. "Second chances are rare, Faith. I'll never have one with my parents. And trust me, you don't want to be in my position, wishing things could be different after it's too late."

She blinked once and nodded. "I'll think about what you said," she promised.

"Good." He drew himself up straighter. They needed to

get the hell out of this room and its memories and get down to business. "Time to work."

"Agreed."

They headed downstairs in silence, for which Ethan was grateful. They settled into two folding chairs over a bridge table he used for the kitchen. By the time she'd pulled out her notepad, the tension over their earlier discussion had eased. She peppered him with questions about his taste.

Colors? Anything masculine looking. Era? Contemporary but not stark. Yes, he liked dark wood. Granite in the kitchen was okay. He took her down to the basement and explained his vision for the media room and she approved. They talked about the house for over an hour. It felt more like five minutes.

"This is fantastic." She patted the notebook in her hand. "What I'd like to do is take some time to put together a proposal for each room along with fabric samples and pictures of the furniture pieces for you to look at and approve. Or not. It's fine for me to go back to the drawing board. You're the one who has to live here, so make sure you like everything before you agree."

"Not a problem. You can expect me to speak my mind," he assured her. He'd never done anything else.

"I figured as much. Now about price and commission—"

"Whatever you say is fine with me." He dismissed the issue with a wave of his hand.

"But . . ."

"No buts. I trust you not to rip me off and to take a standard commission."

She opened her mouth and closed it again.

He grinned. "You're speechless. That's a first," he said, amused by her reaction.

She shook her head. "No, I was just going to say that I appreciate your faith in me." Her cheeks were flushed with color, and he liked his ability to both make her happy and rattle her at the same time.

"Have dinner with me." Ethan's words surprised him only because he hadn't thought before speaking.

"I . . ." She bit down on her lower lip again. "I can't. I have other plans."

Cancel them. That's what he wanted to say. If she really had plans.

Unless she was avoiding being alone with him after what happened in her old room earlier. Rationally he knew she *could* have plans. He hadn't given her much notice.

"With Kate? Bring her along." He knew Faith didn't have many other close friends in town. He'd take her with her best friend if it meant he could see her again.

"It's not Kate. It's an . . . old friend."

Something about the way she hesitated told him all he needed to know. "A date?"

She set her jaw. "No. Nick and I have a lot of catching up to do."

Her old high school boyfriend didn't waste any time moving in. And she obviously wanted to go enough not to make an excuse to Nick to go out with him. Ethan was pissed. Logically he knew he was being irrational expecting her to jump at his command.

But his ego and pride weren't going down easily. "Okay, then. I'll see you when your plans are ready. You can call to make an appointment." Knowing he was acting like an asshole and not caring, he reached for a scrap of paper she'd discarded earlier and wrote down his cell.

She accepted the phone number and shoved it into her bag. "You need to drive me home," she reminded him. "Unless you expect me to walk? In which case you can call a cab and I'll put the expense on your unlimited tab." Her voice had turned frosty.

He didn't blame her. He'd closed himself off first. But maybe it was for the best. After all, she was here to do a job and they'd already gotten way too personal. Because Ethan sensed Faith wasn't just a woman he could fuck and walk

away from. And with his track record in life, it would be
nice if he could prove to family he was trustworthy before
he started thinking about a woman.

Serendipity had one restaurant for date night named
Laguna and it was family-style. Nick insisted on picking her
up and taking her there. She agreed, despite the fact that she
wasn't in the mood for company. She and Nick had business
to discuss, including the terms of her lease and moderate
construction work on the store. She hadn't seen the place
yet, but she already knew she'd need shelves at the very
least. And if Nick held any lingering notion that they'd get
back together as a couple, Faith needed to dispel that too.

She didn't dress up, choosing jeans and a simple T-shirt,
careful to keep herself as casual as her intentions. As they
walked into the restaurant, she realized Laguna hadn't changed
in all the years she'd been gone. The place still looked like a
scene from *Lady and the Tramp*, with red and white checker-
board tablecloths, a wine-bottle-shaped candleholder on each
table, and bread sticks in the center. If Nick asked her to share
spaghetti, she was leaving, she thought wryly.

The maître d' greeted Nick, but when he caught sight of
Faith, his welcoming smile turned to a frown. "Your father
should be ashamed," he muttered under his breath as he led
them to the table.

Nick hadn't heard and Faith wasn't about to cause trouble
by mentioning it. She swallowed the painful lump in her
throat, and by the time she was seated across from Nick
she'd managed to calm down. God, she resented the mess
her father had left behind. No wonder her mother secluded
herself in her house, Faith thought. It would have been easier
to just pack up and leave, but it took courage to stay. Maybe
she ought to cut her mother some slack.

"Is everything okay?" Nick asked her, a smile on his face.

"Of course." She forced her attention to her ex-boyfriend,

achingly aware that not only weren't there sparks, but that she also couldn't stop thinking of Ethan—the intense time they'd spent together in her old room and how he'd shut down when she'd said she had plans. But Nick's voice distracted her and she forced herself to concentrate on him.

An hour into dinner, they'd reminisced about high school, discussed the lease, agreed on a fair price that she could pay when her first job brought in income. She was grateful.

They finished their meal with myriad interruptions from people Nick knew and many Faith remembered. Most people were warily friendly to her, whether it was for Nick's sake or genuine, she'd never know. And only a few dropped a snide remark or two about her father. Not bad for a night out on the town.

Nick drove her home and Faith was eager to get inside and be alone. But he insisted on walking her to the door and an uncomfortable feeling settled in the pit of her stomach. She'd managed to keep the conversation friendly throughout the evening, but the gleam in his eyes as they stood by her apartment made her uneasy.

No doubt Nick, with his dark brown wavy hair and his chocolate-colored eyes, was a good-looking guy. Thanks to the construction business and hard manual labor, he'd filled out since high school. Any unattached female would love to have him gaze at them with that interested expression. Any female who hadn't already experienced Ethan Barron's intense gaze and incredible kiss, that is. Just as he had in high school, Ethan had ruined any chance of her developing deeper feelings for Nick.

Lost in thought, Faith didn't see the sudden dip of Nick's head, so his lips on hers caught her by surprise. She didn't want to hurt his feelings. Didn't want to make him feel like an idiot for the attempt.

So she let his mouth linger for a few seconds. She wasn't tempted by his cologne or body heat. His touch was cool and Faith felt nothing. No warmth. No heat. No desire. Nothing like Ethan's kiss, that was for sure.

Without warning, Nick lifted his head and met her gaze, obvious surprise in his expression.

"What?" she asked softly, resisting the urge to touch her sleeve to her lips.

"Honestly?"

She nodded. She didn't want him to be anything but. Because in a matter of minutes she'd be doing the same to him and probably breaking his heart in the process.

"It was . . . nothing. I felt nothing," he said, more than a hint of disappointment in his voice.

Faith blinked, his comment taking her off guard, and suddenly she burst out laughing.

"Should I be insulted?" he asked.

"No!" She placed a comforting hand on his shoulder. "It's just that I didn't feel it either and I was afraid I was going to have to let you down gently. Yet here you are doing it to me." She grinned and wrapped her arms around him in a friendly hug. "God, I'm relieved!" She stepped back and met his gaze.

His smile was grim but accepting. "Whatever happened to us?" he asked. "I mean, one day we were the most popular couple and the next you were a different person. We broke up, drifted apart. I never expected it," he admitted, speaking of their high school days.

She nodded, understanding how her actions back then could have hurt him. "I'm sorry. I just realized that my feelings for you were more about friendship, and at sixteen I didn't know how to tell you. So I froze you out until a breakup was inevitable." She shivered at the memory, recalling how awful she'd felt ignoring him and being cold all because she hadn't been able to get Ethan's kiss out of her mind.

Then or now.

And she couldn't admit the truth to him any more today than she could have back then.

Nick nodded slowly. "I get it now. I was a little dense back then. Couldn't quite understand how you didn't want to be with a studly football player," he said, laughing. "High school. Aren't you glad that time in our lives is over?"

She smiled. "I sure am. Umm, Nick?"

"Yeah?"

"I know what happened tonight is awkward and every-thing, but it's also been . . . cathartic. I feel like now we have the closure we never had before." She drew a deep breath. "What I'm trying to say is, I don't have many friends in town and I'd be really grateful if you remained one of them." She held her breath, waiting for his answer.

Hoping this whole incident hadn't cost her an ally and someone she liked.

He cocked his head to one side. One hand braced against the wall, he studied her as if seeing her for the first time. "I'd be honored to be your friend, Faith."

Relief poured through her. "That's great!"

"I have a project to finish up, but I can schedule one day next week to meet at the store. My sister can let you in to look around in the meantime. Then we can go in and discuss where you want the shelving you mentioned, as well as any potential repainting, carpeting, et cetera."

Faith nodded. "I plan to keep it to a minimum for both my budget and not to take advantage of you and April. You've been so good to me already."

He waved away her concern. "Don't worry about it. Con-sider it a favor for a friend." He winked at her, clearly relieved they'd cleared the air—she wouldn't hold that kiss against him and they could go on with their friendship.

"I guess now that we've cleared the air between us, I'll have to get used to seeing you with other men," he said.

She raised an eyebrow.

"Kidding! As long as any guy treats you right, I'm all for you dating."

She shook her head and laughed. "I'm not ready to date," she admitted.

Yet she'd kissed Ethan. What was it about him, she wondered. The bad-boy charm? The wounded soul inside? A kindred spirit in some sense?

"Earth to Faith." Nick snapped a finger in front of her face.

"Sorry," she said, startled.

"I should let you go in and get some sleep."

She nodded. "I am tired."

They said good night and she let herself inside but knew sleep would be a long time coming, thoughts of Ethan's bottled-up pain and his fathomless dark eyes keeping her tossing, turning, and awake.

A week after Faith had agreed to take on Ethan's job, she met Nick at the storefront. He'd arrived earlier than she had, and by the time she showed up he was already stacking boxes in the corner of her store.

Her store.

He'd provided her with a standard lease a few days earlier and she'd taken it to the man with the most established shingle in town, Richard Kane. Nash Barron was the other lawyer in town and she wouldn't be going to him. Richard had read through it, made a few changes, and negotiated them with Nick. He'd charged a reasonable fee, she felt like she'd protected her interests, and she'd signed on the dotted line.

So here she was, in her store. "What's in those?" she asked, gesturing to the plain brown boxes.

Nick turned to face her. "You tell me. The UPS guy delivered them fifteen minutes ago. They have your name on them."

She raised an eyebrow and strode over. Carstairs Designs' distinctive label stared back at her from the top of the box.

"Recognize the name?"

"Actually, I do. Joel Carstairs is my good friend. He's a decorator and he's way too generous!" she said, her excitement rising. "He promised to send me samples and books to get me started, but this looks like he's sent me enough to stock this place!"

"That's some good friend." His tone held a question with no note of jealousy.

Some time since that disastrous kiss, they'd become more comfortable with each other. Even more than when they'd been boyfriend and girlfriend.

"Joel's a friend. In fact, he's gay, so there's no possibility for anything more," she said, being honest with Nick. "Which has always taken the pressure off, you know?"

He grinned. "Yeah, I do."

"Coffee for the workers!" Kate's voice rang out from the doorway. She strode inside, a cardboard holder in her hands and the now familiar disposable coffee cups inside.

"Oh, you wonderful person, you!" Faith made a beeline for the caffeine.

"Not so wonderful. Bored. I'm a teacher on summer break and I need to be busy! Put me to work, please!"

Faith laughed. "I thought you were volunteering at the youth center."

"Part-time. I'd love to help you!"

Faith eyed her friend, then shrugged. "Okay, but be careful what you wish for. See those boxes over there? I'd love it if you would start unpacking them. Organize them by fabric, wallpaper, whatever different goodies are in those boxes. We'll decide where to put them once Nick finishes his part.

"Yes, boss!" Kate saluted. "What will you two be doing?" she asked.

"Figuring out where to put shelving, hanging some pictures, and ordering a sign for outside—once I figure out a name for this place." Faith studied the walls, envisioning the prints she'd chosen to take with her before leaving New York.

"I'll brainstorm names with you," Kate offered.

"I'd love that. But first"—Faith pointed to the coffee—"which one's mine?"

"Latte for you." Kate handed her one cup, then pulled out another for herself. "Chai tea for me."

"Hey, what about me?" Nick asked.

"Sorry. I didn't know what you drink."

"Regular, dark, no sugar," he said.

Kate narrowed her gaze. "And you want me to what? Go back and pick you up a cup?"

"Well, since you offered . . ." He treated her to an endearing grin.

Or one Faith would have found endearing if she were interested in Nick. She wasn't. But suddenly she wondered if her best friend could be.

"Well, I'm not serving. But if you'll be here tomorrow, maybe I'll remember to pick up something for you. If you're nice to me."

"For coffee and a pretty woman, I can be on my best behavior."

Faith glanced at Kate, who flushed before turning away and heading over to the boxes.

"What's up with that?" she asked Nick. "You two went to high school together and you've never teased her like that before."

He shrugged. "I don't know. It just happened."

Faith would love for it to *just happen* again, but she kept her thoughts—that they'd make a cute couple—to herself.

"Okay, let's get to work," he said.

Faith nodded.

For the next hour, they each had their jobs. Kate unloaded the boxes, sorting, resorting, and making piles of the books and other supplies Joel had sent over. Then Faith and Nick talked shelving and paint and he headed to the hardware store to pick up supplies. Faith took the time to call the local florist and order a thank-you bouquet to be delivered to Joel. She helped Kate with the sample books and together they sketched out a more detailed plan for where everything should go. Faith had already ordered pieces to stock in her shop that she could use as decorative accents until they sold.

Nick returned with picture hooks and the shelving units she'd requested, and he got to work measuring the wall space and planning where things would go.

The next few days comprised working to get the store ready to open. Kate suggested a simple business name: "FAITH'S!" Storefront sign ordered, Faith turned her focus to business cards and letterhead.

She brought her laptop to the store and was waiting for Nick to come by to help her set up the wireless modem the phone company had sent over. It still irked her that she couldn't figure it out on her own, and she decided to try once more. She called the phone company's toll-free number and followed the computerized voice instructions telling her to shut down the computer, unplug the modem from the wall, then from the computer. She was then instructed to plug in both again and to reboot. No luck.

The annoying voice then told her to make sure she had the serial number of the modem ready for the next available operator. The modem was plugged in beneath the desk and out of view. Placing a pen and pad on the floor, she bent down beneath the desk in a futile attempt to get the serial number without any light.

"Hello?" Nick's voice called out.

"Under here!"

His footsteps sounded as he walked around the desk. "Mind if I ask what you're doing?"

"Trying to get the serial number on the modem," she muttered.

"I said I'd be here to help you!"

"Well, I wanted to figure it out myself." Suddenly aware that her position on all fours beneath the desk exposed her lace underwear (and thank God she hadn't worn a thong), she began to back out of the uncomfortable, small spot she'd wedged herself into.

"Let me help."

She felt Nick's hand on her waist at the same time she heard Ethan's dark voice. "Anyone want to tell me what I'm interrupting?"

Faith didn't know whether to laugh or cry at the absurdity of the situation. She did know she had a situation on her hands.

Ethan should have walked out while he had the chance. When he strode into the small store, expecting to find Faith, he hadn't anticipated discovering her beneath the desk with Nick Mancini bending over her. And though there was probably a good explanation, he couldn't stop the jealousy that exploded inside his head, despite the fact that he had no hold over her and no right at all to be jealous.

Right or not, he heard his voice through a haze. "Anyone want to tell me what I'm interrupting?"

Ignoring Ethan, Nick placed his hands around Faith's waist and helped her up from beneath the desk.

She rose, brushed her half-lifted, extremely short skirt farther down on her legs and met his gaze. "Modem troubles," she said with a too-bright smile.

"And really, what's it to you?" Nick stepped in front of Faith, in male protective mode.

Ethan clenched his jaw, no desire to get into a pissing match with the man. "I didn't know I answered to you, Mancini."

"I take it you two know each other?" Faith rushed around Nick and inserted herself directly between the two men.

"I know he's trouble," Nick muttered, crossing his arms across his chest.

"You don't know a damn thing about me," Ethan said.

"I know that you—"

"Nick, stop." Faith put a hand on Nick's arm, halting whatever words he'd been about to hurl at Ethan midsentence.

At the sight of her hand on the other man's skin, a burning sensation spread through Ethan's gut.

Faith glanced up at Nick. "Ethan and I have business. And we're *friends*. So even though you mean well, you need to back off." She shot Nick a warning glare.

Friends, huh? Ethan had a bone to pick with that description. After the kiss they'd shared in her apartment, he wanted to be a helluva lot more. In the week since he'd seen or heard from her, her silence had him twisted in knots. Like a teenage guy wanting to get into a girl's pants, he couldn't stop thinking of her. Except even as a teen, no girl had denied him what he wanted.

Except this one.

There was that unfinished business between them, rising up to tease, tempt, and torment him.

"I hope you remember his reputation," Nick said, his face flushed. Clearly he didn't like being told to back down.

"People change." Faith spoke with more certainty about Ethan than he felt about himself.

He appreciated her efforts, but he didn't need Faith fighting his battles. And she didn't need him provoking Mancini in her store either and decided now would be the time to ignore the other man completely.

"I brought a down payment for the work on the house. I figured it would help you get started," Ethan said.

"Thank you!" She was obviously, pleasantly surprised.

They hadn't spoken about contracts, pricing, or anything specific, but he knew she had limited funds and he wanted to help her any way he could.

Nick stood watching them both like an overprotective brother. Or boyfriend.

Faith cleared her throat. "Nick, do you want to get to work on the modem? Ethan and I have business to discuss."

Her look told Nick any more comments about Ethan wouldn't be welcome.

Ethan wanted to applaud, but that would only set off things between him and Mancini again.

Nick's scowl indicated exactly how he felt. "Tell you what. I have to check on my crew at one of my sights, so how about I just stop by later to set up the modem?" he asked, his gaze on Faith.

She nodded. "That would be great. Thank you."

"I'm pretty good with electronics, so why don't you call first?" Ethan suggested. "She might not need your help after all."

Nick's shoulders and jaw tensed. "Just be careful." He slid a glare Ethan's way, then kissed Faith on the cheek and headed out of the store.

After he'd gone, Ethan realized his hands were still clenched into tight fists over that kiss, one no doubt meant to piss Ethan off.

And it had.

He forced himself to relax before meeting Faith's gaze.

Her hair was tousled and messy from her stint under the desk, her cheeks flushed, and desire licked through him, the flame burning hotter inside him now that they were alone.

"Sorry about that. Nick was a little too overprotective," she said.

He raised an eyebrow. "A little? The man wants you for himself."

"Actually, he doesn't. We settled that question already." The color in her cheeks deepened, giving away way too much information.

"Settled it *how*?" he asked, his voice a low growl.

She perched her hands on her hips. "Frankly, that's none of your business."

She was right. That didn't make the need for answers go away. "Okay, what about us? You and me? Is that any of my business?"

She opened her mouth and closed it again.

"I'll take that as a yes." He stepped in closer until he felt her body heat and inhaled her intoxicating scent. "So tell me something. You told Nick we were *friends.*"

She didn't back down or break eye contact. "I thought we were."

"Do you kiss all your friends like you kissed me?"

Her tongue darted out and swept across her lips. "I was drunk."

"I remember. So maybe we need to clarify things again now that you're not," he said, dipping his head and capturing her lips in a kiss.

Seven

Faith wasn't drunk or tipsy and she'd remember everything about *this* kiss. Ethan cupped his hands over her cheeks, holding her head in place while he thoroughly devoured her mouth. At the first touch of his tongue to her lips, she let out a moan and couldn't find it in herself to be embarrassed.

He felt too good.

He ran his tongue back and forth over the seam of her lips until she couldn't stand it another second and opened to let him inside. Eager to taste him, she slid her tongue over his, and the next groan came from deep in his chest. She took a heady pleasure from the effect she had on him, from knowing she wasn't in this crazy web of desire alone.

And understanding it was equal, she wound her arms around his neck, kissing him back and pressing her needy body against his, seeking closer contact. Since the night he'd brought her home, she hadn't been able to get him out of her mind, her thoughts, or her dreams. And this is what she'd been dreaming about since last time.

Him.

Her.

Their bodies locked together tight.

He pulled her closer, her breasts pressed tight against his chest, his hard erection wedged between their bodies. Her heart pounded harder. Her desire for him grew, the emptiness inside her yearning to be filled. As if he knew, he levered one knee between her legs, raising his thigh so he applied weight at just the right spot, pumping his leg up and down, building the pressure inside her until waves of sensation crested and eased, crested and eased.

She clenched her fists in the back of his shirt, bunching the material, silently begging him not to stop.

He murmured coaxing words, urging her on as his lips trailed moist, wet kisses over her cheek, her throat, reaching her collarbone where he paused to graze at her skin. One part of Faith was lost in sensation, another part unable to believe she was riding his leg seeking an orgasm he seemed intent on giving. She arched her back, thrusting her pelvis forward with the same rhythm he'd found, enabling her to grind into his hard, unyielding leg. Suddenly she was close, panting and closing her eyes as the brightest stars exploded behind her lids, taking her entire body along for a ride that never seemed to end.

As the sensations ebbed and reality came back, Faith realized what she'd just done.

And what he hadn't.

And she knew she wasn't prepared to open her eyes and deal with him just yet. Not when her underwear was damp and her body still quaked with little after shocks. Not when she felt warm and sated and while she still clung to him.

Slowly she loosened her grip on his shirt. Even more slowly she forced her eyelids open. Just as she'd expected, he stared at her with those deep, fathomless eyes.

"Was it good for you?" A sensual smile raised the corners of his mouth, but unfulfilled desire still pulsed in his gaze.

"It was okay." She couldn't hold back a grin of her own. They both knew it had been spectacular.

A pulse still pounded in the base of his throat, and she wanted to lean in and kiss him there. Somehow she refrained.

"Have dinner with me tonight," he said, his tone indicating this time he wouldn't take no for an answer.

She swallowed hard, knowing that *this time* dinner would involve a lot more than just food. There was so much unfinished between them, not just from this interlude but because there was so much more about him she wanted to explore. He might not be a bad boy anymore, but to her he was still the rebel in her dreams and she wanted to find out just how good it could be between them.

Any why not? She was single. He was single.

"Okay."

A mixture of surprise and relief flickered across his handsome face. "Not going to make me work for it this time?" He brushed her hair off her cheek.

"I think you just did." She ducked her head in embarrassment, putting space between them.

But his laughter followed her as she attempted to pull herself together, though she knew she'd spend the rest of the day looking as frazzled as she felt.

She finally met his gaze. "Thank you for the check," she said, bringing him back to what really had brought him here. "It wasn't necessary since we haven't even agreed on anything yet."

He raised an eyebrow. "How about I wanted an excuse to see you?"

Pleasure wrapped around her at the admission. "Well, if you aren't comfortable, you can hang on to the money until you see and approve my ideas."

His hand came down on her shoulder. "Here's the check." He reached into his pocket and handed her a folded piece of paper. "Cash it and don't argue, okay?"

She nodded. "Thanks." Joel was allowing her to use his

name and credit with key accounts until she'd established herself, but the cash infusion would allow her to set up credit on her own. " I've been working on some ideas I can show you tonight."

"Sounds good. Instead of going out, why don't you come over? I know Rosalita would love to cook for you." His eyes twinkled with mischief.

She shook her head and laughed. "You know I can't turn down one of her home-cooked meals." And he didn't hesitate to use it to get his way.

"Then I'll pick you up at seven." He started for the door and she raised her hand in a silent wave.

What in the world was she doing? Faith asked herself once she was alone. She was single for the first time as an adult. She barely knew who she was and what she wanted out of life. For a woman coming off an ugly divorce and not interested in a relationship with any man, she seemed to be diving into *something* with Ethan Barron way too fast.

By the time Ethan picked up Faith and she returned to the house, Rosalita was long gone. She'd left a set table and dinner ready to be served, something Ethan did an admirable job of handling on his own.

Faith was impressed.

There was something inherently sexy about a man at ease with serving a woman dinner. Of course there was something even more sexy about the man himself. He wore a simple white short-sleeved collared polo shirt and a pair of khaki-colored pants, yet she couldn't tear her gaze away. There was nothing simple about the way he filled out the clothes either.

As delicious as the paella tasted—she'd always loved Rosalita's signature dish of Spanish rice and seafood, she could barely concentrate on what she was eating. She was distracted by Ethan and thoughts of what they could very easily end up doing together after they finished the meal.

Despite the easy flow of conversation, she couldn't help noticing that he was preoccupied too, only with what seemed like more than just the company.

Like right now.

They'd finished eating, but he turned his fork over and over, lost in thought.

"What's going on?" she asked at last.

He glanced up, meeting her gaze. "What do you mean?"

"Up here." She pointed to her head. "Every once in a while, I lose you. What's got you so preoccupied?"

He treated her to an apologetic grin. "A business problem that I shouldn't have brought with me to dinner."

She shrugged, unconcerned. "Obviously you couldn't leave it at the office. So? What's going on? Sometimes if you put it out there, it's easier to forget about for a while."

He groaned and leaned back in his chair, bracing his hands behind his head. "You know I'm in weapons software development, right?"

She nodded.

"Well, I'm working on a bid for a new government contract. Both the software and the bid itself are proprietary. But someone's funneling information to my competitor."

"Ahh. That explains your distraction."

"Don't tell me you thought I wasn't interested in you . . ." He snagged her gaze and the heat in his eyes promised her that wasn't the case.

"No, I think we've already established that you are." She felt the blush rush to her cheeks. "I just figured something important was bothering you."

"I appreciate your asking."

And she was grateful for any insight into who he was, what he did for a living, anything that made him tick. Up till now, he'd been closed about himself and she was curious.

"So tell me. How'd you get into weapons development of all things?" she asked.

He leaned forward in his chair. "Didn't know I had the brains, did you?"

She grinned. "Hey, I didn't say that. Now spill."

Ethan laughed, seemingly more relaxed than he'd been all evening. "Let's see. I didn't last six months on my own. I woke up on a park bench one day and realized I was on the road to nowhere. I passed an army recruiting center, walked in, and signed up."

"You were in the army?" she asked, stunned. She couldn't see the younger version of Ethan succumbing to anyone's rules.

"You sound surprised. What's wrong? Don't see me obeying orders?" He chuckled.

She shook her head. "That's an understatement." He was so on target he might just be reading her thoughts.

"The army was exactly what I needed. Someone had to kick my ass and get me to shape up. I actually got a scholarship through their ROTC program. Uncle Sam paid for my education and I gave him three years."

She blinked, looking at him in a whole new light. "So you finished your military obligation, what? Three years ago?"

"Exactly. Luckily for me I was a computer simulation gaming freak. Bet you didn't know that about me either."

He winked at her and her stomach curled into a delicious knot.

"Anyway," he continued, oblivious to the sexual sparks he'd fired up with that one wink. "The army put my skills to good use, so I ended up at a military base Stateside. In my free time, I started working up weapons software specs."

"Wow."

He shrugged. "I know it sounds nuts, but this stuff comes naturally to me. But I needed to support myself, so after my tour was up, I took a job at Lockheed Martin. Heard of them?"

"Yes, but I couldn't tell you what they do," she admitted. Leaning forward on her hands, she waited for him to continue his story. His history was fascinating to her and she wanted more.

"Lockheed is a global security and tech info company, but by then I'd had it with rules and regulations."

She grinned. "Big shock."

"Exactly. It wasn't a good fit so I turned independent. Luckily I had connections and I'd already been working privately on a system that would revolutionize the capabilities of our country's next fleet of military jets. An old army buddy turned up and together we nailed the glitches in my software. Dale Conway and I started Magnum, our weapons software development company. We secured our first government contract, and bingo. Here I am." His hand swept around the house with pride.

Until he met her gaze and obviously remembered from whom he'd bought the house. The house and the moment clearly reminded her of their change in status. They were still far apart on the food chain, they'd just reversed positions.

His expression sobered and he cleared his throat.

"So you and Dale are still partners?" she asked, eager to return to his past before he could hop onto her own.

With the way he'd skipped over the year his parents died, he wasn't so keen on delving into painful history either. Hopefully he'd take the hint and keep discussing himself.

"Nope. I had to buy him out pretty quickly after we made the government deal. Dale wasn't always the stablest nut in the tree," he explained.

She nodded, taking it all in. "And where's your main office?"

"Manhattan and a smaller base in D.C. But with the wonders of technology and FedEx, I can work from here just as easily."

"I'm impressed," she said, referring to his success. Regardless of the fact that he now lived here—and she didn't—he'd made something of himself on his own.

"Thanks. But frankly, until my brothers come around, these kinds of accomplishments don't mean as much."

Having seen how one of his brothers treated him, she understood. As much as she wanted to question the dynamics of his relationship with them and why he blamed himself for so much, she knew better. Bringing it up would only ruin the comfortable byplay between them, and she was selfish enough to want him at ease with her.

"They will. Now that you're here, they'll come to see how much you've changed. Not that you were so bad to begin with," she said with complete honesty.

He eyed her with wonder. "Why do you do that?" he asked.

"Do what?"

He pulled his chair closer, so their knees touched as he looked into her eyes. "Try so damn hard to see the best in me?" he asked gruffly.

She blinked, taken off guard by the question. Why did she? "I don't know."

All she knew was what she felt—and those feelings extended back ten long years—to when she'd taken that bike ride because she'd wanted to know him better. And to a kiss she'd never been able to forget.

"Whatever the reason, I'm grateful."

She swallowed hard. "I don't want your gratitude." She wanted more.

His eyes darkened, making her wonder if he was somehow able to read her mind again.

She'd always felt a secret connection to him that made her want to believe he was good despite what the rest of the world thought. What *he* thought. She hadn't turned him down ten years ago because of him, she'd turned him down because of herself. She hadn't been ready.

Now she was.

They were both adults, both wanted sex without making apologies for it. She just wasn't ready to invest her heart, but he wasn't asking for it. From all the signals he'd sent so far, he had sex on his mind.

"So what do you want?" His compelling gaze, his taut expression all told her he already knew.

She swallowed hard. "I want you."

"That's what I hoped you'd say." He leaned in and his mouth touched hers.

Want, need, desire, all the things she'd been missing for so long, collided inside her. His lips lingered, a teasing torment, a prelude for what was to come.

Then, suddenly, chimes rang out, and she knew his kiss wasn't setting off these particular bells. They were too familiar. "Doorbell," she whispered against his lips.

Ethan muttered a low growl, followed by a curse. No one in this damned town even liked him. "Who the hell would come ringing my doorbell now?"

He stood and Faith rose with him.

"Might as well see." She sounded as disappointed as he was with the interruption.

"Whoever that is, I'll get rid of them." He grabbed her hand and headed for the door.

Now that he had her in his home, ready and willing, no way would he allow some visitor he couldn't give a damn about to stop them from finishing what they'd started.

He reached the large wood door and opened it wide. In front of him stood a stranger, a woman about his own age, maybe a few years younger. "Can I help you?" he asked, not bothering to hide his irritation.

The woman, a brunette, glanced back over her shoulder. "Tess. Get over here now."

Tess?

Ethan didn't know anyone by the name of Tess.

Suddenly a teenage girl—a sullen teenage girl—stepped up beside the other woman. Folding her arms across her chest, Tess glared at Ethan, looking no happier to see him than he was to find either of the women on his doorstep.

He braced one hand on the doorframe. "I don't know who you are or what you want, but it's not a good time." Ethan started to swing the door closed.

"Just see what they want," Faith suggested from behind him.

He had no choice. The older of the two had shoved her sneakered foot in front of the door, preventing him from shutting her out anyway.

"Not so fast. I'm Kelly Moss and this is my sister . . . well, my half sister, Tess. Tess is your sister too."

Ethan narrowed his gaze. "Hey, lady, I don't know what kind of scam you're running, but I can assure you I don't have a sister."

Two brothers who wanted nothing to do with him? Yeah, he had those. "There are no females in my family, so you can go find some other sucker to play."

The teen just glared, looking for all the world as if she didn't give a shit about whatever was going on around her. Having perfected that facade once, Ethan had a hunch there was a helluva lot more going on beneath the mask of indifference. Not that he cared. No way was she his sister.

The brunette rolled her eyes. "Not everything in life is about money. Does the name Leah Moss sound familiar?" She was nothing if not persistent.

"No." He was tempted to swing the door shut again when the name suddenly rang a bell. "Wait." He searched back in time until he finally remembered why. "My father's secretary," he said.

An uneasy feeling crept up Ethan's spine as childhood memories came flooding back. His father being away on business, arguments behind closed doors when his dad had been home and in town. An awareness that things between his parents weren't quite right and the fear his family unit might be falling apart.

"Bingo." The woman snapped her finger in the air. "Leah Moss is our mother." She gestured back and forth between herself and the teen, who, Ethan realized, had short black hair with a streak of purple in the front.

"And what's that got to do with me?" Ethan asked.

Behind him, he felt Faith step closer, offering silent support, as if she shared his unease.

"Tess's father died when she was four." The woman deliberately paused. "Ten years ago."

Ethan's mouth grew dry.

"Like your father did, right?" the woman asked.

Ethan clenched his jaw. "So you did your research. Everyone in this town knows about that."

"I didn't have to dig further than this." She pulled a piece of paper from her purse. "Tess's birth certificate naming your old man as her father. My mother had no reason to lie."

And though Ethan had no reason to believe her, he'd always known his family hadn't come from a Normal Rockwell painting. As the oldest, he'd been keenly aware of his father's absence; Ethan's early troubles had been an attempt to get his father's attention, keep him home with his family more. Not that his extreme behavior had worked.

Ethan stared from the woman to the teen she claimed was his sister. *Had* Mark Barron been having an affair with his secretary? Ethan had overheard his mother accuse his dad of fooling around. Mark and Alicia Barron hadn't had the best marriage, and Mark sure as hell wouldn't be the first man to knock up his secretary.

"Where is your mother?" Ethan asked.

The woman shrugged. "Your guess is as good as mine. We haven't heard from her in almost a year. Tess came home from school one day to a note telling her she ran off with some man."

The teen didn't flinch at her sister's description. Her walls were damned high, Ethan thought.

"I'm sorry," he said, meaning it. "It's a sad story. But if you're looking for a handout . . ."

The brunette pinned him with a disgusted glare.

Behind him, Faith poked him in the back. Obviously neither was happy with his assessment.

"Look, I don't need your money. Tess here doesn't need your money. What Tess needs is a firm, guiding hand. A male guiding hand. Look at her."

Ethan's gaze traveled back to the girl. The shrubbery lighting that lit up the path gave him a solid view and for the first time, he really looked. Black T-shirt, black pants, black combat boots, along with the black hair, added to the overall look. A step closer revealed that black eyeliner ringed her eyes and she had a ring piercing her eyebrow.

"From your stunned expression, I see you finally realize what I've been dealing with." The brunette looked none too pleased to have made her point.

And the uneasy feeling in Ethan's gut returned, magnified.

"She's out of control—drinking, smoking, running with a dangerous crowd, and I can't handle her anymore. I definitely can't work and raise a rebellious teenager. I have a job to get back to, so it's your turn."

"Excuse me?"

"I said it's your turn. Step up and play big brother. I'll come back at the end of the summer before school starts and we'll figure out what to do next. In the meantime, get to know each other and see if you can handle her any better than I can."

Ethan clenched and unclenched his fists. She couldn't possibly mean to leave the girl here. "Just because your mother wrote my father's name down on a piece of paper doesn't make it true."

Faith groaned.

"I told you this was a fucking mistake." Tess folded her arms over her chest defensively.

Ethan winced. Even as the words spewed from his mouth, he *knew* he was out of line, especially to say it in front of the kid. But he just wanted this mess to go away.

"I figured you'd say that." Only the older sister hadn't reacted to Ethan's words. "Luckily for you, my mother was smart enough to grab some of his DNA," she said. "Toothbrush," she continued before he could ask. "She had the tests run. I had them repeated." She handed him another envelope from her purse. "Read it and weep."

He wanted to.

Because if her story was true, Tess *was* his sibling. Another person he'd deprived of a parent. Another person he owed for his past mistakes. And she looked pretty screwed up too.

He met the brunette's gaze. "Look . . . what did you say your name was again?" He winced as he spoke.

"Kelly Moss, but the only name you have to concern yourself with is Tess." As if from nowhere, the older sister produced a large duffel bag from the darkness and tossed it onto his front step.

"Kelly." Ethan heard the apology in his tone. Hopefully she'd caught it too. "You took me off guard. Come on in and we'll talk about this, okay?" He reluctantly gestured for them to come inside.

His chance at being alone with Faith had long since been shot to hell, but he still wasn't ready for the responsibility Kelly Moss intended for him to take.

She shook her head. "Nope. Took me over an hour to drive here from the city. I have a long drive back so I can be at work in the morning. But Tess would be more than happy to come inside, right, Tess?" She stepped closer to the teen and nudged her in the back.

"Bite me," the girl said in a clearly pissed tone.

She glanced at Ethan. "*You* can get her to come inside. Oh, and one more thing? Her juvenile probation officer knows she's going to be living with you. His name is on here." She held out a card.

Stunned, Ethan couldn't make his hand move.

Faith accepted the card for him.

"Make sure you check in with the man," Kelly said.

"Probation officer?" he finally blurted out, feeling as if he were in a nightmare from which he couldn't wake up.

Without warning, the woman abruptly turned and hugged the teenager—the first sign that she cared since Ethan had opened the door.

When she spoke, her voice quivered. "Be good. Be smart . . . smarter anyway, and be safe. I love you. I'll call you every night, okay? And I'll see you at the end of the summer."

The teen stood with her arms stiff at her sides. She didn't return the hug or utter a word in reply, but suddenly Ethan knew that for Kelly, dumping her sister on his doorstep hadn't been easy. In fact, it suddenly seemed like a desperate last-ditch effort on the girl's behalf.

But that made her Ethan's problem and damned if he knew what to do with a hostile teenager, and a girl no less. He'd barely survived those years himself.

Ethan suddenly had a family crisis on his hands. Which meant, he realized, he needed to call a family meeting. He nearly laughed aloud at the absurdity of that thought. He and his brothers were far from being a family, but with this new sister, Nash and Dare would have no choice but to come over and deal with the new family reality.

Whether they wanted to or not.

Eight

Faith stood in the empty living room area of Ethan's house, her mind whirling with all that had occurred. On top of the obvious—Ethan had a troubled sister dumped on his doorstep—Faith realized he also had an empty house that needed furniture much faster than either of them had thought.

He strode back into the room, cell phone in hand, his expression tight.

"Are they coming?" Faith asked about his brothers.

He'd called them both. She'd heard him explaining that they needed to come over, that it was important. She'd forced Tess into the kitchen when an argument seemed imminent. Forced because Tess hadn't wanted to move, not when asked politely and not when ordered to do it either. Only when Faith had told her she could come and eat now or starve for the rest of the night had the teen stomped her way into the kitchen, where she'd refused to engage in any conversation at all.

Ethan's jaw tightened. "Yeah. Once I told them it wasn't about me, they each agreed to show up."

Ouch. "At least they're coming."

Faith had stood by his side during the revelation about Tess and kept her busy while Ethan placed calls to his siblings. She'd done what she could. But she couldn't imagine how difficult he found this whole situation, and he didn't need her observing his family drama any further.

"Where's Tess?" he asked.

Faith glanced at him. Exhaustion was evident in the lines around his eyes and she had a hunch it was about to get worse.

"She's in the kitchen. I gave her some of Rosalita's finest," she said, leaving out the details about how rude, obstinate, and difficult the girl had been. He'd learn soon enough.

Faith placed a hand on his shoulder, finding it difficult to believe that just a little while ago, she thought they'd be heading up to his bedroom. "I really should get going before your brothers get here."

"Why?" he asked.

"Seriously? Because it's going to be difficult enough to break the news to them without a stranger in the midst."

"We're all strangers," he muttered. "And I'd like you to stay." He reached out and clasped her hand.

She wondered if there was a hint of desperation in the request when without warning he spun her toward him. "Do not for one minute think I forgot about what we were about to do before we were interrupted." The heat in his gaze promised her he hadn't.

Her body trembled at the thought of being with him. "I haven't forgotten either."

But she had a hunch he wouldn't be free to act on his sex life for a while. A pang of disappointment followed that thought.

"Are you sure you want me here?" she asked.

"Positive." He dipped his head for a quick kiss.

"Eew!"

Faith flung herself out of his arms.

"Get a room." Tess stomped in, further making her presence known.

"Jesus, kid. Relax," Ethan said.

"Did you finish dinner?" Faith asked her.

Tess bit her nails before finally muttering an answer. "Yeah."

"Did you put your plate and things into the sink?" Faith automatically asked.

Tess braced her hands on her hips and cocked her head to one side. "No. I left it next to both of yours on the table. Are you telling me a place like this doesn't have a maid?"

Ethan expelled a long breath of air.

At least he was showing restraint and patience, something he'd need for the long haul, Faith thought.

When the doorbell rang, Ethan's knowing gaze met hers. She wondered if he considered his brothers a reprieve from being alone with Tess or more like being in front of a firing squad. Neither possibility appealed.

"I'll be right back," Ethan said, heading for the door.

Faith turned to face the girl. "That's probably your other brothers," she explained. "There are two more of them."

"Big whoop." Tess folded her arms and glanced around. "So what's with this place? It's like a goddamn empty museum."

Faith bit the inside of her cheek. "Ethan just moved in."

"What happened? He spent all his money on the house and couldn't afford furniture?" Tess returned to gnawing on her nails.

Black chipped polish, Faith noted. Lovely.

"Faith." Ethan stood in the doorway, his two brothers waiting behind him. "Can you hold down the fort in here?" Ethan asked. "I need to talk to them first."

She nodded, forcing a bright smile. "We'll be fine," she promised him.

I owe you. He mouthed the words.

She grinned, deciding it might be nice to make him pay.

* * *

Ethan led his brothers into the kitchen, the only other place in the house with furniture other than his room. The tension was so thick he could slice it, but there was a kid in the next room who needed them to pull it together like a family.

He set his jaw, counted to ten, and turned to face his younger siblings.

"What's so important that we had to show up when you snap your fingers?" Nash, the middle brother asked.

Unlike Dare who, along with Ethan, had inherited their father's dark hair, Nash favored their mother, his coloring and hair lighter.

Ethan braced his hand over the back of a chair and met his brothers' gazes. "There's no easy way to say this, so I'll get right to the point. There's a teenage girl in the other room. Her name's Tess, and I just found out she's our sister."

Both men looked at Ethan as if he'd lost his mind. Sometime in the last hour, he figured he definitely had.

"Remember Leah Moss, Dad's secretary?" Ethan asked. Nash nodded.

"Sort of," Dare said. As the youngest, he'd find it the hardest to remember.

"Well, according to the woman who dropped off Tess on my doorstep, and this piece of paper, we all share the same father." He held out the envelope that held the DNA test and birth certificate Kelly had given him.

"You're saying Dad had an affair?" Dare asked, sounding appalled, angry, and disbelieving all at once.

"I'm not saying it. This paper is." He waved it in the air once more.

Nash, the attorney, grabbed the envelope, pulled out the papers, and did a quick examination. "Could be forged. I'll check it out."

Ethan nodded. "Good. In the meantime, assuming it's

all real"—and Ethan's gut told him it was—"Tess is here and she's ours."

"Who dropped her off?" Dare asked.

"A woman named Kelly Moss. Says she's her sister. Leah Moss is her mother too."

"And what kind of sister drops a kid off with a stranger and leaves?" Nash asked.

Ethan had wondered that himself—until he'd seen the hug and flash of tears in the other woman's eyes. "The kind who can't handle her anymore." Exhausted, Ethan ran a hand through his hair. "Prepare yourselves. Our little sister is a pain in the ass."

More like an out-of-control juvenile delinquent, but let his brothers see for themselves. "Kelly said it's time for me to step up and play big brother." He deliberately paused for impact. "Which means it's time for all of us to do the same."

"What you're really saying is she's *our* problem because you don't plan on being there for her any more than you were there for us." Having said his piece, Dare narrowed his gaze, his expression bordering on disgust.

Ethan bit the inside of his cheek to keep from hitting his own brother. "What I'm saying is that she'll be living here with me. You two ought to meet her. And since you both have such strong views on someone who'd bail on a kid, I'm assuming you'll be around for her too."

That seemed to silence the duo for the time being, so Ethan continued. "Consider my house your house. Come by when you can. The kid's a mess. She needs all three of us."

Nash's expression changed from suspicious to merely wary while Dare looked at Ethan like he wasn't sure what to make of him and didn't want to bother figuring it out. Which had all been well and good *before* Tess had entered the picture.

"She's in the living room. Are you coming to meet her?"

The two men glanced at each other and nodded.

"Let's go." Ethan headed for the other room without bothering to make sure they followed.

He entered the living room and found Faith pacing, Tess leaning against the wall, her expression hostile and bored. He wasn't buying it. She'd just been dropped off on his doorstep and didn't know a damn thing about him. She had to be scared and intimidated, not that she'd show it. The kid had perfected the defensive wall she'd put up around herself.

He met Faith's gaze for a quick second, grateful she'd stayed, that he had one ally in what felt like a viper pit, not a family gathering.

"Tess, this is Nash and Andrew. Everyone calls him Dare." Ethan pointed out each brother.

The three of them stared at each other. Ethan wondered if they'd noticed that beneath the black eyeliner, Tess's blue eyes resembled their father's.

Nash stepped up first. "Hi, Tess," he said awkwardly.

"Where are you from?" Dare asked her.

She set her jaw and refused to reply.

"Tess, say hello to your brothers," Faith said into the silence.

The girl glared. "Hello, brothers."

Since the little hellion wasn't going to cooperate, Ethan decided to focus on the adults. "And Faith Harrington, these are my brothers, Nash and Dare." Again, he gestured between the three.

"Harrington?" Nash asked.

Faith straightened her shoulders. "Yes, Harrington," she said in her most formal—wary—voice.

Shit, Ethan thought. *Now what?* "I'm assuming you remember each other from high school?" He strove for familiar ground.

"I know who she is." Dare stepped forward and shook her hand. "I heard you were back in town."

She nodded.

"I heard too." Nash didn't bother with a polite handshake. Instead, he crossed his arms over his chest. "From my clients," he added coldly.

Faith pasted a smile on her face, one Ethan recognized as forced. "And what clients would those be?" she asked too sweetly.

Nash had already thrown the first punch. Faith was readying her defense.

"I'm an attorney. I represent the people in this town your father screwed over." His brother's arrogant gaze raked her over. "Hardworking people who didn't deserve to lose their homes or their retirement funds. People like my adopted parents."

Ethan shook his head in disbelief. If asked, he'd have said the night couldn't possibly have gone further downhill.

"Oh man, you're a *lawyer*?" Tess asked in disgust. "And what does this one do for a living?" She jerked a finger Dare's way.

"I'm a cop." Dare met her gaze, almost challenging her to comment.

"Fucking swell."

"Watch your mouth," all three brothers said at the same time.

At least we agree on something, Ethan thought.

Tess leaned back against the wall, her face once again a sullen pout.

Nash stepped closer to Ethan. "You asked me to come and I did. But this is a family matter, so what's she doing here?" He tipped his head at Faith.

She flushed red. Anger or embarrassment, Ethan couldn't be certain. By the way she folded her arms inward, she was definitely hurt.

Ethan had forgiven his brothers their bad attitudes toward him. He wouldn't allow them to treat Faith the same way. "Who is she? She's my guest and my friend, and I expect you to treat her with respect. She's as much a victim as your clients, so back off." It was the first time he'd raised his voice at his brothers since his return.

Damn, it felt good.

Faith shifted from foot to foot. "I told you I should have left earlier." She started for the door, when suddenly Tess darted around the room and stopped her.

"Hey. Don't leave me with them!" Her voice trembled. "I don't know them and who knows what'll happen to me here?" She faced Faith, treating her to the first expression of emotion they'd seen.

Damned if it wasn't panic. Ethan couldn't decide if this was an act or if she really was afraid of being alone in the house.

With him.

"You don't know me either," Faith reminded the girl. But she grasped Tess by the shoulders and met her gaze. "They're your brothers and you need to get to know them. It might actually be kind of nice having older brothers, not that I'd know. But you should give them a chance."

"Yeah, but one's a cop and the other's a lawyer! And I don't know what *he* does"—she pointed to Ethan—"but it's probably something else I'll hate," she muttered, back to angry and moody once more.

"For a kid with her own juvenile probation officer, you should be glad to have a cop and a lawyer on your side."

"A what?" Dare shouted at Tess.

Ethan shrugged. "I don't know the details on that either. Her sister dropped the bomb along with the guy's card. That's something else we need to get information on."

"I'm a cop and she's a juvenile delinquent." Dare let out a choking sound.

"He's a laugh riot," Tess muttered. "Fine. So go on. You ditch me too," she said to Faith. "Story of my life."

Faith studied the girl, as if trying to figure her out. Finally she dug into her bag and handed her what looked like a business card. "My cell number's on here. If they give you any trouble, call me, okay?"

Tess bit down on one of her nails before grabbing the card. "Whatever."

"I'll call you tomorrow to talk about the decorating," she said to Ethan, obviously ready to leave.

"You don't have to go." Ethan refused to let Nash run her out.

"Yes, I do." Faith looked at Nash, who didn't ask her to stay.

His brother was a fool. From what Ethan could tell, Faith might be the only one who could get through to Tess. Not to mention that Ethan wasn't finished with Faith, despite the fact that their night had imploded hours ago.

But she clearly no longer wanted to be here and he didn't blame her. "I'll walk you out." Ethan turned to his now *three* siblings. "Can I trust you all alone together?" He aimed for a joke.

"We'll manage," Dare deadpanned.

With a shake of his head, Ethan placed his hand on Faith's back and led her to the front door, joining her outside on the porch for privacy. "This sure as hell wasn't how I planned for this night to end."

"I can't even imagine how you must be feeling."

"I'm reeling," he admitted. "And I don't have a clue what to do with her. She's fourteen and pissed off at the world. I'm a stranger who doesn't even have a bed to offer her."

She laughed. "That's easy. Give her yours for tonight. First thing tomorrow I can arrange for a bed to be delivered same day. Do you think she'd want to pick out the rest of the furniture in her room?"

"Do *you*?"

Faith shook her head and sighed. "Good point. Okay, I'll just come up with something that will get here fast. As far as the rest of the house, you're going to need a lot more furniture a lot faster than we'd planned. Do you want to meet to go over some ideas?"

"Do I want to see you tomorrow? Yes. Do I care what furniture you pick out or what you put on the walls? Hell, no. As long as the kid has a place that feels like home, that's all I care about right now."

An unexpected, wide smile tipped her lips. A warm, sexy smile.

"What?" he asked, confused by her reaction.

"You're wrong," she said sofly.

"About what?"

"You *do* know what to do with her," she said, referring to his earlier declaration that he didn't.

Admiration filled her gaze and, as usual, her faith in him took him off guard. "I just hope you're right."

"I am. I'll come by tomorrow with books and decorating plans anyway. You might not be in the mood, but you should still have a say in the furniture and look you're going to have to live with."

As long as he could see her, he'd pick out curtains if he had to.

"You should get back inside," she said, and he realized he'd been staring.

Acting on instinct, he reached for her, intending to pull her into a kiss—one that would hold him over and make up for what they'd missed tonight—but she backed out of reach.

Surprised, he narrowed his gaze. "What's wrong?" Unless he was mistaken, they'd been about to sleep together just an hour or two before.

Okay, so the notion of him having a sudden family under his roof wasn't ideal, but that didn't mean he'd changed his mind about her.

She took another step back. "Your life just did a one eighty. You won't have time for a fling, so let's not set ourselves up for something we can't have."

She was backing away and he had no idea why. "What's going on, Faith? Why the change of heart?"

She waved a hand, telling him she wasn't going to discuss it. "I'll see you in the morning. Good luck with Tess. And your brothers." She started down the path.

"Uh, Faith?" he called into the darkness.

She turned.

"I drove you here," he reminded her.

In the end, Dare drove Faith home, leaving Ethan to deal with Tess, who refused to take his bed, insisting the floor was no big deal.

Ethan disagreed but didn't win the argument. Or any other one during the night. He had a feeling his version of "no big deal" and his new sister's version were worlds apart.

Needing someone to talk to, Faith wrapped her hand around her cell phone, planning to call Kate as soon as she walked into her apartment. She stopped herself before she could dial. As much as she wanted to confide in someone, she couldn't admit to her best friend what she could barely admit to herself.

She'd seen sides of Ethan tonight that surprised her. True, she'd been defending him to Rosalita and Nick, but even she'd been surprised by his softer side.

As long as the kid has a place that feels like home, that's all I care about right now.

The idea of having an affair had been appealing for many reasons. Like Kate had said, she could dip her toe back into the dating game without a major commitment with a man who did it for her in a big way. But tonight Faith realized he wasn't just a hot guy, he was a hot guy with a heart, and that scared her. Because a guy with a heart, who would open his home to a fourteen-year-old girl and put her priorities first, was a man she could fall for. And she wasn't anywhere near ready. She'd backed off fast, but she hadn't fooled Ethan or herself. This unresolved thing between them was far from over.

If they were the only two people involved, she'd find it easier to wrestle with her personal demons and discover a way to be with him, but there'd been another reason she'd backed off tonight. Nothing meant more to Ethan than mending his relationship with his brothers. He'd said as much himself. Not even the successful business he'd built and the money he'd acquired meant more to him than Nash and Dare.

And Nash had made his feelings about Faith perfectly clear. He disliked her father and Faith by extension. As long as Faith was in the picture in any personal way, she'd be another obstacle standing between Ethan and his goal of reuniting his family. His new sister gave him an in with his brothers, a reason for the three of them to be together in a meaningful way.

Faith was grateful to Ethan for standing up for her, but she couldn't live with herself if she came between them. If that meant she had to give up an affair with the one man she'd always wondered about, so be it.

At least she'd be able to look in the mirror and know she'd put someone else's needs in front of her own.

Ethan woke up, took a quick shower, dressed, and headed downstairs to find Tess. His stomach was growling and he didn't have much in the way of food. He figured they could eat at the diner and then go grocery shopping together. He had no idea what a teenage girl liked to have in the house.

Nothing about Tess had been easy. She refused to talk to him and had insisted on crashing on the floor in the carpeted family room, unwilling to take his bed.

He walked into the room in silence in case she was still asleep. The blanket he'd given her lay in a heap on the floor, but no Tess. He tried the kitchen second. No Tess there either. He strode from room to room, his stomach sinking with each unsuccessful attempt.

"Son of a bitch." He couldn't take care of her for one single night.

The kid didn't know the town, so he couldn't imagine where she went. Then he remembered her begging Faith not to leave.

He grabbed the phone and made the most embarrassing call of his life.

"Hello?" Faith's voice did little to soothe his panic.

"I lost her," he said into the phone.

"Ethan?"

He gripped the receiver harder in his hand. "Yeah. I lost Tess. Woke up and she was gone. I searched the entire house. Any chance she came to find you?"

"No, but don't panic, okay?"

"Easy for you to say. I'd call the police—"

"Except they'd make you wait twenty-four hours before filing an official report," she pointed out logically.

"And my brother Dare would have more proof of why I'm not worth believing in," he muttered under his breath.

"He'd be wrong," Faith said, her voice filled with a certainty he couldn't feel.

Dare had taken the job of looking into Tess's past. Nash had agreed to check into the family connection, and Ethan was supposed to look out for the kid.

Helluva job he'd done so far.

He grabbed his car keys. "I'll take a ride and see if she walked to town. Call me if by some miracle she shows up at your place?" he asked Faith.

"Of course. She's probably just testing you."

If so, he was failing. He broke the connection and hung up. Cell phone still in hand, he started for the front entrance. He'd left the car outside after picking Faith up last night, so he didn't need to go through the garage.

He opened the door . . . and nearly tripped over his missing sister, sitting on the front porch, smoking . . . "Is that a joint?" he asked, shocked down to his toes.

He shoved the phone into his back pocket and stared at the kid. "What the hell do you think you're doing?"

"Getting fresh air, what's it look like?" Tess scowled at him. "Is there a law against sitting in the great outdoors?"

"There's a law against possession of marijuana." He

reached out and snagged the joint from her hand. He snuffed it out beneath his shoe, grinding the rest of it into the ground.

She jumped to her feet. "Hey! That stuff's expensive!"

And he was sure he didn't want to know where she'd gotten the money to pay for it. But he did. He needed to know everything about her if he had any hope of turning the kid around.

Ethan pulled in a deep breath before dealing with her. "I thought you ran away."

She eyed him warily. "I considered it."

He raised an eyebrow. "What happened?"

"Kelly's smart. She left me with no cash, no credit card, and you sleep with both right next to your head. I figured I wouldn't get far." She shrugged. "So I came outside for a hit instead."

He shook his head in disbelief. "Sit," he ordered.

She folded her arms across her chest in blatant defiance.

"Sit down, Tess." He took a step closer to her, hoping his size would force her into complying.

To his shock, she did.

Begrudgingly, but she lowered herself to the stoop, glaring at him the entire time. "What now?"

"Now we talk."

Nine

"How does a fourteen-year-old end up with a juvenile probation officer?" Ethan figured he'd start with the easy questions and work his way up.

"How do you think?" Tess kicked at the stone paving beneath her feet.

"I'm guessing you got into trouble. Want to explain?"

She shook her head. "Not really."

This was going well, he thought, memories of stonewalling his own parents returning to haunt him. "Vandalism? Got caught smoking pot by the wrong people? What?" he pushed Tess for answers.

"What's the difference? End result is the same."

She had a point. He glanced out at the lush green shrubbery surrounding the massive house he now owned. A world away from the small track house on the outskirts of town where he'd grown up, where he hadn't wanted to face that his family was falling apart. Tess was just confirmation of something he'd known all along.

He studied her hard profile. "You know, I was always

getting in trouble when I was your age. Drinking, stealing, racing cars."

She raised an eyebrow. The ring pierced through her brow glimmered in the sun. "You're so full of shit."

"And you need to watch your mouth." Okay, so she didn't want to talk. Dare would get the information they needed and he'd figure out what to do with Tess then. "Let's go get food," he suggested.

"Sounds good." She jumped up. "Where are we going?"

"Got the munchies?" he muttered.

She glanced at him, surprised. "You know about that?"

He nodded. "I'm old, but I'm not that old. We'll get a decent meal at the diner in town, then we'll pick up groceries so we have something to eat in the house."

"Fine. Whatever," she said, back to her sullen self.

An hour later, they'd eaten at the Family Restaurant, the only diner in town. He'd gone to school with some in the family who now ran the diner, but despite going way back with them, Ethan had no idea if they'd treat him with disdain for running out on his siblings. To Ethan's surprise and relief, considering he had Tess with him, he'd been welcomed and treated with respect by the Donovans. The other patrons either ignored him as a stranger or stared inquiringly.

Either way, he'd take it, even if it was his money and current status as Harrington mansion owner that gave him a pass. He didn't care why as long as his new sister wasn't subjected to the *he's nothing but trouble* feeling shared by many people in town.

He didn't have much time to mull over how that little bit of acceptance felt because during their meal, Dare called to inform him that Tess's juvenile probation officer had been full of information about their new sister. Despite being arrested for breaking and entering, she'd skated serious trouble this time. Now all she had to do was behave for the next six months and the charges would be dropped. If she stayed out of trouble until she turned eighteen, her arrest record would be expunged. Ethan had had her with him for less than twenty-four hours. The next four years loomed long ahead of him.

They finished eating in silence, Tess still not in a talkative mood. For now, Ethan let her be. He paid the bill, leaving a nice tip.

Before stopping at the supermarket, Ethan took a detour to Faith's shop. A large truck was outside, indicating the awning and signs were being delivered, filling him with an unfamiliar tug of pride. She was accomplishing her dreams, and he applauded her for it.

"Let's go see what's up," Ethan said.

"Where are we?" Tess tipped her head up to see.

"Faith's." He watched Tess for any reaction.

The most positive response she'd had thus far had been to Faith, and if he had a prayer of getting the kid to open up, he had a hunch Faith was the key.

"What does she do?" Tess asked, sounding more intrigued than she'd been by anything except his disposing of her pot.

"Interior design. We need to get your room ordered and make sure you have a bed tonight." He steered her inside before she could argue.

He didn't see Faith, but Kate was stacking books on newly installed shelving and Nick was talking to the delivery guy. He was also stealing covert looks at Kate's ass as she bent over to retrieve items from boxes on the floor. The other man's interest loosened the hold on Ethan's chest.

"Is Faith around?" Ethan asked.

Kate whirled around, startled. "Oh, hi." She settled a curious gaze on him. "I'm not sure we've been introduced."

"Not officially, no. Ethan Barron." He extended his hand for a shake.

"Kate Andrews."

As he shook her hand, Ethan felt a distinct male presence come up behind him.

"Relax, Mancini. I have an appointment with Faith." In

actuality, Faith thought Ethan would be stopping by the house later, but details were none of the other man's business.

"She's out. So you have no reason to be here," Nick said, keeping up the overprotective act, even when Faith wasn't here.

"Don't you have work to do? An awning to help put up?" Kate asked him too sweetly.

"Are you always so pleasant?" Nick studied Kate with the look of a man seeing a woman for the first time.

"Since when do you give me a second thought?" Kate asked. "Go worry about something you can control." She dismissed Nick with a wave of her hand.

The man let out a low growl. "I'll be right outside if you need me."

Kate grinned. "I won't," she assured him.

For some odd reason, Ethan decided Nick was tortured enough and opted not to provoke him further by flirting with Kate. He got his satisfaction in the way Kate bossed the other guy around and did his best not to laugh out loud.

"You just watch yourself around him," Nick warned, before storming out.

Kate chuckled, then turned her attention to them. "So, this must be Tess? Faith told me she met you last night."

"Tess is my . . . sister," Ethan said, testing the word on his tongue for the first time in public.

Kate treated the girl to a big smile. "Hi, Tess. I'm Kate. I'm a friend of Faith's."

Being Tess, she narrowed her gaze and let out a put-upon sigh. "Big—"

Ethan cut her off with an elbow nudge to the ribs. "We're working on Tess's social skills," he said tightly.

Kate grinned. "I'm a middle school teacher," she said, as if that summed up her understanding.

Ethan supposed it did. "Where's Faith?"

"She's out getting coffee, but she should be back any

minute. You're welcome to wait." She gestured to the chairs in front of a small wood desk.

"Have a seat," he said to Tess.

To his surprise, Tess stomped over to a metal folding chair and lowered herself into it.

"Need help?" he asked Kate.

She shook her head. She returned to her job of stacking and organizing the shelves. "So, what are you going to do with her for the summer?" Kate asked, referring to Tess.

Ethan began handing her books from the floor, speeding up her task. "I'm not sure." He spoke low, so Tess wouldn't overhear.

A glance over told him he needn't have worried. She'd put her iPod ear buds on. His guess was that she was blasting music, tuning him out along with the rest of the world.

"She's obviously got issues," Ethan said to Kate.

"Well, I work afternoons at the youth center. They have different programs ranging from regular summer day camp to service programs for troubled teens. Your brother actually works one night a week with a group of kids."

"Youth center?" Ethan asked. "I don't remember there being one of those." He'd certainly qualified as a troubled teen, so if there had been programs around, he hoped his parents would have mentioned it.

"The town community center is fairly new. As a matter of fact, every once in a while, budget cuts threaten to shut it down. The existing structure is pretty old, but at least it offers a place for these kids to go."

Ethan nodded in understanding. "Definitely something to consider." Since he knew he'd have to keep her busy and out of trouble. Figuring out what was at the root of her acting out and getting her under control were also on the agenda.

A youth center sounded like just the place for a kid like Tess. Assuming he could get her to even walk in the door with him, let alone stay for a couple of hours.

* * *

Faith walked into the coffeehouse, which was empty
except for a few people sitting behind computers and headed
for the counter, where Lissa waited to greet her.

"Good morning!" Faith said brightly, hoping that Karaoke Night had smoothed things over between them.

"Says you." The other woman seemed unhappier than
usual. Her eyes were bloodshot, her hair matted. Even her
clothes looked slept in.

If she were anyone else, Faith would ask what was wrong.
There was nothing Faith could say to Lissa the other woman
wouldn't take the wrong way.

"My ex called last night. He's getting married," Lissa
said, taking Faith off guard. For some reason, she obviously
decided to open up. "To a twenty-two-year-old heiress. Did
you know there was such a thing as a twenty-two-year-old
heiress?" Lissa let out a sudden, harsh laugh. "Look who
I'm asking—the princess herself."

Faith glared at her. "And here I thought we might start
getting along. Stupid me." She leaned across the counter
and deliberately got into Lissa's face—the only language
the other woman would understand. "Do I look like a princess to you?"

Faith gestured to her hair, pulled into a ponytail, a denim
skirt that April had sewn together from a combination of
Levi's jeans and pieces of her other clothing, and her new
sneakers to make walking around town easier. "Now, I'd
like to get coffee." She pulled out a piece of paper with her,
Nick's, and Kate's orders.

Lissa braced a hand on the counter. "Do you realize how
easy it is to hate you? Your old man screws the world, your
family loses everything, yet you come back to town and
open a goddamn business while I'm writing the obits for the
newspaper, wishing I could get a journalistic break and
pouring coffee to make ends meet."

Faith bit the inside of her cheek. She had no idea Lissa was an aspiring journalist. Given how Faith perceived the profession, she shouldn't be surprised this piranha was one of them, Faith thought wryly. Although Faith understood the other woman's frustration, it wasn't her fault that Lissa's life hadn't turned out the way she'd hoped and dreamed.

Faith curled her fingers around the edge of the counter. "Jealousy only hurts you, Lissa. Not me. But for the record, my life isn't exactly peachy keen right now. I caught *my* ex screwing his assistant. He only married me for my father's connections, and when it came to the divorce he tried to hide our assets. I walked away with little but my pride."

Lissa raised an eyebrow, but Faith sensed she was listening.

"The only reason I have a business is because I have friends who are willing to help me out until I get on my feet. But if I'm going to make a go of it, it'll be on my own hard work and talent." Faith paused for a breath and straightened her shoulders, deciding to end this bickering once and for all. "Frankly, I'm getting sick and tired of you treating me like I still have a silver spoon in my mouth," she said, her voice rising. "Now back off and fill my damn coffee orders!"

Then she braced herself for the fallout.

To her never-ending surprise, Lissa snagged the list of coffee orders out of her hand and headed back to work without another word, returning with the three iced coffee drinks.

"Here." She placed them on the counter.

"Thank you," Faith said.

Lissa rang up the order and Faith paid, dropping a tip into the jar by the register.

"Maybe I could cut you some slack," Lissa finally said.

"Gee, thanks," Faith muttered, smiling because despite all odds, she'd broken the ice with Lissa Gardelli.

Faith picked up the cardboard tray holding the drinks, ready to leave.

"I heard you're seeing Ethan Barron," Lissa said, her words stopping Faith from turning and walking out.

Faith sighed, damning small-town gossip. "Where'd you hear that?"

"I didn't hear as much as see it for myself. At Karaoke Night."

Faith frowned, not wanting people to get the wrong impression. "You saw wrong. He just helped me get home."

"I'm betting he did more than that considering you were wrapped up against him like a bitch in heat." The satisfaction in Lissa's voice sliced through Faith.

"Just when I thought I might be able to like you." Faith's head spun from Lissa's constant mood changes. She picked up her coffee and headed for the door.

"Wait."

Faith paused but didn't turn.

"I'm sorry. I know I'm a bitch."

Faith pivoted slowly. "I don't know how the hell you have any friends."

Lissa let out a laugh. "Me neither. Look, I know Ethan from way back. He could charm a girl out of her panties, but he doesn't know the first thing about sticking around."

Faith narrowed her gaze. "Careful, Lissa. That almost sounds like friendly advice." Or jealous nastiness.

Too bad there'd been a definite ring of truth to the other woman's words.

Faith left the shop, grateful to get away from Lissa. Even the hot, humid air was preferable.

Temperatures had been over a hundred for the last two days, and the air conditioner in her apartment was on the fritz. Add to that, she hadn't been able to stop thinking of Ethan and her body heat was at an all-time high. She'd barely slept last night, thoughts of what might have been keeping her awake, tossing and turning on top of the covers.

She turned the corner leading to her new store, stopping where Nick and the awning guy worked on installing her sign. The teal-colored writing read FAITH, and a burst of pride and excitement soared through her at the sight.

She handed Nick his coffee and headed inside where it was cooler, only to find her best friend and her—she didn't know what to call Ethan—working side by side and chatting like they were old friends.

In his worn jeans and faded light blue T-shirt, he was sexy as sin. He handed Kate books and she stacked them on the shelves, their heads bent together, whispering as they worked. Faith couldn't hear the conversation, but a stab of jealousy struck her in the heart anyway. Not something she was proud of, but there it was anyway, Lissa's words about his inability to stick reverberating in her head.

Faith knew so little about Ethan and what had happened after he'd left town. What drove him to run? What demons kept his guilt so high? Had he had any relationships in the intervening years? Or was he still the love-'em-and-leave-'em type?

And why did she care? She was just beginning to stand on her own for the first time. And she knew she'd only be a hindrance to his making peace with his brothers, especially Nash. So why was she racking her brain, trying to understand him now?

Because she was drawn to the man. No matter how hard she fought it, she wanted him for herself. Just one time, she wanted to be with him and explore that unfinished business.

Could they have sex and still work together? Could she sleep with him and keep her heart intact? And was it possible to do all that and not come between him and his brothers?

Talk about mood swings, Lissa had nothing on Faith.

Faith didn't know the answers to any of her questions, but now wasn't the time to figure it out. She tore her gaze from Ethan and Kate, noticing Tess for the first time. The teenager sat, head down, at Faith's desk, pencil and paper in hand.

Faith stepped up to the desk. "What are you busy with?"

she asked, placing the coffee holder on the wooden surface.

Tess didn't answer and Faith realized an old iPod sat on the desk, its ear buds in the teenager's ears.

"Hi." Faith waved her hand in front of Tess's eyes.

Tess shot her an annoyed glare.

Faith gestured for her to remove the ear buds. When Tess returned her gaze to the paper, pretending not to understand, Faith tugged on one of the long white wires, dislodging the earpiece.

"Hey!"

"Hey yourself. I asked what you're busy with."

"None of your business." Tess snatched the paper and crumpled it in her hand.

But not before Faith caught a glimpse of the page and the sketches the teenager had been working on. "Seems like a waste to crinkle it up and throw it away. I wasn't going to ask to see. I was just curious what you were doing."

"Drawing. Duh."

The fact that she had an interest in artwork was encouraging, in Faith's opinion. It meant that she could be distracted by something positive and made a mental note to mention it to Ethan.

Faith nodded. "Nice. Next time, there's empty computer paper in this drawer. You don't need to use the back of an invoice." That now sat in a ball in Tess's hand.

"I didn't hear you come in!" Kate walked over, Ethan following behind.

Faith glanced at her friend. "You two looked busy. I didn't want to interrupt." Faith cringed inside, knowing how juvenile she sounded. "Here's your coffee." She handed Kate her drink.

"Thanks." Kate shot her an odd look, which Faith ignored.

"I was just telling Ethan about the different programs down at the youth center," Kate said.

Faith immediately felt bad for her earlier jealousy.

"Thanks for the coffee." Kate picked up her cup. "I'm going to finish up the last box before I have to leave for the day." Kate raised her coffee cup in a salute and strode back over to the shelves.

"Those programs had better not be for me," Tess muttered.

"I don't see any other *youths* around," Ethan said. "You didn't think you'd sit around all summer smoking pot, did you?"

Faith's startled gaze swung to Ethan's. He gave her a subtle nod.

Okay, so his hands were even fuller than she'd thought.

Tess's expression turned frosty. "I shouldn't be surprised. Less than twenty-four hours and you want to get rid of me already. What else is new?"

Ethan set his jaw and shook his head. "Finding something constructive to occupy your time isn't getting rid of you," he said in a surprisingly even voice.

"So, what are you two doing here?" Faith asked, changing the subject.

Facing her, not Tess, Ethan grinned, his smile warm and welcoming and obviously meant for her alone. "Making your life easier. I figured we could come here to talk about furniture and decorating Tess's room instead of you having to take a cab ride out to us."

Faith interpreted that to mean he needed to get out of the house and keep the kid busy. Still, he had a point about how she'd get to his house and she already realized she would have to dig into her savings for a car if she was going to run a business that entailed visiting other people's homes.

She pulled a chair around to sit beside Tess. "What's your favorite color?" she asked the teen.

"Black," the teen said as she bit on her nails.

"Not happening," Ethan immediately said.

Faith shot him a warning look. "Actually I can use black

accents." She knew Ethan feared a Goth-style room, but she had other ideas. "Pick a second color," she encouraged the teen.

Tess looked past Faith to Ethan. "I don't give a shit," she said, clearly testing him.

He clenched his hands at his sides. "That's it. I've had it with your fresh mouth."

"Guess what?" Kate returned just in time, placing both hands on the desk.

"What?" Faith asked.

"I'm finished here and I need to get to the community center for my shift. How about I take Tess with me and show her around?" Kate glanced at Faith, seeking her okay.

Faith thought it was a great idea. Kate had a way with kids and Tess clearly needed someone who knew how to deal with her.

"I don't think that's a good idea," Ethan said.

"I'll go," Tess countered, a defiant grin settling over her face.

Faith stepped closer and put a hand on his shoulder. "Kate's a good chaperone." And he clearly needed a break to think and plan how to deal with his new sister.

"Great! Let's go. I'll introduce you to kids your own age and to the community service director." She met Ethan's gaze, silently asking for his approval.

He treated Kate to a nod. "You will behave," Ethan said to his sister.

Tess merely opened her hand and closed it again, mimicking him talking. "Let's blow this joint," Tess said.

Faith cleared her throat. "Since you're taking her, Ethan and I need to shop for some things for the house. I'll call you when we're back and he'll pick up Tess then?" Faith asked.

Kate nodded. "Good by me. Let's go," she said to Tess.

The young girl marched out without a good-bye. Still wearing those black combat boots in one hundred degrees, topped by what looked like an old army surplus jacket.

"I don't know if Kate's brave or just plain stupid," Ethan said after the duo had departed.

Faith stared at him in silence. Last night she'd rebuffed him coldly. Today she'd been jealous in a way she'd never experienced. Far different from the angry betrayal she'd felt on walking in on her husband and his mistress. She hadn't been jealous then, just hurt. Right now she found it difficult to hold on to her resolve to stay away from Ethan and her chest ached.

She needed something tangible, something she could understand to take her mind off the building need. "You really found Tess smoking *pot*?" she asked.

"Yeah. And Dare found out why she's got a juvenile probation officer."

"Bad?" Faith asked.

"Actually could've been a lot worse." His shoulders lowered slightly and he drew in a deep breath. "Her sister wasn't kidding. Tess ran with a rough crowd. The boys were into vandalism and had moved on to breaking and entering and arson. Tess was arrested with two guys and another girl, and accused of all three crimes. To make a long story short, the probation department investigated, looking into Tess's home and school behavior, which, though out of control, didn't rise to the level of many of her friends'."

Not yet anyway.

The obvious thought settled between them.

"At the hearing, Tess's lawyer presented evidence that Tess and the other girl were in the house but didn't have advance knowledge of intent nor did they start the fire. The boys were remanded to a detention facility. As for the girls, the judge ordered an adjournment in contemplation of dismissal. If she stays out of trouble for the next six months, the case will be dismissed."

"That's something, I guess," Faith said.

But Ethan's troubled expression told her how unlikely he found the possibility.

"Assuming we can keep her out of trouble, you're right. It is something."

"When I came in earlier, Tess was sketching on a piece of paper. She got really embarrassed and defensive when I asked her what she was doing, but it got me wondering if art wasn't a way to reach her," Faith said.

Ethan raised an eyebrow. "Interesting. I'll see what I can do to draw her out."

Faith smiled, having every confidence he'd accomplish his goal.

"So, what's this about us going shopping?" Ethan asked next.

"I already ordered a bed for Tess. Delivery between three and five today. But I figured the easiest and fastest way to get her bedding, towels, and other things she'll need is to make a run through Target. There's a superstore in Monroe."

He thought for a moment and nodded. "Lead the way."

SuperTarget was the megastore of all megastores. Even for a man who loathed shopping, Ethan had to admire the fact that anything he needed, he could find here. Definitely worth the twenty-minute drive. What he couldn't get over was the surreal feeling of walking through Target with Faith as if they were a couple shopping for *their* home.

In order to get that thought out of his head, he grasped for another as he pushed the cart toward the bed and bath department. "So I have to ask. Have you ever been in Target before?"

"Wise guy." She laughed.

He appreciated her sense of humor about the subject. More so, he was glad the cool Faith from last night was nowhere to be found today.

"As a matter of fact, Kate took me here when I moved in. I was able to buy everything I needed at an unbelievable price. This place actually makes me wish I'd come in here

a long time ago. Stop." She pointed to the BEDDING sign.
"This is what I was looking for. Bed in a bag."

"What's that?"

"I went online last night and did some preliminary
browsing. The best buys are these bed-in-a-bag sets—
comforter, two pillow cases, a top and fitted sheet. And look
at the selection of colors." She gestured to the variety of sets
lining the shelves.

"I don't know that it matters. She won't like anything we
pick out."

"True, but we can still accommodate her taste without
putting you over the edge."

He nodded. "Nice of you to take that into consideration."

She laughed. "Hey, you're paying the bills. So, what I'm
suggesting is we look at anything with black somewhere in
it. There's plenty of black and white, black and gray."

"No. Let's find something that at least says *girl*."

"No emo chic?" Faith asked.

He placed a hand on her arm before she could go forward.
"What's emo?"

Faith turned to face him, a grin on her pretty face. "Don't
feel bad. Kate had to teach me the term. I guess it's similar
to what we think of as punk, only different. It's her short
black hair, the piercings—"

"There's more than one?" he asked, horrified.

Faith shrugged. "I don't know. It's just the style."

He cringed. "How am I going to get through to her?"

Before Faith could answer, a high-pitched, female voice
screeched through the aisle. "Faith? Is that *you*?"

Ethan turned to see a woman wearing a Jackie O–
inspired head scarf and big dark sunglasses. She was as
inconspicuous as a nun in a porn shop.

"Mother?" Faith asked, obviously shocked.

Talk about a mood killer. The woman hated Ethan when
he'd only been seventeen. He could imagine how she felt
about him now that he lived in her mansion.

"What are you doing in Target?" Lanie Harrington asked on a stage whisper, pronouncing the store name with a fake French accent. "And what in the world are you doing with the likes of him?"

Here we go, Ethan thought, stiffening. Nothing like a woman's disapproving mother to bring him back to the bad boy he'd been.

With a forced smile, he met the woman's gaze. "Nice to see you too, Mrs. Harrington." He threw the first shot and steeled himself for her reply.

Ten

Faith's mother raised her small nose, which her daughter had inherited, into the air and turned her back on him, facing Faith instead. "Well? What in the world are you doing here?" her mother asked again, ignoring Ethan completely.

"I'm shopping, Mom. What are *you* doing here?"

"Picking up a few necessities," Lanie said in another hushed whisper. "This budgeting business isn't for me."

Ethan swallowed a laugh he knew would be unwelcome.

Faith rolled her eyes. "Welcome to the real world."

Her mother straightened her shoulders. "You didn't answer my other question." She clearly intended to avoid Faith's comments. "What are you doing with *him*?"

So he'd been wrong. She wasn't going to ignore him, just insult him.

"Really, Faith. A Harrington has to show some class."

"Like Dad did?" Faith asked.

Her mother sniffed, clearly offended. "That comment was uncalled for. You know your father has been maligned and misunderstood."

"Actually, I know no such thing," Faith said.

"Good point." Ethan added his unwelcome opinion.

"Thank you." Faith actually sounded pleased.

Ethan grinned. He hadn't realized his little tigress had teeth and he found himself wishing she'd use them on him, not to reprimand him the way she had her judgmental mother, but in bed.

"And by the way, *he* has a name," Faith said to her mother. "It's Ethan Barron and since I'm here with him, it means I like him. So I would appreciate it if you'd show some respect. Or ignore me along with him." She'd taken a page from his book the other night when he'd defended her against his brother.

Man, they were a pair.

Her mother let out a prolonged sigh. "I thought you gave up temper tantrums when you got married."

Married? This was the first he'd heard about it, and the idea threw his stomach into crippling knots.

"This is a waste of time." Faith gripped the shopping cart handle hard enough to turn her knuckles white. "We have shopping to do. And so do you." Faith dismissed her parent.

Lanie raised her nose farther in the air.

If the woman lifted her chin any higher, she'd be looking at the ceiling, Ethan thought.

"Fine. But we will discuss this," her mother said, and walked away.

"When? Next time you call me, which is never?" Faith muttered at her mother's back. She turned to Ethan, regret etched in her face. "I'm sorry about that. She's horrible."

"No more than my brother was to you." He shrugged it off, truly not bothered. "And you're not responsible for what she says."

Blue eyes met his. "Thanks. So where were we?" she asked, obviously eager to put the scene with her mother behind her.

He propped a hand on the shelf behind her. "We were

about to discuss the fact that you're *married*?" He raised an eyebrow and waited for an answer.

"Divorced."

The knot in his stomach unwound a bit. "Better. But not perfect."

The corners of her mouth lifted in amusement. "What? You thought I was a vestal virgin?"

No, but he couldn't bear the thought of another man's hands on her naked body. Especially when he hadn't had *his* hands on her yet.

"Relax, caveman." She poked him in the chest. "It's over."

Not for Ethan. He needed to know more. "What happened?"

"Do you really want to have this conversation in the aisle at Target?"

It was better than not having the conversation at all. "Yep."

"Fine." She hitched the strap of her purse higher on her shoulder. "I married a man my parents approved of. It turned out he only married me for my father's connections, but I was too naive to realize it. Once my father was arrested, Carter had gotten all he could from our marriage. I caught him in bed with his mistress."

"Asshole," Ethan muttered.

"*Our* bed."

"Son of a—" Anger at that kind of betrayal flooded Ethan's veins.

"It's over," she said again, more softly this time. "And it should have been finished long before that. Now can we get back to business?" She pointed to the colored comforters lining the walls.

Ethan wanted more information. He wanted to know if she'd been happy with the man. If she'd loved him. But he knew better than to push. He had his own walls, didn't he?

"So how do we choose for Tess?" he asked.

She released the breath she'd obviously been holding. "If you ask me, it comes down to these. There's this floral"—she touched a pink and black flowered pattern—"which I don't see as an option." She looked to him for confirmation.

He nodded. "I agree there."

"So it's one of these animal prints." She swept her hand over the green, purple, pink, or regular black and white zebra stripes. Shockingly, Ethan could live with one of those.

"She seems to like purple," he said, recalling her awful colored hair.

Faith laughed. "Exactly what I was thinking." She turned and reached high to grab the right size comforter, causing her denim skirt to ride up on her thighs and reveal a flash of what he thought was bare flesh. A second look showed a dusky pink color covering and almost blending with her pale skin.

Ethan's mouth grew dry. Thoughts he'd managed to keep at bay most of the day came flooding back now. Wanting her. Needing her. His groin hardened at the thought, thrusting against the rough denim of his jeans.

"Let me," he muttered, reaching for the plastic covering and pulling the blanket into his hands.

"Thanks!"

"No problem." He shifted his jeans, trying unsuccessfully to get more comfortable. "Queen." He read the label. "Is this the right size?" he asked gruffly.

"Yes. I thought we'd give Tess my old room, and it's definitely big enough for a queen." She narrowed her gaze. "What's wrong?" she asked, perceptively reading him.

He glanced around. Once assured they were alone at the end of the aisle, he wrapped an arm around her waist and pulled her close, her back facing the wall. "What's wrong is you wearing barely there underwear beneath that skirt."

"What? It's a full bikini!"

He slid his hand around her thigh and inched his fingertips upward until he cupped her thinly covered cheek. "The color of your skin," he said thickly.

"It's light mauve," she whispered on a sigh as he glided his finger over the damp spot between her legs.

"Do not wear these things with a skirt ever again." He barely recognized his voice.

"Would you prefer I wear armor?"

He punished her sarcasm with a glide of his finger over her mound.

At his touch, she shuddered and let out a soft moan. "I forgot all about the skirt when I reached up for the comforter."

He'd never forget the sight or the feel of them in his hand. Knowing he'd gone as far as he could in public, he freed his hand, then sucked in a ragged breath, attempting to relax his body.

"What else do we need to buy?" he managed to ask, all the while wondering when he could have her.

How he could possibly carve out time for them alone.

"I have a list," she said as she adjusted her outfit.

For the rest of the day, they shopped up a storm, accessorizing Tess's purple and black room. Faith managed to get him to let her order black lacquer furniture for the teen because it would help convince Tess that Ethan actually heard her when she spoke. That he cared about what she wanted. And they never mentioned the incident in the aisle.

But somehow, some way, Ethan was determined to finish what he started with Faith.

Trunk loaded with shopping bags, Faith settled into the passenger's seat of the car beside Ethan. "Success!" she said, pleased with the items they'd bought for Tess.

"You did good." He slipped his sunglasses on and headed back to Serendipity.

Faith glanced at her watch. "The mattress is going to be delivered in an hour. Is Rosalita there?"

He shook his head. "She usually works mornings, but she asked for today off. Don't worry, though. I can be there for the delivery."

"And set things up afterward?" She grinned. "If you don't mind driving me back later, I can wait with you and then put the sheets and comforter on the bed. That way you can surprise Tess later."

He slid an appreciative glance her way. "That'd be great."

"Part of the job," she assured him, knowing it was much more. She wanted to help get the girl's room put together so the teen felt like she belonged there. "The wallpaper in the room clashes horribly with the new bedding," she pointed out.

He waved a hand through the air. "Carte blanche," he reminded her. "Order whatever you think is best."

She nodded. "I will. Did you speak to Rosalita and tell her about Tess?"

Ethan groaned. "Did I warn her, you mean? Not yet. I need to do it in person."

With a shrug, Faith shifted in her seat. "She handled my parents. One teenage girl will be a piece of cake for her. As a matter of fact, I think she'll be good for Tess."

"She won't put up with any of her BS, that's for sure." A sexy grin lifted the corner of his mouth.

She sighed, unable to look away. Gorgeous face, strong hands on the steering wheel. God, what the man did to her.

"What do you think of asking Rosalita to work full-time?" She forced herself to keep her mind where it belonged. "Having her in the house will free you up to come and go and not worry about keeping an eye on Tess. And there will definitely be more mess with a teenager living there. Not to mention laundry."

"Another good idea. Think she'll do it?"

"Her kids are grown, she's widowed . . . I don't see why not."

"Good."

They arrived back at the house and Ethan pulled up the long driveway to find an irate delivery driver waiting for them.

Faith climbed out of the car and met him by the cab of the truck while Ethan pulled the car into the garage.

"I was just getting ready to leave," the man muttered.

Faith deliberately glanced at her watch. "You're early."

He lifted a baseball cap and scratched his head. "And you're complaining? Most people hate sitting around all day."

"When you give a window, that means people can leave the premises before or after the time you're supposed to be there. Anyway, we're here now." She gestured toward the house.

"Let me unpack the mattress," he muttered.

"Thanks. I'll have a cold glass of water for you waiting inside," she said, flashing him her brightest smile.

"I'd appreciate that," he said, his gruff attitude lessening.

The driver disappeared into the back of the truck. Once in the house, Ethan and Faith separated, Ethan heading into his office to make phone calls and handle business. Faith threw the new linen into the washing machine while the driver unpacked and unloaded the delivery. He carried the mattress, box spring, and headboard Faith had ordered into the house and set up the bed in Tess's new room.

She watched with mixed feelings as the man finished putting a bed together for another girl to live in Faith's old room. She'd had some great memories growing up here, and if she let go of the pain of her father's betrayal, she could admit she'd been a lucky, fortunate kid. So was Tess, if only the girl would give her brothers a chance and let them in, Faith thought.

Once the driver had finished and handed her his water glass, she tipped him and walked him to the door, ignoring the surreal feeling of being a stranger in her own home. A home that was no longer hers.

She shook off the pain inherent in that thought and returned to work. She switched the linen from the washer to the dryer and while waiting, she made some calls of her own. First Faith called Kate, who assured her that Tess was fine, she shouldn't worry, and then rushed her off the phone so Kate could get back to work.

Next up, Faith needed to speak to Joel—more as a designer than a friend. He gave her ideas of places with quality furniture whose managers would work with her to deliver pieces in way under the normal six-week period of time.

Her next call was to Nick. Faith had a vision of dark wooden built-ins for the family room walls, and as a contractor, Nick had the ability to make her idea come alive. His crew could also handle any other work the house desperately needed.

As Faith expected, he fought the idea, citing his dislike and distrust of Ethan. It took some arm twisting along with very valid arguments to change his mind. Faith merely asked whether in this economy Nick could really afford to turn down a job that would keep his men busy and paid. Nick relented and Tess had hired herself a contractor.

When the dryer buzzer sounded, she gathered the items and headed upstairs to make the bed and ready the room for Tess. Ethan had already carried the Target bags and other items they'd purchased upstairs, including some temporary accessories. Faith put the black plastic table beside the bed and set out the purple iHome alarm clock and iPod holder. Next came the sheets and the comforter, topped by pillows to sleep on and matching zebra print throw cushions to match. The pièce de résistance was an oversized purple beanbag in the corner with a pocket to hold Tess's iPod.

If Faith ignored the mismatched carpet and wallpaper, all of which she'd fix soon, the room was ready for the teen.

Unfortunately, Faith knew that even if Tess loved the room, there was no way the girl would admit as much to herself or to Ethan. So Faith settled for admiring her handiwork instead.

Ethan walked into Tess's room just as Faith bent over to smooth wrinkles on the bed. A glance at her bare feet and from her long legs up to the flash of *light mauve* underwear, and his ability to hold himself in check snapped. He strode up behind her and wrapped his arms around her waist, pulling her to him ass first.

She squealed, then relaxed and let her buttocks ease into him. At the sweet pressure, he let out a harsh groan and slid his hand beneath her shirt, flat against her smooth stomach.

"Didn't I warn you not to wear these underwear around me?" He barely recognized his voice.

"I thought you said not to wear them with a skirt ever again?" she asked, obviously teasing him.

"That too." He nuzzled the space between her neck and shoulder, inhaling her fragrant scent, arousing himself even more.

"Well, it's not like I've been home to change." Without warning, she turned to face him, sliding her arms around his neck and meeting his gaze. Her eyes twinkled with mischief . . . and desire. "This is such a bad idea."

He brushed her hair off her shoulder, leaned in, and nipped her soft skin. "Why?"

"So many reasons." She leaned her head to one side, giving him better access.

"Name one," he challenged. But not one to turn away a good thing, he licked the sweet spot he'd nipped earlier and was rewarded when she shuddered in his arms.

She glided her tongue over her lips, then said, "Your brother hates me."

Ethan laughed at that one. "My brother hates *me* too."

She swallowed hard. "I work for you."

Also weak, he thought, not too concerned since she wasn't exactly pushing him away. "You're decorating my house. Hardly an employer, employee relationship," he countered. "No sexual harassment here." His hips jerked forward and he felt cushioned in feminine heat.

Another minute and he'd explode.

"No, I wouldn't call it harassment," she agreed with a needy sigh.

"Any other reasons?" he asked, wanting to sum up this conversation and get them into his bed.

She paused in thought. "I'm coming off a really bad relationship," she finally said.

He grinned. "All the more reason to dive into a good one."

"Not looking for a relationship," she clarified.

Neither was he. But looking for something with her? Most definitely. "How about good sex?" He eased his hand beneath her skirt and cupped one cheek in his palm. Then, for added incentive, he urged her closer. "Are you looking for good sex?"

"Oh, yes."

Her moan shook him to his core. "Then does my bed sound good to you?"

Another "Oh, yes" followed. So he played caveman and picked her up and carried her to his room.

Some mistakes were meant to happen, Faith thought, and the seeds of this one had been planted that day long ago on Ethan's bike, when he'd tried to get into her pants—or cheerleading skirt as it so happened—and she'd said no.

Today she was saying yes.

She'd deal with the consequences later. And she had no doubt there would be consequences.

But not now. Now she could experience everything she'd dreamed of since saying no that fateful day.

Ethan kissed her the entire way down the hall to his room. He kissed her as he laid her down on his king-size mattress. And he kissed her as she scooted to the headboard at the top of the bed until she leaned up against the pillows.

Faith wasn't the temptress type. She'd never set the stage for seduction, not even with her ex-husband. But she was already in Ethan's bed and she wanted to see his reaction, to know she had the power to entice him as much as he did her.

Bracing her arms at her sides, her breasts thrust up from beneath her tank top. He noticed, his eyes drawn to her cleavage and glazing over with need. Pleased, she inched up the hem of her tank, exposing a strip of skin on her stomach.

He groaned at the sight, then lowered his head and pressed a long, openmouthed kiss against her belly button. Heat spiraled inside her, her stomach rippling under the assault.

"God, you taste good," he murmured, his hands sliding to her thighs.

"You feel good," she said of his warm lips on her flesh.

She'd never experienced this heady power over a man and realized she liked it, knowing he was taking equal pleasure in her body just as she was reveling in the feel and sight of his. But when he reached beneath her skirt and pulled her panties down her thighs, thoughts fled because he had talented fingers that inched their way up her thighs.

"I want to see." He lifted her denim skirt and settled himself between her legs, his face inches from her pulsing heat.

She swallowed hard, feeling open and exposed.

"And I want to taste." His voice was rough. Sexy. Aroused.

And a low moan escaped her throat. She no longer cared who was seducing whom. She just wanted him to stop talking and act. But he was obviously intent on taking his time, admiring and making her squirm with need. Okay, so maybe she should care who was seducing whom.

And then he lowered his head, his mouth covering her, his lips tasting her, his tongue laving her slowly. Lovingly. Outer lips, inner lips, he devoured her like he couldn't get enough. She curled her fingers into the comforter, her hips undulating, her body writhing. With every lap of his tongue, sensation and waves of unbelievable need grew inside her. Heat pummeled her from inside out. She was so close to the edge, close but not yet there.

She bent her legs and arched her back, seeking deeper contact, which he seemed only too happy to give. He lifted his head and met her gaze. Eyes gleaming, he covered her with his hand, inserting one finger inside. It was good, not as good as *he* would feel, but *good,* and when he pressed his thumb over exactly the right spot, stars flickered behind her eyes and the most intense climax beckoned.

She was lost, close, seeking something just out of reach when his deep, sexy voice added to the sensations buffeting her body, except she couldn't hear his words.

He swirled his palm against her mound, hitting the right chords. "Come," he commanded and her body reached higher. "Come for me, princess."

That she heard and flew up and over, her climax surging. She rode it out, wave after wave that seemed to go on forever, encouraged by the circular motion of Ethan's hand and the husky sound of his voice.

After, the sensation subsided slowly and she kept her eyes closed, waiting to catch her breath. A distinct crinkling sound caught her attention. A glance at Ethan told her all she needed to know.

"You're prepared," she said, pleased.

"I have been since I discovered you were back in town."
He loomed over her, a sexy grin on his face.

"That confident, huh?"

He let out a laugh. "Hardly. I was confident I'd do my
damndest to convince you."

And he had.

She bit the inside of her cheek before saying, "I'm on the
pill."

His eyes dilated even more. "You have nothing to worry
about from me," he promised her.

"I'm safe too."

He reached for her skirt first, then her bra, pausing to
worship her breasts, first with his gaze, then with his hands,
cupping them in his palm and treating each stiff nipple to a
long, thorough wet kiss. She was squirming by the time he
finished and finally made short work of unbuttoning her
skirt and pulling the rough denim down her legs.

Her skirt hit the floor. His shirt followed. In a few seconds, he was standing in front of her gloriously male, completely nude, and thoroughly aroused. He lowered himself
to the bed and she reached for him, wanting to hold his
thickness for herself. Needing to give back after the ride
he'd taken her on.

He shook his head. "Touch me and it's over."

She felt herself smile. "Isn't that the point?"

"Not unless I'm inside you."

His words caused liquid to pool between her thighs.

He tumbled her back onto the mattress, sealing his lips
over hers. She loved the way he kissed her, as if he couldn't
get enough. As if he wanted to own her body and soul, and
though her rational self would run, she was too connected
with him, too swept away to care. With every thrust of his
tongue, he took deeper possession of her body and she
wanted more of him.

All of him.

Lifting his head, he looked into her eyes. Braced his hands on either side of her head and teased her moist entry with the head of his penis. She closed her eyes and sucked in a ragged, needy breath.

"More."

His eyes darkened and she realized she'd spoken out loud. Before embarrassment could hit her, he gave her what she'd asked for, edging his thick, hard member deeper inside her but not all the way home.

He looked into her eyes. "Enough?" he asked, his arms shaking from the obvious restraint.

She shook her head and he edged himself farther into her.

Her body screamed for his. She ached for him to fill her. She tossed her head from side to side, bending her legs, trying to pull him into her.

"Now?" he asked.

"No," she said, the word sounding more like a cry. A plea.

"Then tell me what you want." He spoke as if his life depended on her answer.

The neediness consuming her demanded a reply. *"I want you,"* she begged, writhing beneath him, twisting her hips, seeking that deeper, intense contact only he could give.

Her words released something primal inside him and he thrust inside, all the way, until he touched the deepest, most private part of her. He slid out, then in, picking up an intense rhythm that matched the desire building inside her once more.

As she watched his face, the play of emotion and expression connected her to him and need rose quickly, the crescendo building as he gave her everything she'd asked for and more. Harder and deeper, he played her body like he'd known it forever, fast thrusts followed by slow, lazy glides, their synchronicity bringing tears to her eyes as she realized sex had never been like this.

"Good?" he asked.

The question took her by surprise, but she forced an easy

smile, not wanting to give away the intensity of emotion rushing through her.

"Worth the long wait." They both knew she was referring to years, not the days since they'd met up again.

"I'm glad." A sexy smile edged his mouth. "I'm also not finished with you yet."

He picked up the fast tempo again and her nails dug into his shoulders. Once he began, he didn't stop, pounding into her with the force she'd craved, yet there was that *connection* between them that took this from rough sex to raw lovemaking. Their bodies collided and so did their souls, Faith thought, seconds before she came, her body racked with tremors of bliss that seemed to go on forever. Her orgasm triggered his, and he shouted her name, causing yet another quaking tremor to take hold. She rode out the consecutive wave, holding on to Ethan as he took her over the edge once more.

She didn't know how long they lay entwined, catching their breath, not saying a word. After such an intense experience, Faith figured silence was golden. She could barely grab hold of her thoughts. It was those thoughts—the ones during and the ones rushing at her fast and furious now—that had her scrambling to withdraw.

Two loud beeps disturbed her thoughts. Beeps she recognized. And from the way Ethan dove off her, beeps he recognized as well.

"Someone's here," he muttered, shooting her a concerned look.

"Ethan? It's Kate!" Which meant she had Tess with her.

God, this couldn't be worse. Faith groaned. "How'd she get in?"

"I gave Tess a key." A symbol of belonging, he'd thought.

"Go! Bathroom!" Faith pointed to the doorway in the corner.

He grabbed his clothes and bolted while she scrambled, pulling her underwear on first, her skirt, bra, and tank top. Ethan burst out of the bathroom, fully dressed.

"Ethan? Are you home?" Kate called again.

"I'll be right down!" he called to her. He turned to face Faith, but she wasn't ready for conversation and glanced away.

"You should go down. I'll be there in a few." After she'd pulled herself together.

Convinced herself this had been sex and only sex.

That she could go back to seeing him, working with him, and not want to jump his bones.

Or want things from him she shouldn't.

Eleven

Ethan didn't want to leave Faith alone with time to think and regret. He'd seen her withdrawing even before Kate showed up. He'd been blown away by what just happened between them too, but as he'd promised himself, he was finished running from things that scared him or that he didn't understand.

He'd deal with his guest and as soon as Kate was gone, he'd sit Faith down and make sure things between them were okay.

He jogged down the stairs to find Kate waiting for him as he reached the bottom.

"What are you doing here?" he asked her. "I thought I was picking Tess up from the center. Speaking of Tess, where is she?" Ethan glanced over Kate's shoulder, but his sister wasn't standing behind her.

"Tess! Come here and face your brother," Kate called to the open front door.

Tess didn't appear.

"Uh-oh. What'd she do?" he asked, dreading the answer.

"I introduced her to a group of nice kids. I got called into a meeting and when I came out she was hanging out in the back of the building with a different bunch that we're having some issues with, smoking cigarettes."

"Tess!" He bellowed, and to his surprise the teen stomped into the house without his having to ask a second time.

"What? You've got a problem with cigarettes too?" she asked, glancing down at her feet instead of looking him in the eye.

He leaned against the wooden banister. "Apologize to Kate. She was nice enough to take you for the afternoon and you thanked her by giving her aggravation. Nice going."

Tess set her jaw.

Silence filled the house, broken only by the sound of Faith's footsteps on the stairs. He figured she'd caught the gist of what was going on because she didn't say a word, merely stepped around him, to stand beside Kate.

A quick glance told him Faith had dressed and fixed her tousled hair, but it was obvious, to him anyway, exactly what they'd been doing. And from Kate's raised eyebrows, she knew it too.

"Tess. Apology. Now." Ethan folded his arms across his chest, forcing himself to concentrate on what mattered at the moment.

"Sorry."

"Thank you," Kate said to the teen. "I'm there every afternoon if you want to give it a try again."

"Very generous of you," Ethan said, acknowledging Kate's offer with a forced smile.

Something had to give with this kid and soon. No wonder her sister had dumped Tess here. "Kate, do you happen to have the names of some child psychologists?" he asked.

"No fucking way am I talking to some stranger." Tess wrapped her arms around herself, pulling her coat further around her like a shield.

"Yes, way. Did Kelly ever take you to a shrink?" he asked.

Tess shook her head violently. "No. She knew I wouldn't go." She raised her chin in a defiant gesture, sure she now had the upper hand.

She was about to find out differently. "Well, you now have three brothers who can pick you up and carry you into the office if that's what it takes."

Tess let out a choking sound.

Faith broke her mask of indifference for the first time and treated him to an approving smile, which helped release the vise that had been squeezing inside his chest.

Kate nodded in agreement. "I'll get the numbers to you ASAP," she said, surprise in her tone.

No doubt she thought Ethan wouldn't know what to do with a kid like Tess. Maybe Kate even believed he wouldn't care. Based on his past, he knew everyone figured he'd run at the first sign of trouble.

Well, they were all right about one thing only. He *didn't* know what to do with Tess. He only knew what seemed right. What nobody had done when he'd been wild and out of control, he realized suddenly and filed that thought away for another time.

"I hate you," Tess said, whirling past him and storming up the stairs, deliberately adding a loud stomp with each step.

Join the club, kid.

Kate sighed. "I'm sorry. I didn't mean to bring her back here and interrupt . . ."

"You didn't," Faith interjected, the desperation in her tone making a lie of her claim.

Kate shot her an *I know better* look. "I just thought bringing her right home would make a stronger statement than letting her stay and think she got away with something."

"It's fine," Ethan assured her. "I appreciate the trouble you went to today."

"It wasn't trouble. I feel sorry for her. Therapy's a good idea. Any way you can show her that no matter how much trouble she causes, it won't change the fact that she's your sister, should help. But it'll take time."

"I hear you." Ethan ran a hand through his hair, wondering how he'd get through it. "I was also thinking I'd have Dare take her on a tour of the jail and juvenile detention facilities. Scare her a little. Because right now, she doesn't seem scared of a helluva lot." Which frightened him to no end.

Kate raised her eyebrows. "Another good idea. Maybe I misjudged you," she allowed, her expression softening.

He laughed. "You wouldn't be the first and you won't be the last."

His gaze slid to Faith, who was still antsy, moving from foot to foot and unwilling to meet his gaze. That wouldn't do.

"I should get going," Kate said.

"I'll go with you. Can you drop me off at my place?" Faith asked, taking him off guard.

"I can take you back as planned," he said.

"That's okay. We're . . . finished and Kate's going now." *Finished. Ouch.*

But he heard the desperation in her tone and knew even if she stayed, he wouldn't get anywhere with her now. Better to give her breathing room. And if he were honest with himself, he could use some too. To deal with Tess and to process what the hell had gone on between them upstairs.

Because he'd had sex many times in his life. And that hadn't been just sex.

Faith remained tight-lipped on the car ride home, and Kate, good friend that she was, didn't push. She dropped Faith off at her apartment because she had to get back to the center, and Faith was grateful for the time alone.

Not that she wanted to think. She didn't. So she threw herself into her to-do list, starting with buying a new car. She no longer wanted to be on anyone's schedule but her own. Ironically, she'd need Kate to take her to a dealership to look for a vehicle, but then she'd have wheels and freedom.

Feeling the beginnings of a headache coming on, Faith realized it was almost dinnertime and she hadn't eaten anything in hours. She called Tony's Pizzeria and ordered up a small plain pizza for delivery. An hour later, she'd eaten, showered, and watched some mindless television. By ten o'clock, she could no longer avoid the inevitable and she let her mind wander to this afternoon.

To Ethan.

At sixteen years old, she'd wanted him. She just had no idea what that really meant. At twenty-seven, with boyfriend experience and a marriage behind her, she thought she'd been prepared. But how could she have anticipated anything like the explosive chemistry they'd shared? She'd never craved any man like she did him. No man had ever made her bold enough to ask for what she wanted in bed. None had made her scream out loud. And none had ever taken her to such unbelievable heights of passion. He was alternately tender and giving, strong and demanding, taking everything she had. And she'd willingly complied, both emotionally and physically.

What in the world has happened between us?

She wasn't sure, but she knew it threatened the very fragile, new foundations of the life she was building for herself. And that she couldn't allow.

Her phone rang, rescuing her from herself, and she eagerly picked up the receiver. "Hello?"

"Hello, princess."

It was as if she'd mentally connected to him and he called. Her stomach curled with warmth and pleasure while her mind rebelled against wanting something that frightened her so much. Just a few short days ago, her independence had been all that mattered to her. Jumping back into another relationship had been the last thing she planned because in her mind, relationships equated to giving up pieces of herself and her needs for someone else. Until she'd cemented who she was, she couldn't let a man distract her.

"I just thought I'd say hi," he said.

His sexy voice blanked out every objection she ought to have.

She swallowed hard. "Hi. How's Tess?" She grasped for a safe topic. "Did she like her room?"

He let out a groan. "Tess is Tess. And I have no idea how she feels about her room. She's not speaking." She heard the frustration in his tone. "But I didn't call to talk about her."

"Oh." Faith's mouth went dry. "What did you call to talk about?" *Please say your house, furniture, something safe,* she thought.

"*Us*—as if you didn't know." His low laughter reverberated in her ear.

Us. With that one word, heat washed over her body in undulating currents.

"And before you say there is no us"—she figured the man must be a mind reader—"let me assure you there definitely is."

His rich voice oozed through her like maple syrup on Rosalita's pancakes, warm, gooey, and delicious, one taste making her crave so much more.

"Ethan—"

"Don't worry. I'm not asking for a lifetime commitment. I'm not even asking for that pesky relationship you don't want. I'm just saying it's pointless to lie to yourself and say there's nothing when whatever it is was so damn good."

That did it. Liquid fire settled between her legs and she squeezed her thighs together, only serving to heighten the tension, not ease it.

He was right. Whatever it was, was damn good and too potent to ignore. They were both adults who could indulge and walk away when it was over.

"I know you're there. I can hear you breathing," he said lightly.

She clenched the receiver tighter in her hand. "I'm here."

Adult, she reminded herself. *Go with it.* "You're right," she said to him. "It's something."

He exhaled hard. "Good."

She nodded. "Good."

"Night, princess."

"Night," she said, a lump in her throat, but she didn't know why.

He'd offered her exactly what she could handle at this stage in her life. She ought to feel good. Then why did she feel so empty and abandoned inside instead?

Faith awoke the next day, determined to keep building her life. She and Kate went car shopping, resulting in her buying a white Volkswagen Jetta. The car fit her new lifestyle and didn't put a major dent in her savings, especially thanks to Ethan's house job. She frowned at the notion. Everything came back to Ethan. Her thoughts, emotions, and now even her financial state.

No more.

She picked up her new car a few days later and her first stop was the newspaper office where she intended to purchase an ad for her business. The classified editor recognized her name and tried to push for information about her father's time in prison, something Faith wouldn't know anything about. She still hadn't spoken to her father and didn't intend to. Nor did she plan on filling this little weasel in on her personal life.

The editor in chief, upon learning she was in the building, came out to attempt to coax her to sit for an interview about being the daughter of the town's most well-known felon. Again, she declined to comment. He wasn't happy.

Nobody appreciates the high road, Faith thought.

After dodging the small-town press, she managed to take out an ad for Faith's, hoping to drum up business.

Next she distributed her business cards to local shops

like April's Consign and Design, asking her to recommend Faith to people who came into her store.

She called Kate and informed her that she wanted to join her monthly book club and then headed to the coffee shop to let Lissa know in person that she'd better accept her because Faith wasn't going anywhere. Lissa seemed to appreciate Faith more when she was outspoken than when she meekly allowed the other woman to verbally abuse her. So a wary truce was formed, and Faith felt like she'd taken a further step toward inserting herself into the fabric of Serendipity.

A few days later, an older woman walked into Faith's. Since it was the first person who'd come in off the street, Faith took heart. Although she hadn't been in business long, it seemed obvious the people in town weren't flocking to Faith Harrington's new venture.

As the woman came closer, Faith recognized her. "Mrs. Bretton!" Faith rose from her desk where she'd been busy planning the schedule for construction on cabinets and wall units in Ethan's house.

The dark-haired woman had been a friend of Lanie Harrington's for as long as Faith could remember. Unable to have children of her own, Caroline Bretton had been one of Lanie's country club friends who busied herself with tennis, golf, mah jong, and whatever other social activities could keep her busy.

"Faith, dear, welcome back to town," Caroline said.

Faith smiled. "Thank you."

Faith was surprised to see her. These days, she didn't know if Caroline was one of the women who'd abandoned her mother or whether Lanie had just frozen her out as she had her daughter. Her mother was tight-lipped about her postscandal personal life.

"So what are you doing here?" Faith asked.

"I saw your ad in the paper. It just so happens I'm ready to redecorate my family room. I thought I'd give you a chance!"

Faith blinked, stunned. "Really? That's wonderful. Thank you!"

"If it works out, I'll hire you for the rest of the house." She patted Faith's hand.

Faith's heart beat faster inside her chest. "I don't know what to say." Faith was grateful for the other woman's generosity.

"I know you haven't had an easy time. It's the least an old family friend can do." Caroline smiled.

So her mother's friend hadn't turned her back on the Harringtons. Lanie just hadn't informed her that Faith had opened her own business. Faith was hurt but not surprised. Her mother had already made her feelings on Faith's business clear.

"I hope my mother knows what a good friend you are."

The older woman shook her head and met Faith's gaze. "No. She doesn't. But you knew that already."

Faith sighed. Her mother hadn't had many real friends that Faith could recall, just people who had wealth and status in common, but she remembered Caroline had always been different. She'd called the house, seemed interested in Faith whenever she saw her, and even her mother knew she could count on Caroline. Lanie didn't know how to return friendship any more than she knew how to be a real mother. Yet Caroline had seemed to accept her mother for who and what she was, and apparently that hadn't changed.

Maybe I ought to take a lesson from her, Faith thought. "Mrs. Bretton—"

"Please, call me Caroline. We're going to be working closely together, after all."

Faith nodded. "Caroline, how is my mother *really*?"

"In complete and utter isolation. Yes, most people in our social circle ostracized her, thinking she knew about your father's illegal activities or afraid they'd catch the scandal by breathing the same air. But there were those like me, who knew better. Your mother was too concerned about her lifestyle to worry or think about where that money came from."

Faith bit the inside of her cheek and nodded. "That about sums her up," she agreed. "I don't believe she knew either. Which isn't to say she shouldn't have, but like you said, she wouldn't look too deeply as long as her life was going along the way she wanted it to."

"Exactly." Caroline's hazel eyes bored into hers. "I always liked your mother. Despite the fact that she could be so superficial, she was also smart and honest. I respect a woman who tells it like it is. And give her one martini and she became an excellent listener. Just not anymore. Now she's holed up in that house on the outskirts of town, refusing to have anything to do with real friends like me."

"So she has no one?" Faith asked, surprised and a lot guilty.

She'd reached out to her mother, but it was superficial, doing her duty as a daughter, Faith admitted. A phone call here and there to tell herself she was trying.

"No, but that's her own choosing," Caroline said. "Don't beat yourself up over it."

Faith disagreed. How could she not? She was an adult, but she still viewed her mother through a child's eyes. Instead, she should have looked deeper, should have made an effort to push herself into her mother's life, to see what was going on.

"I appreciate your honesty," Faith said. "I know my mother is who she is, but I'll try harder to reach her."

Caroline fingered her overly large pearls. "Just don't expect too much or you may be doomed to disappointment. I still call her weekly, but she shuts me down and never returns the gesture."

"I'm sorry." Faith didn't know what else to say.

"Oh, no. Never apologize for someone else. She's your mother, but you are your own person. You don't know how much I admire that. If I had a daughter, I hope she'd be as strong as you." Caroline's voice softened.

Warmth spread inside Faith. It surely wasn't a sentiment her mother had ever thought about her. But Faith realized she had to be more like Caroline, accepting Lanie for who she was instead of being angry at her for her inability to be who Faith wanted her to be.

"That's one of the nicest things anyone's said to me," Faith told Caroline.

"I'm sure since your return there haven't been many pleasant things said to you at all. Our set of friends don't know how to rally around someone when they're down."

"I appreciate you saying that."

Caroline straightened her shoulders. "Well then, back to business! When can you come over and look at the room? I have some ideas I'd like to discuss with you."

Faith was grateful for the subject change and returned to her desk. She pulled out her appointment book. They agreed on a date and time and Caroline walked out.

She'd given Faith a lot to think about where her mother was concerned. Lanie was the only family Faith had. And while Faith was watching Ethan's struggles with his family first hand, she'd been ignoring her own. In Faith and her mother's relationship, Faith was more the adult, Lanie more the child. If anyone was going to make a true overture, it had to be Faith.

But right now, Faith had something else to think about and celebrate. A new client.

"Woo hoo!" She hung her head back and let the blood rush to her head, spinning around in her chair. She understood the importance of Caroline's offer. If Faith got this job right, a reference from Caroline would open all sorts of doors.

Faith had wanted independence and now she was on her way.

* * *

For Ethan, the weeks after he'd slept with Faith were all about Tess. Both his business and his personal life took a backseat to settling the teenager into his life and finding a routine. He followed up on Kate's recommendations and narrowed down the list of therapists, calling each and choosing the one he thought sounded like a good fit for Tess. Ethan met with the doctor by himself first to make sure his phone impression held up to real life.

He liked Dr. Tina Sinclair. About his age, she was young enough that Tess would be able to relate to her and seemed "with it" enough not to turn the teen off with too conservative views. That set, he took his silent, fuming sister for her first appointment.

Dr. Sinclair's first suggestion? Ethan and his brothers needed to form a tight-knit unit, setting up a schedule and a family the teenager could rely on. Easier said than done, Ethan knew. Yet his brothers were coming tonight for their first family dinner, cooked and served by Rosalita. His housekeeper had reacted to hearing about Tess just as Ethan expected.

She'd folded her arms across her chest and huffed. "You're a bad boy, Mr. Ethan. I'm not surprised you have a bad sister."

But this time Ethan thought he caught a twinkle of amusement in her eye, then decided he knew better. She still hated him.

"Tess is misunderstood, like me. Give her a chance," he'd said.

Rosalita had agreed, the woman having more integrity than to judge a child by her looks. Rosalita had extended her hours, coming in around ten and staying until dinner was served and the dishes cleaned. Of course, his housekeeper and Tess had gotten off to an expectedly rocky start, arguing over everything. But like Faith had promised,

Rosalita dealt with the angry teen just fine, and her firm hand was exactly the help Ethan needed.

Then there was Faith, whom Ethan had given a bullshit line to about not wanting a relationship when everything in him screamed in protest. He damned well wanted something more than casual—because, so far, casual meant Ethan hadn't seen or heard from her since the night he'd found heaven in her body.

Except for an e-mail exchange about fabric and colors in the family room, she'd gone silent. So no, casual wasn't working for him. As soon as he survived this family gathering, he'd turn his focus to bringing Faith back into his orbit.

Ethan didn't kid himself that his brothers' willingness to come over meant they had forgiven him. But other than his promise to stick around, he was at a loss how to handle them. Just like he was at a loss how to handle Faith. Or his business, since Franklin had called earlier with the news that Ethan's onetime partner, Dale Conway, was sniffing around Amelia, Ethan's executive assistant, in his Washington, D.C., office. Since Amelia handled all the government contracts—sensitive information—transferred from the office in New York City to D.C., Ethan knew he was in trouble. The PI was now monitoring Amelia and promised to report back soon.

The doorbell snapped him out of his thoughts and brought him right into the present.

His brothers had arrived.

Ethan had instructed Rosalita to bring them right into the kitchen. No sense pouring drinks when they didn't want to give Tess the idea that they approved of drinking. Not to mention the fact that it would only lead to three men standing around, glasses in hand, in awkward, angry silence. Might as well have an awkward, angry meal instead. Though hopefully Nash and Dare would bury their real feelings for Tess's sake, he was about to find out.

He met them in the kitchen. Like Ethan, who'd dressed

in jeans and a crew-neck shirt, Dare too was casually attired in worn, faded jeans and a New York Yankees T-shirt. Nash, the professional, wore a pair of khakis and a short-sleeved polo shirt. They couldn't look more different, but they stood shoulder to shoulder, facing Ethan.

"Thanks for coming," he said to them.

"We're here for Tess," Dare said.

Didn't Ethan know it.

Nash nodded. "DNA tests confirmed it," he said, repeating what he'd already told Ethan on the phone. "Where is she?"

"Miss Tess right here." Rosalita gave the girl a not-so-gentle nudge in the back, forcing her into the room.

"Hey, watch it," Tess muttered.

"You need to learn how to speak to people," Ethan said. "Thank you, Rosalita."

The other woman nodded and headed to the working side of the kitchen.

Dare walked over to Tess. The more casually dressed of the brothers, he'd have more of a shot of relating to Tess on an overall looks level—except that she knew he was a cop. Ethan doubted she'd cut either brother any slack.

"So, how are you doing?" Dare asked Tess.

She folded her arms across her chest, which had the effect of hugging that damned jacket closer around her slender body. "What's it to you?"

Ethan was about to reprimand her, but Dare shot him a warning glare, accompanied by a shake of his head. A silent *Stay out of it.*

"You taking your coat off for dinner?" Dare asked, ignoring her attitude.

Ethan hadn't seen her remove the old surplus jacket ever. She merely glared.

"Chicken and potatoes," Rosalita said, rounding the counter, arms laden with dishes.

Grateful for the diversion, Ethan grabbed a seat and everyone followed. Ethan sat at the head and Nash and Dare united on one side of the small rectangular table across from Tess on the other.

Rosalita served them and they all began to eat in uncomfortable silence. Ethan didn't know where to begin to break the ice.

"So how come you didn't invite your girlfriend to this gig?" Tess asked, having no problem finding a subject to discuss.

"What girlfriend?" He decided to play this deliberately obtuse.

She rolled her eyes. "Faith Harrington. Unless you've got another girl on the side?"

"Of course not!" He gritted his teeth, unable to believe what a challenge this kid was.

"I thought Faith Harrington was just a *friend*." Nash's disgusted tone indicated what he felt about Faith having even that status in Ethan's life.

Girlfriend wouldn't go over well. And Tess knew it, the little stinker, Ethan thought, catching the evil gleam in her eye. Of course it was hard to be sure with the black liner circling her lids, but Ethan was certain she was playing them, using the information she'd learned the one and only night they'd all been in the same room together. The night Tess had arrived.

"I thought tonight was about family," Ethan said. "And all of us getting along. That can't happen if we're making digs and deliberately bringing up subjects to piss one another off." He snagged Tess's gaze once more.

"Sounds to me like she fits right in," Dare muttered under his breath.

"What the hell did I do?" Tess asked, shoveling chicken into her mouth. "I'm just making conversation since none of you wanted to do it."

She'd picked up on the obvious.

"Don't talk with your mouth full," Dare said. "And watch the language. We're here, so let's make the best of it."

Ethan appreciated Dare's take on things, but his brother refused to meet his gaze so Ethan could acknowledge it or tell him so. Fine.

"How have you been keeping busy?" Nash asked the teen.

"He sends me to the community center to hang with other juvenile delinquents," she said, gesturing to Ethan with an elbow.

Ethan groaned. "The community center has good programs for teens. She's been working with Kate Andrews."

"She's *Faith's* best friend," Tess said between gulping her drink.

Ethan ignored her. "Tess and I met with a therapist," he said to his brothers. That particular appointment had been extremely enlightening and he needed to share the information, since helping Tess would be a group effort.

Without warning, Tess threw her silverware onto the table, the fork and knife hitting the plate with a loud clatter. "I'm outta here," she said, rising from her seat. Apparently she didn't like the tables being turned and her being the focus of discussion.

"Sit down *now*," Ethan said, taking charge of this fiasco.

"Hell, no," she said, and stormed out of the room, leaving the brothers alone.

Dare and Nash looked at one another, some silent understanding passing between them that left Ethan out in the cold.

"What?" Ethan spat, annoyed.

Nash wiped his mouth on the napkin. "She follows orders just as well as you ever did."

Dare's mouth lifted in a grim smile.

Ethan blew out a long, frustrated breath. "Don't you think I've grown up since I've been gone?"

Nash rose to his feet. "I don't know. Have you?" he asked in definite challenge.

With Tess gone, the gloves were apparently off.

Ethan pushed his chair back, and stood, meeting his

middle brother's angry gaze. "Maybe if you came around more, you'd find out." Ethan was finished tiptoeing around his past mistakes.

Nash shoved his chair beneath the table hard. "Tess aside, give me one other good reason I'd want to be here. Because it sure as hell wouldn't be to get to know you. You gave up being our brother the day you left."

Without being asked, Dare silently stood, standing beside Nash, united against Ethan in every way.

Twelve

Ethan braced one hand over the back of the chair, gripping the handle tight. "I was eighteen and fucked up," he reminded them. "Do you think I knew what I was doing back then?" Not that it was an excuse and they all knew it.

"Apparently not since you got our parents killed," Dare joined in with a lethal blow.

Shooting pain seared through both Ethan's head and heart. It was one thing to blame himself, another to hear his youngest brother say it out loud. To know his siblings held him responsible was a hell of a lot worse than to merely fear it, and Ethan felt a ten-ton weight settle on his chest.

He could barely catch his breath. "They were killed by a drunk driver," he managed to say, repeating the logic he'd heard over the years. The same logic the army shrink had tried on him when nightmares drove him to seek help. It hadn't helped him then and it sure as shit wouldn't smooth things over now.

"And you were the reason they were out on that goddamn road." Dare stepped forward, spine straight, face red. "And

even then, you couldn't step up and be a man. You ran."
Dare's voice filled with disgust while Nash gripped his
younger brother by the shoulder.

Holding him back or comforting him, Ethan didn't know.
Didn't care. He had no excuses, no words to make it better.
He'd thought the same things over the years, hating himself
and the kid he'd been. But his brothers' loathing and disgust
ripped him in two.

"I made a mistake," he said through clenched teeth.

"A decade-long mistake," Nash said. "You never called.
You never came back. You just blew out of town and disappeared from our lives without a goddamn thought about
what might happen to your brothers."

Ethan couldn't deny Nash spoke the truth, and his heart
threatened to pound out of his chest. Holding his ground,
he knew all he could do was to somehow hang on to the
shreds of pride he had, though at this point there wasn't
much left. "I'm sorry," he said.

But it seemed they wanted more. They wanted blood and
damned if they didn't deserve it, he thought, now clenching
and unclenching his fists.

"Tell me something," Nash said. "Did you ever wonder
what the hell kind of life you abandoned us to?"

Ethan didn't answer. Didn't have to. They'd tell him anyway. Knowing he'd spent nights beating himself up, wondering the same thing wouldn't make a difference to either of
them. And Ethan needed to hear about the past from their
mouths.

"We were split up," Nash finally said. "Separated. No
one would take us together." His brother gripped his hands
together, twisting them in an obvious effort to contain his
anger.

Ethan couldn't even swallow.

"I went to the Rossmans, a good family on the *right* side
of town," Nash said, no pleasure in his words. "They could
have afforded to take in both of us, but they only wanted

one son—to replace the one they'd lost to a drug overdose a few years before, and I happened to be the same age as their kid when he'd died."

Nash paused for air.

Dare glared at Ethan, who couldn't bring himself to speak.

"And Dare?" Nash asked. Finally ready to go on, he gestured to their youngest sibling. "He went to the shittiest foster home you can imagine. Remember the Garcias?" This time he waited for Ethan to process the name and reply.

It didn't take long. Ethan recalled the family who'd always taken in more kids than they had room for, happy for the state checks. He had a vivid recollection of the Garcias' foster children with clothes that didn't fit, sitting alone because nobody would hang with them. Other kids would rather abuse them than befriend them.

Nausea filled him. He folded his arms across his chest, but he couldn't deflect the internal blow. "I remember."

Nash's eyes, normally their mother's medium blue, darkened in anger. "He was only fifteen." He gripped his brother's shoulder once more. "I snuck him food and I brought him my old clothes. Where the hell were you?" Stepping forward, Nash poked Ethan in the chest, deliberately pushing him.

"I was in the army."

No surprise flickered in either brother's gaze.

Ethan had no doubt Nash and Dare had done their research on him. Afraid of what he'd find, Ethan hadn't let himself do the same for them.

"So here we are," Nash said. "We'll show up for Tess. We'll make sure she has what she needs, but don't ask us to do anything for you." His middle brother made their current position perfectly clear.

Nash's words rang in Ethan's ears. He distantly heard the alarm beeps and the door slam, but the noise barely registered.

"Do we understand each other?" Nash asked.

"Perfectly," Ethan said, his hands digging into the seat back.

"So what does Tess need from us?" Dare asked.

Ethan couldn't think, couldn't breathe. Even speaking was beyond him. But he managed to remind himself that a teenage girl needed him to act like an adult. And as much as he wanted to run far and fast, he stood firm. Because running was what his brothers expected of him, and for that reason alone, he managed to look them in the eye now.

"Tess needs to feel she's part of a solid unit, and we're the best she's got." Ethan let out a wry, sarcastic laugh because their best was pretty damn pathetic. "We need to set a good example of behavior, and the doctor suggested we implement rules so we all know what we can and can't expect from one another."

"Fucking swell," Dare muttered.

Ethan narrowed his gaze. "You may not like me, but right now we're in this together. You treat me like shit in front of Tess and she'll think it's okay to do the same. And vice versa."

"Is that shrink talk, or are you coming to these brilliant conclusions on your own?" Nash asked.

Ethan set his jaw and silently counted to five. "Both. I've been the adult in her life for the last three weeks or so. It's time to pull together on this."

"What did you have in mind?" Nash asked, in a more conciliatory tone.

Ethan's ears were still ringing with their words, anger, truths. Yet he had to keep them together like the doctor said. "I was hoping we could eat dinner as a family a few nights a week. Let her know she can expect us and count on us. You two up for that?" Ethan asked.

To his surprise, they both nodded.

"Too many kids come into the station and the center with no stable family unit. Just name the days and I'll be there," Dare said.

Ethan barely let out a breath, realizing that *Dare* knew just what it felt like not to have that same family unit. Ethan's mouth grew dry. "Rosalita's off Mondays. Tuesdays, Wednesdays, and Thursdays work for you?" he managed to ask.

"Yeah," Nash said.

"Me too," Dare added.

"I can take her to work one day next week. Give her a tour of the county jail, let her see what juvie's like," Dare offered. He paused. "Unless you want to give her an insider's tour?" As soon as the words were out, he shook his head, his dark head bowing. "It'll take time to get used to not knocking you with every breath," he muttered.

Ethan ignored that. He was already raw and bruised inside. A few more hits couldn't do any more damage. "I'll get Tess's community center schedule from Kate and we'll coordinate with yours."

Dare nodded. "Fine."

Nash raised a hand. "I can take her to the sidewalk fair tomorrow night and she can stay for dinner. And maybe I can get her working filing some papers in the office to keep her busy when she's not at the center."

Ethan was grateful for their suggestions, not that he'd say so. They didn't care how he felt about anything. "It's a good idea for her to get to know you one on one." He kept the focus on Tess.

"She can stay over," Nash said, and Dare nodded, indicating the same.

"Let's see what she's comfortable with, but it's fine with me," Ethan said carefully.

And so it went as they awkwardly hammered out a schedule, each writing down dates and times and agreeing to revisit the schedule in a few weeks. As for school, Kate had already promised to explain how and when Tess would need to be registered. By the middle to end of August, her sister, Kelly, would return, and the four of them could discuss the future.

Right now, the brothers had accomplished all they could. In fact, they'd had more of each other than any of them could handle. *Or stand,* Ethan thought.

Long after they were gone, Ethan stood in the center of the kitchen, more alone, lost, and disgusted with himself than he'd been since he'd left home at eighteen.

"Mr. Ethan, Miss Tess, she's gone!" Rosalita came running into the room, her large body heaving. "I thought she was in her room, but she's not there!"

Ethan ran a shaking hand through his hair. "Did you check outside?" he asked, recalling where he'd found Tess last time, smoking a joint.

Rosalita nodded. "She's not out back or on the front porch."

Ethan recalled hearing the door beep earlier but thought it was Rosalita. "Was that you who went out while we were in the kitchen?" he asked her.

She shook her head. "I make myself scarce in the laundry room."

Ethan groaned. Tess must have walked out. Probably after hearing the yelling and accusations in the kitchen. Ethan's cell phone rang suddenly and he yanked it out of his back jeans pocket, pausing to glance at the number.

Faith.

An hour ago, he'd have been thrilled to hear from her. Now? He couldn't stand his own company. He wouldn't be subjecting her to his.

"Maybe she knows where Miss Tess is," Rosalita said.

He pressed send. "Hello?"

"Ethan, it's Faith." Her soft voice was a soothing balm to his senses, one he didn't deserve. And she definitely deserved better than him. "I have Tess," she said quickly.

He let out the breath he hadn't been aware of holding and nodded at Rosalita. "She's with Faith," he told his housekeeper, who immediately crossed herself.

"She came to you?" he asked.

"Not exactly. I went outside to throw out the trash, glanced over the railing, and she was outside. Making out with a boy in a corner of the empty parking lot," she said, her voice now a whisper.

"I'll be right there."

Faith let Tess watch TV while they waited for Ethan to pick her up. The teenager had already given Faith an earful about what went on in the house and why she'd run off, and Faith's stomach churned at the accusations Dare and Nash had thrown at Ethan. At first she'd been surprised the teen was talking in full sentences, but clearly Tess wanted to share the discoveries she'd made about her new family.

And Faith knew Ethan well enough by now to realize he already blamed himself for the deaths of his parents, and his brothers hadn't cut him any slack. None at all.

When her doorbell rang and she let Ethan inside, one look at his dark, tormented eyes told her all she needed to know. Nash and Dare had done serious damage to his psyche.

"Hey," she said gently. "Come on in."

He stepped inside and his gaze immediately snagged on Tess. "Let's go."

The teenager didn't shift her gaze from the television screen and the MTV *Cribs* show she was watching.

"Why don't you come sit down and we'll talk?" Faith asked.

He needed to calm down before he took his mood out on Tess. And he looked like he needed someone to be there for him. As much as she'd tried to pull away these past few weeks and focus on herself and her business, he'd never been far from her mind. Sleeping with him wasn't something she could forget.

"It's not a good time," he said coldly, then looked past her to Tess. "Tess, I said move it!" he barked.

There was no warmth, no vestiges of the man who, while intense, had always shown interest in Faith whenever they as much as breathed the same air. She didn't take it personally, but she was really worried about how deeply he'd drawn into himself.

"Chill," the teen muttered, taking her time rising to her feet.

"I don't think you're in a position to be calling the shots," he said to his sister.

"Ethan . . ." Faith reached out and touched his shoulder.

He flinched and pulled away. "You don't want to be near me right now." His dark tone was a warning she ought to heed.

Tess strode up to her brother, her bravado not faltering. "It's not my fault you screwed your brothers over," she said, then stormed past him and headed out the door.

Ouch, Faith thought. The kid needed to learn when to back off.

"Out of the mouths of babes," he said under his breath.

"You weren't much more of one yourself," she reminded him. "Don't let Nash and Dare get under your skin. You're here now."

His startled gaze met hers. "Tess overheard the fight?" he asked as if his worst fear was confirmed.

Faith nodded. "I'm sorry."

"And she took great pleasure in filling you in," he said flatly.

"Actually I think she feels bad for you. She just doesn't know how to express her feelings. Cut her some slack now and maybe she'll do the same." Faith didn't know anything about raising a teenager, but she sensed something in Tess that was desperate to reach out to her brother.

He raised an eyebrow. "Just because Tess decided to open her big mouth doesn't make any of this your business."

Faith bit the inside of her cheek. Though she knew why he was lashing out at her, she wasn't about to take it. "I wouldn't be so quick to alienate me. You don't have many people on your side."

"Obviously that's the way I like it. You should have gone with your gut instinct and stayed far away from me." He pulled his car keys from his pocket and stormed out the door.

Faith stood watching out the window as they climbed into the car and Ethan tore out of the parking lot, obviously thinking he'd made a clean escape. The problem was, she couldn't let him go.

Ethan had taken a beating no man deserved, especially not one who was already punishing himself for mistakes he'd made in the past. Tess needed Ethan, but he needed someone too. He couldn't be alone tonight, angry and brooding.

Heaven help her, she was the only one who could get through to him now.

Ethan gripped the steering wheel hard, not trusting himself to speak to his sister just yet. The bruising his brothers had given him was still fresh. And seeing Faith in her gray sweatpants, loose T-shirt, and high ponytail, like she'd just rolled out of bed, with those soft, caring eyes, he was barely holding it together. He wasn't in the mood to spar with the mouthy teen.

"Man, you really were a screwup, weren't you? Guess we have something in common after all," Tess said, sounding pleased with herself and him.

He bit the inside of his cheek. "Does that mean you'll give me a break and behave from now on?"

"Hell, no." She burst out laughing, taking him off guard.

He slid a glance her way before returning his attention to the road. With her unexpected smile and light in her eyes, he realized she was actually a cute kid. Pretty, even. He knew better than to mention it.

"Fine," he muttered. "Then how about a truce for just one night? We'll discuss your behavior in the morning."

She folded her arms across her chest. "Only if we can talk about what I overheard too."

He gripped the wheel harder. "This isn't a democracy," he told her.

"No, it's a fucking dictatorship." She shifted her entire body ninety degrees and faced out the window, turning her back to him.

He opened his mouth to tell her to watch her language, then shut it again.

He was done for the night.

They returned home. Rosalita was still cleaning and informed him she would stay until she'd finished some extra laundry she'd thrown into the machine. He appreciated her more than she could imagine or was able to express at the moment.

Without another word, he and Tess went to their separate rooms.

An hour later, Tess had finally stopped blasting heavy metal music, and the light went out beneath her door. He'd looked out at least five times, checking on her. He already knew he didn't have to worry about her escaping through the window. It was a straight drop from the second floor to the ground below.

He returned to his bedroom, washed up, tossed his shirt into the hamper, and unbuttoned his jeans, his bed beckoning. It had been a long day he couldn't wait to put behind him.

The beep beep of the door told him Rosalita had left for the night and he was finally alone in his house. He sat down on his bed and ran a hand through his hair. When his bedroom door cracked open slowly, he couldn't have been more surprised.

"Come in, Tess," he called out.

"It's not Tess." To his shock, Faith, dressed as she'd been earlier, which he for some reason found sexier than a string bikini, stepped inside. "Rosalita let me in on her way out."

His heart staggered inside his chest. Putting up emotional distance was hard but necessary. "Why bother?" he asked coldly.

Faith shut the door to his bedroom and turned the lock, leaning against the closed door. "I was worried about you."

He admired her courage. At his darkest, he wasn't someone to mess with. "Well, don't be. I'm fine."

"You don't look fine. Your eyes are flat. Dead." She stepped closer, slowly making her way across the room. Toward him. "There's no life, no twinkle," she went on.

And she obviously thought she could put it back. A few hours ago, maybe she could have. Right now, he was back where he'd been ten years ago. Nobody could save him. Not even Uncle Sam.

"Your brothers aren't being fair. People change. I've seen how you talk about wanting a relationship with them. You're here. They'll come to realize that."

"Don't psychoanalyze me or my family. You don't know anything about us."

"True. And you knew nothing about me and my father, but that didn't stop you from giving me advice." She stood toe-to-toe with him.

He smelled her fresh scent, teasing him, tempting him, making him want to lose himself inside her until he couldn't think about who he was.

But he felt the anger at Nash and Dare simmering inside him and he knew he wouldn't be gentle with her. He couldn't. Didn't have it in him to think about her when it was all he could do to put one foot in front of the other and get through the night to face Tess tomorrow. And his brothers the day after that.

So if Faith pushed him now, yeah, he'd take her up on what she was offering—but it would be sex. And she wouldn't like him much afterward. He wouldn't like himself either, but that was pretty much a given.

She reached out and stroked his cheek with her delicate fingers.

Fire licked across his skin.

"Someone has to look out for you," she said.

He cocked his head to one side. "And you want that someone to be you? For the last three weeks you didn't want anything to do with me."

Something deeper flickered in her golden gaze. "There's no way you want to have this conversation now."

"You're right. I don't."

Her fingers still touched his face and she cupped his jaw. "Talking's overrated anyway." She leaned in, pressed her lips against his, soft and willing. Giving him the escape he desperately needed.

He deepened the kiss, thrusting his tongue inside her mouth. She moaned, her hands coming to his shoulders, her nails digging into his skin as she kissed him back, easing her body closer until her breasts crushed against his chest. Her thin T-shirt might as well have been nonexistent. He felt the rasp of her nipples and his body hardened. She sighed and climbed on top of him, bracketing him with her thighs, straddling him in heat.

Thrusting his hand into the back of her hair, he pulled her head back till he looked into her eyes. "Be sure, Faith." Because this was going to be no gentle lovemaking.

"You need me," she said simply.

He didn't argue.

She pulled her shirt over her head, baring her braless breasts. With a groan, he cupped them in his hands, dipped his head, and curved his lips around one distended nipple.

Nipping, laving, losing himself in tormenting her. Her cries of pleasure aroused him beyond reason and he switched breasts and repeated the process, drinking in her taste and scent.

She slipped her hands to the waistband of his jeans and impatiently tugged at the zipper. "Help me," she said, frustrated.

He gripped her around the waist and lifted her off him so he could yank her sweats down, gratified when her underwear went with them. Faith kicked the clothes into a heap while he rid himself of his jeans. With an eager smile, she wrapped her arms around his neck, clearly ready to climb back on top of him.

Instead, he turned her around and sealed his body against hers. His front against her back, he soaked in her heat from behind, his erection a hard ridge between them and he thrust his hips forward, immediately feeling her body tense.

"Relax for me, princess." He slid his arm around her waist, letting his hand trail down her smooth flat stomach to her slippery heat. He eased one finger into her dampness, finding her pulsing center.

She whimpered and tried to turn in his arms.

"Uh-huh." He brushed her hair off to one side, kissing her neck, dampening her skin, grazing her flesh lightly with his teeth.

Ethan couldn't take it anymore. He needed to be inside her.

Now.

"Bend over," he said gruffly. Intentionally rough.

She hesitated.

He waited.

He wanted to shock her and he was sure he had, certain her ex-husband and past high-society lovers had never pushed her for anything that made her uncomfortable. He hoped like hell she'd comply because as much as he wanted her, he refused to give himself the pleasure of looking into her beautiful face while he lost himself inside her. He wanted release but refused to accept anything more.

She'd always been his shining star, the ultimate representation of all that was good. He didn't deserve her and had been deluding himself in thinking it didn't matter. Tonight with his brothers had proven otherwise, putting him back in his place. So here he was with Faith, pushing her boundaries, hoping she would run and prove to him he was the bastard he thought he was.

To his surprise, she suddenly bent over, holding on to the bed with both hands—taking his breath and humbling him at the same time.

With everything inside him, he knew he should run far and fast because even without seeing her face, he knew he was in trouble. She was offering herself to him, giving him what *he* needed.

A better man would call a stop. He'd never been that man, he thought, gripping her hips and thrusting into her feminine heat. From this angle, he was tighter, deeper, than he'd been before. He felt everything she was, everything she was giving him.

Unable not to move, he slid out, then pushed back into her, out and in, only to find her immediately picking up his rhythm, her gasps and moans telling him she was building to a fast and furious climax. She wasn't alone. He pumped into her, doing as he wanted, as he needed, losing himself and the painful memories as he found heaven inside her willing body.

She clenched her inner walls tighter around him, milking him for all he was worth as he came in one last, powerful thrust. And though she followed him over, she continued to shudder in his arms, and he kept up the tempo of their joining until he was certain he'd wrung every last contraction out of her body.

When it was over, he didn't allow himself to remain inside her or find pleasure or comfort after. He separated them, his earlier gut-wrenching pain returning, multiplied tenfold, eating a hole in his chest.

She'd come to him, but he'd accepted, planning only to use her body to find meaningless release. Instead, he'd discovered that with Faith, there was no such thing.

Thirteen

"Faith—" Ethan spoke, reaching out to her.

She shook her head. "Don't say anything, okay?" She didn't want him to speak and ruin what had been the most intense experience of her life. She'd have plenty of time to mull things over and ruin it for herself later.

Still naked, she turned around and met his gaze. His eyes didn't hold any more life than they had earlier, but she'd briefly taken away his pain, even if it had returned now.

Faith had no regrets. She did, however, have plenty of reasons why she now knew to stay away from this man, the feelings he engendered inside her, and the choices he compelled her to make.

"I should go before Tess wakes up and realizes I'm here."

He nodded, not arguing. "I'll walk you out." He bent down and picked up her clothes, handing them to her.

She deliberately kept her concentration on putting one leg at a time into her sweats and not on his magnificent body as they dressed in silence, neither saying a word.

He wasn't pushing her, choosing instead to withdraw into

himself. She understood. After the confrontation with his brothers, he'd obviously decided he had enough going on in his life without adding her to the mix. She could definitely say the same.

She was glad she'd come to him and given them this one more night because there wouldn't be another. They walked downstairs, tiptoeing past Tess's bedroom. Funny, but already she thought of this as Ethan's house, no longer associating her old memories with these new ones.

They reached the front door and she turned. "I need to get into the house tomorrow or the next day with Nick. He needs to firm up some more measurements."

"Rosalita's always here. Feel free to come by." He paused, a frown wrinkling his forehead. "How did you get here anyway?" he asked.

"Oh, that's news. I bought myself a car," she said, knowing she sounded ridiculously pleased by such a normal act. "I decided I was finished relying on others to get where I needed to go." A sentiment she needed to apply to all aspects of her life from now on.

"Good for you." For the first time all night, his lips curved into a smile.

She couldn't contain a grin in return. "Don't torture yourself, okay?" The words slipped out before she could stop them.

"Don't worry about me," he said, back to giving orders.

Unwilling to make promises she couldn't keep, she merely said, "Good night, Ethan."

"Night, princess."

She stepped into the humid darkness and headed for the car. And though he didn't shut the front door, keeping an eye out until he heard the beep of her car doors unlocking, the slam still reverberated in her ears. Because he'd shut her out as thoroughly as she knew she needed to close the door on her relationship with him.

The drive home was short, but her mind was finally

churning with the thoughts she'd been holding for when she was alone. She pulled into the parking lot behind her apartment and rested her head on the steering wheel, mind reeling with how overpowering Ethan Barron was.

The men she'd dated and later the one she'd married had been oh-so-respectful in bed. Too respectful, never leaving her completely satisfied, yet she hadn't asked for or expected more. Despite that lack, she'd still turned herself inside out to make her husband happy. She'd buried her needs in favor of being the perfect lawyer's wife and companion, and on walking away, she'd promised herself that she'd never lose herself in a man ever again.

Then came Ethan.

She'd always been drawn to his hard edges and the bad boy inside him. But she understood on a fundamental level that her feelings for him threatened the identity she was trying to build and the independence she needed. She'd promised herself she'd steer clear, and yet at the first sign that he needed her she'd put her needs aside and gone to him.

He'd taken her, dominated her, and in doing so, he'd fulfilled a fantasy, one she'd never admit to a living, breathing soul. But she'd learned how easily she could submit to a strong, powerful man like Ethan. Though he and her ex-husband couldn't be more different, Faith realized now that Ethan posed that same risk—and she refused to lose her identity to another man.

Even one she was drawn to like no other.

After a sleepless night, Ethan woke up to face certain facts. Last night he'd let his brothers vent their anger, and though the fallout had devastated him, he had no choice but to deal. But he'd had no right to inflict his pain on Faith. It didn't matter that she'd come to him, cornering him when he'd have preferred to have been alone. Well, that was a lie. Being with her had been just fine, as long as it had been on his terms.

He'd used her to obliterate his feelings and she'd let him, which only made him feel worse. That they were both adults and he'd warned her about his mood wouldn't make facing her any easier. But she'd been there for him in a way no one ever had. Not his parents, not his brothers, not even his army buddies had pushed past one of his black moods or self-destructive bents, and last night he'd been on a big one.

He hadn't thought anyone could pull him out of it, but he had to admit, looking at things in the light of day, she'd gotten to him. And now she probably, rightfully, hated him. Since, at the moment, there was nothing he could do to fix things with her or his brothers, he turned his attention to the youngest family member.

He showered, dressed, and headed downstairs where he found Tess eating cereal out of the box in the kitchen, her concentration on her sketch pad.

As soon as she saw him, she hugged the pad to her chest, hiding her work from view. He didn't push, understanding they hadn't reached any level of trust just yet. But he was curious and knew she'd reveal her work when she was ready.

"Come on," he said to her. "You can bring the box in the car."

She glanced up from her Lucky Charms. "Where are we going?"

"You'll see." He took a look at her usual dark, heavy clothing, noted it was already ninety degrees out, and paused. "How about you leave the jacket home? It's hot as hell out there."

She raised a pierced eyebrow at him. "Where are we going?" she asked again.

Give and take, he thought. "Okay, you don't like surprises. We're going television shopping. We're also buying an Xbox."

"Nice!" she said before she caught herself and schooled her face back into an uncaring facade. "I'd rather have a Wii," she muttered.

Interesting. Whether she was being obstinate or not, he saw a chance here. "Take off the jacket and you've got yourself a deal."

She stared at him as if assessing his sincerity and his sanity. Finally, she shrugged and let the too-big jacket slip off her shoulders. Beneath it she wore dark khaki cargo pants and a black T-shirt. She looked about to drop the jacket on the floor, thought the better of it, and hung it over the back of a chair.

Progress, he thought, but understood if he made a big deal of her removing the jacket, he'd lose what little ground he'd gained. So he merely nodded and walked toward the garage, knowing she'd follow.

Twenty minutes later, they reached the Target he'd visited with Faith a few weeks ago. He parked the Navigator he'd driven instead of the Jag and walked into the store, Tess by his side.

"Grab a cart," he said to her.

For once, she did as he was told. "So why are you so interested in televisions all of a sudden?" Tess asked.

Because he'd been up all night tossing and turning, fighting the urge to run and make all his problems go away.

When he was younger, he'd lost himself in gaming systems, shutting out his mother's crying or his parents' fighting with the bright lights and sounds. He hadn't thought about how they could afford those items then. Looking back now, he realized his father had brought them home something from every trip he'd taken. A way to assuage his guilt, Ethan realized now, since he was probably spending his time away with Tess's mother.

So Ethan had the first Nintendo and the first Sony PlayStation on the market and he would play for hours, his mind always seeming to be light-years ahead of what he saw on the screen. As he got older, running with the wrong crowd had been a bigger draw, a way to catch his father's attention at first. Later on, the troublemaking aspect of his personality had just been stronger than the computer geek.

As an adult, he had better control of his impulses, mostly thanks to army training, and he knew he had to find something to lose himself in when the urge to escape became strong, like now.

He also needed to find common ground with Tess.

"Hey, I asked you a question!" Tess snapped her fingers in front of his face. "Where'd you go?"

He surprised himself by laughing. "Just lost in thought. The reason we're here is because of you."

"Huh?" She wrinkled her nose at him.

"I saw you watching TV at Faith's last night. I figured you'd like to have one in the house. Plus, since I moved in, I haven't had a chance to make the house a home. I know Faith's working on that, but I didn't want to wait for all her furniture orders to come in before we started enjoying the place." Not to mention he had to make the house more than just a prison for Tess if he wanted her to stay put. "You like TV, right?"

She nodded. "I guess I wouldn't mind being able to watch."

Yeah, right. Her eyes were wide as she took in the big screens surrounding them. She was practically salivating at the thought.

"How come you want Xbox? I thought you were an *adult*." She said the word *adult* like she thought he was no better than the devil himself.

At least she was keeping up the questions and not shutting down, talking and not cursing at him.

"Grown-ups can like video games. That's how I got into what I do for a living." He went on to explain to her about his job and how becoming a pro at computer simulation enabled him to build a future, when in reality, he should have had none.

To his surprise, she seemed to be paying attention.

"You're saying you'll play those games with me?" she asked, hopefully.

He brought the cart to a stop. "I'm saying I'll beat you at whatever game you choose." He winked at her and turned his attention to a huge flat-screen TV. "How about this one?" He looked to her for approval.

She shifted from foot to foot, obviously uncomfortable. "It's not up to me. It's not my house."

"What if I said it was? Do you like that little thirteen-inch? Or would you prefer this bad boy?" He wanted her to feel important, in control.

She folded her arms around herself, forming a cocoon without the help of her jacket. "I don't give a shit."

"And I don't believe you." Obviously she didn't understand that he really wanted to include her in the decision, that his house was her house, her home. "Okay, fine. If you're going to be a brat about it, I'll decide. I want this big one." He made a mental note of the make and model so he could ask a salesperson to get it for them later.

Without another word, he strode down the aisle, headed for the gaming stations at the far end. He found the Xbox 360 Live first and placed the console in the cart. Then he began searching for the Wii.

"What are you looking for?" Tess asked, cautiously.

He glanced at her out of the corner of his eye. The poor kid was torn between hope and fear, wanting to be excited yet afraid to express herself at all.

"I'm looking for the Wii. Isn't that what you wanted?"

She continued to brace her arms around her thin body. "You're still gonna get it for me?" she asked in a small voice.

"Yeah."

"Why? I was just a brat, like you said." She sounded defensive, but her body language said she felt more defeated than angry.

He swallowed hard, uncomfortable, not knowing the right thing to do to reach her and make her trust. "Because we made a deal and you held up your end." He met her gaze, deliberately holding it, wanting her to see and hear the promise he was about to make. "I promised you a Wii, and I'm a man of my word. If I tell you I'm going to do something, you can believe it."

He was referring to more than the Wii. Would she believe him? Or had past experience taught her not to trust the adults in her life? He didn't know enough about her past to judge.

"Are we cool?" he asked her.

"Nobody says 'cool,' " she muttered, but the edges of her lips turned upward in a grin. "Yeah, we're cool."

He resisted the urge to hug her, knowing he'd made enough progress for one day.

They found the Wii selection a little farther down the aisle from the televisions. There were white consoles, black consoles, ones bundled with sports software, exercise software, and Super Mario Bros. Eventually they agreed on the black— of course—and the Guitar Hero bundle. Then Ethan spoke to the nearest sales associate and asked for the television he wanted. The man offered to have it delivered, but Ethan wanted to take all of his purchases home with him instead.

The house was already wired for cable and satellite, and he wanted everything set up today. He'd gotten the name of an electronics guy from Nick, who was grudgingly doing the work around his house at Faith's urging. Ethan had already called the man first thing this morning, and he'd agreed to meet him back at the house later this afternoon to set up whatever items Ethan purchased.

Together he and Tess made their way to the register.

"Ethan?" she asked, as he put the systems on the conveyor belt.

"Yeah?"

"Thanks," she said, unable to meet his gaze.

He grinned. It was enough that she was polite and as happy as he'd seen her ever get. "You're welcome."

They picked up sandwiches, soda, and chips on the way

home, and by 4:00 P.M., Ethan and Tess had their family room set up with the biggest, baddest television in Serendipity, complete with two state-of-the-art gaming systems.

And for a while, they were both able to forget their problems and find peace.

Faith spent the day pulling in favors, getting earlier-than-expected delivery dates set for Ethan's furniture and arranging for the painter and paper hanger to get to work. First thing next week, the old wallpaper would come down and Faith's vision for the house would begin, starting with fresh paint and new paper.

Faith had arranged to meet Nick at Ethan's house at four o'clock and she was running late. April had begged Faith to meet her at Faith's apartment so she could show her new designs and pick up some things.

April unveiled the newest pieces she'd made using parts of Faith's couture items and vintage pieces of her own.

"These are incredible," Faith said, fingering delicate lace and rough denim that somehow came together to make the most amazing-looking jacket.

Today April's hair was a deeper red, almost burgundy, and still she looked put together and bright. "Thank you." April grinned. "Pretty darn good if I do say so myself, right?"

In her arms, her Yorkie let out a yip of agreement.

Faith petted the little guy's head.

"You said you have more clothing I can use, right? Things you won't be wearing anymore?" April asked.

"See for yourself." Faith gestured toward the big boxes stuffed in a corner behind the couch. "Take whatever you want."

April's eyes warmed. "Thank you so much. I had an offer from a boutique store in SoHo. They want to take my pieces from this collection on consignment."

"It's the opportunity of a lifetime!" Faith said. "You should definitely go for it."

April eased herself onto the arm of the couch and curled her puppy into her arms, making herself at home. That was the thing Faith loved most about Nick's sister—her ability to just *be*.

Faith admired the other woman's self-confidence and hoped she was finally building some of her own.

"I have a proposal for you. Since the designs came from your clothes, I figure you should get a cut of the commission on whatever sells."

Faith shook her head. She couldn't possibly have anything to do with April's success. "Oh, no. They're your designs, your talent."

"And I intend to take credit, believe me. I have too much of an ego not to." April laughed. "But I couldn't afford to buy clothes like these and that's half the reason these particular items are coming out so well, why an upscale store wants to carry them. You'd be my silent partner. Come on, what do you say?" She deliberately nudged Faith in the arm with her elbow.

Faith remained silent, unsure. She understood the logic of what April was suggesting. After all, hadn't Faith brought the items to April's consignment store to make money? Just because she'd never expected the design element to come into play didn't mean she couldn't benefit from April's talent now.

"Did I mention you've been my inspiration on these designs?" April asked, before Faith could tell her she agreed.

"Inspiration?" Faith asked, confused.

April nodded, petting the Yorkie as she spoke. "Designs for the Independent Woman. That's what I call this collection. And *you're* that independent woman!"

"I'm stunned. And honored."

"And my silent partner?" April asked.

"Yes. Yes!" Faith nodded. "Thank you." It was all she could manage.

April pulled her into a hug. Warmth was something the talented redhead gave easily.

Independent, Faith thought wryly. It was ironic, considering she'd just abandoned a promise to focus on herself in order to give Ethan what *he* needed last night. And that urge to be with him, be there for him, hadn't dissipated. She still wanted him when she knew for certain that wasn't what was best for her. For her future.

She forced herself to look at April. "Listen, I need to get going. I'm late for a meeting, but feel free to stick around and go through those boxes, okay?"

"Thanks, I will."

Faith gathered her papers, samples, and measurements for Nick and grabbed her car keys just as her phone rang. "Damn." She'd never get out of here.

"Want me to get it?" April offered. She'd just bent down to open the first box.

"No, the machine can pick it up." But Faith waited to hear if it was anything important before heading out.

"Faith? It's your mother." Lanie's voice sounded shrill through the machine.

April shot her an *I pity you* look.

"How many years do you want to take off of my life?" Her mother continued. "First, I find you at Target with that *man*, then you open a shop in town, and now you're *working* for Caroline Bretton? You're a Harrington! We hire, we don't—" Thankfully the answering machine let out a long beep and cut her mother off before she could go on berating her.

As if I'm sixteen again, Faith thought, and shook her head.

"See you soon!" Faith called to April and headed out before the other woman could open a conversation about Faith's mother.

Outside and alone, Faith decided it was time to deal with her own demons. She opened her cell and dialed her mother, who answered on the first ring.

"Hello, Mother."

"Faith!"

"I'm in a rush, so I only have a minute." Unwilling to be subjected to a lecture by a woman who'd yet to accept the fact that she was not, and had never been, in a position to judge others, Faith spoke quickly. Before her mother could. "Since I can't talk now, come by my shop tomorrow morning at ten. Thanks, Mom. Have to run. I have an appointment with Ethan Barron. Bye," she said, and clicked off, the little devil on her shoulder compelling her to torture her mother a bit in return.

Tomorrow was soon enough to begin dealing with her own family drama. Right now she was headed to Ethan's, where she was certain another kind of drama awaited her.

Rosalita answered the door to Ethan's house. An eerie feeling of déjà vu settled over her, but she reminded herself this was the bright light of day and she was here to meet Nick on business, not Ethan.

"Is Nick here yet?" Faith asked Rosalita.

"No, he called and said to tell you he can't make it. He's busy on another project," Rosalita said.

Faith frowned. "Why didn't he call me before I came here?"

"No sé."

Swell, Faith thought.

"Come in anyway. You look skinny. I give you a piece of cake I just finished making." Rosalita placed her firm arm around Faith's shoulders, reminding her of when she'd come home from school and the older woman would lead her to the kitchen for milk and cookies.

Faith smiled at the memory. "Thanks, but it's not my

house anymore, remember? I can't just come to your kitchen for meals and snacks."

"Bah." Rosalita waved away that notion. "You said it yourself. *My* kitchen. You eat."

Maybe she would gauge the lay of the land first. "Is Tess here?" Faith wanted to see how the teenager was doing.

"She in the den with Mr. Ethan. They playing."

"Playing?" She had to have heard wrong.

"Sí. Come."

Faith followed Rosalita to the large den in the back of the house. The closer she got, the louder the rock music sounded. Hard rock and guitar sounds.

Faith paused in the entry to the room, stunned to see Ethan and Tess standing in front of a huge flat-screen TV that would wreak havoc with her plans for this room. Ethan held an electric guitar in his hands, playing to the music and beats on the screen, Tess shouting distracting words at him trying to get him to mess up. Apparently they had some kind of competition going.

Faith wasn't sure if she was more shocked by their inter-action, the fact that they were having fun, or that both Ethan and Tess were smiling and laughing. For real. The sound came from the depths of their being and they were enjoying themselves and each other. Faith's heart soared at the sight. She realized Rosalita had quietly slipped away, leaving her alone to watch.

Faith couldn't tear her gaze away.

The teenager wasn't wearing her army jacket. Instead, her thin arms stood out beneath her short sleeves and cargo pants. She hopped up and down, more animated and excited than Faith had ever seen her. The transformation permeated Tess both inside and out. She glowed, her eyes sparkling with delight, and a lump settled in Faith's throat at the amazing change.

Like his sister, Ethan looked different too. His careful control had been stripped away, revealing a younger-looking man, more impossibly handsome and carefree in a way he'd obviously never been. If she'd been drawn to his darker intensity before, his charm and magnetism were impossible to resist now.

Both were so engrossed in the game, neither noticed her. When the song finally ended, Faith couldn't stop herself. She clapped her hands, applauding his efforts.

Both Ethan and Tess turned her way.

"Faith!" Tess acknowledged her first, excitement in her flushed cheeks, her guard completely down. "Want to play? I've been kicking Ethan's butt!"

Ethan's dark gaze met Faith's. "I just showed you up, Twerp," he said to Tess, but he never broke eye contact with Faith.

"Ha! That's because I haven't taken my next turn yet. Hand over the guitar and I'll show you both what I can do."

Ethan handed the guitar over and Tess grabbed the instrument and swung the strap over her head and shoulder.

"If I win this round, you have to take me to the beach tomorrow," Tess said.

Ethan narrowed his gaze. "And if I win this round, you have to ditch the heavy dark clothes and let Faith take you shopping."

He met Faith's gaze and she gave him an imperceptible nod. Of course she'd take the teenager shopping. She didn't blame him for offering up her services. Who else could he ask?

Tess stopped her fidgeting and paused, obviously thinking over his end of the deal.

No way will she agree, Faith thought.

A mischievous smile lifted the corners of Tess's mouth. "You're on," she said at last.

Faith swallowed hard. Something was going on here, some major change between these two she didn't understand or fathom.

"Ready?" Tess asked.

"Do me a favor and practice, okay? I need to talk to Faith for a few minutes. I'll be right back and the competition is *on*."

As soon as Tess nodded and started the music, Ethan grabbed Faith's hand and pulled her toward his office, not giving her the chance to think or argue.

Fourteen

"What are you doing?" Faith asked, stunned by his actions.

"Talking to you." He reached out and stroked her cheek, the caress sending delicious shivers through her body. "What I did last night was unforgivable," he said, taking her off guard.

"Excuse me?" She felt as if she'd been slapped. "You're sorry we slept together?"

"No!" His jaw tightened. "Never that."

Her heartbeat slowed to a more normal rhythm. The more she tried to distance herself from this man, the more she seemed to be drawn deeper.

To care. "Then what?"

"I took my mood out on you. I was rough with you and—"

"It wasn't like that for me." Her cheeks burned at the admission. "It was good. Can we just leave it at that?"

A very male smile worked its way onto his face. "Just good?"

"Beyond good. Amazing. Speaking of, what in the world

is going on with you and Tess?" She deliberately changed the subject.

He let her. "We found something we have in common."

"Music?" she guessed.

"And television and computer games. I needed a distraction and I figured she'd appreciate it." He shrugged. "I'm just glad it worked."

"You also found a way to reach her."

He grinned, the impact devastating as usual. "It's called bribery."

Faith laughed. "Well, whatever you're doing, it's working. She looks more . . . human. Vulnerable. Not to mention happy." She paused. "So did you. Does that mean you're over what happened with your brothers?"

Ethan didn't want to spend another minute overthinking something he couldn't control. Not when he had Faith back in his house and he could make up for acting like an unfeeling ass last night. No matter what she said, he could have handled himself better.

"As far as my brothers are concerned, I'm moving forward. I have no choice."

She nodded in understanding. "I've been there myself," she murmured.

"So you have." He stepped closer, backing her up to the desk. Undeniable sexual tension arced between them. He threaded his fingers through the back of her hair, cupped her head, and pulled her toward him. "I meant it when I said I'm sorry," he said gruffly.

She swallowed hard. "And I meant it when I said there's no need to be."

He gently brushed his lips over hers, gliding his mouth back and forth in the most delicate way imaginable.

"Mmm." She sighed into him. "You make it so damn hard."

"What?" he asked.

"Keeping my distance."

He couldn't suppress a laugh. "Then don't."

Ethan tugged on her hair and she bent her head, the long strands of her hair falling to one side. Acting on instinct, he pressed a kiss to her soft skin, nuzzling her silken flesh. She smelled like peaches and sunshine and he wanted a taste, so he took one, nibbling lightly, stopping before he marked her. No need to give Tess something to talk about.

"Ethan." Faith tried to reprimand him, he knew, but her voice trembled along with her body, making her point moot.

Especially since all that held her upright was the pressure of his body leaning into hers.

"Why fight what feels good?" he asked.

"I can't let myself get so lost in you that I lose sight of me."

"Eew! Not again!" Tess's voice interrupted anything he might have said.

"Would you stop sneaking up on people?" Ethan muttered, stepping away from Faith but keeping his back to his sister. At least until he could turn around and not give himself away.

"I thought you said this is my house too," Tess remarked, *teasing* him.

Wow. "Wiseass," he muttered. "Okay, who's up for a round of Guitar Hero?" He looked from Tess to Faith.

She shook her head. "I came to meet Nick, but he told Rosalita to tell me he couldn't make it. I should get going."

But she wouldn't. He saw the yearning in her eyes, the desire to stay.

"Come on, play with us, Faith!"

"Well . . ."

"I bet I can beat you," Tess said, urging her.

And just like that, Ethan didn't have to say a word. There was no way she'd turn down this suddenly happy Tess.

Faith smiled. "Well, who can resist a challenge like that?"

"Yes!" Tess bolted for the other room, leaving Ethan to grin at Faith and follow her into the family room for Guitar Hero.

Ethan won the original round he'd bet Tess. Not by much. He had to admit, the kid was good. But he had more at stake than her. He wanted her out of those awful Goth clothes, and so he'd concentrated like mad. And he won.

He didn't mention the bet or the clothes, deciding to trust Tess to come to him when she was ready. The kid had honor. He bet she would. If not, he wasn't above reminding her in a couple of days. He didn't want to ruin the progress they'd made today.

And to ensure they didn't, he turned to his new sister. She'd asked for the beach, knowing that meant she'd need to wear a bathing suit. That had to have been a huge request. "We're still going to the beach tomorrow," he said.

Tess's eyes glittered with something unique. Gratitude.

While Faith's beaming approval caused something deep and meaningful to unfurl in his chest. No wonder she was afraid of losing herself. He was afraid he was halfway gone himself.

They spent another half hour including Faith in the fun. He wasn't surprised when she found her groove and was able to compete with them. By the time they finished playing, they each collapsed on the floor laughing from the heckling and insults they'd tossed one another's way.

Ethan couldn't remember the last time he'd had so much fun. Hell, he couldn't remember the last time he'd had *any* real laughter and fun. These two people, who'd come into his life at the same time, gave him that. He knew better than most that good times didn't last, but he planned to enjoy it while it did.

"Dinnertime!" Rosalita strode into the room. "I set a place for Miss Faith," she said before turning her back and walking out.

Faith pushed herself up from the floor. "I think I've overstayed my welcome. I should get going."

"Why? So you can go home and eat alone?" Ethan asked her point-blank.

She shot daggers at him with her eyes.

Tess, as if sensing this didn't involve her, remarkably stayed silent.

He knew he was pushing her. Based on what she'd said earlier, she was afraid of losing her sense of self, like she had in her marriage. Well, he wasn't thinking that far ahead. He wasn't a long-term planner, not in the emotional sense anyway. He just knew that right now, being with her felt good. And he'd spent too much time feeling bad.

"Dinner," she agreed. "And then I need to get going."

"Fair enough."

They settled into the kitchen and indulged in a delicious meal. Rosalita still might not be his supporter or ally, but she knew how to cook.

He'd just put his napkin on the table when the phone rang. A glance at the number told him he couldn't ignore it. "Franklin. What do you have for me?"

Ethan listened to the PI's summary of his investigation and knew he had trouble, including the fact that Dale Conway was having an affair with Amelia Treadway, Ethan's *married* executive assistant in Washington, D.C.

"I'll take a flight out tomorrow," he told Franklin.

He hung up the phone, his mind preoccupied with business and all the ramifications of Franklin's news, to find Tess staring at him with wide eyes.

Shit. He'd forgotten he had responsibilities beyond business.

"What about me?" she asked, her voice hard, her jaw set. She was visibly withdrawing back into herself.

"I wouldn't go if someone else could handle it," he said, but he knew his words were hitting her well-built shell.

Just as his had every time his father left the house on business, Ethan suddenly remembered.

His gaze strayed to Faith's, but she looked as lost as he was, not knowing what to say.

"I'll call Nash and Dare," Ethan said. "They already said

they wanted you to spend time with them. One of them will take you until I get back."

Tess didn't answer. Instead, she bent her knees and wrapped her arms around them. A rude position at the dinner table, but he couldn't point that out to her now.

He opened his cell to search for Dare's number. His younger brother struck him as the easiest of the two to deal with right now.

"Dare? It's Ethan."

"Don't bother asking. I'm not staying with either of them. They don't have any more time for me than you do or Kelly did."

Ethan frowned. "I'll call you back," he said to his sibling.

He placed the cell phone on the table and leaned on his elbows, closer to Tess. "*I* want you." It shocked him to admit how true that statement was.

She slammed her feet to the floor. "Yeah, right. And we're going to the beach tomorrow too, right? You're so full of it!" she yelled at him.

He ran a hand over his face, knowing she had every right to feel angry, hurt, and betrayed.

Just like his brothers did.

"I'll make it up to you."

"Don't bother." She folded her arms across her chest in that defensive way that made his heart ache.

"Umm, Tess?" Faith spoke up suddenly.

"What?" She glared at Faith as if she too had suddenly become the enemy.

Instead of getting annoyed with her attitude, Faith softened her features. "I can stay with you while Ethan's gone."

Surprise rippled through him.

"You'd do that for me?" his sister asked, obviously as stunned as Ethan was.

"Yeah, I would. I'm guessing you'd be more comfortable with me than with your brothers—at least until you get to know them better?" Faith asked.

Tess blinked.

Ethan thought he saw a hint of moisture in those dark-rimmed eyes but he couldn't be sure. He knew he had a lump of gratitude in his throat so huge it threatened to choke him.

"At your place?" Tess asked.

"Sure, if that's what you want. Or here if that's better for you. That way you won't have to uproot yourself all over again." Faith waited, her gaze on Tess.

The girl nodded slowly. "That'd be okay. If you'd stay here, I mean."

"Then here it is."

Ethan knew how difficult it would be for Faith to stay in her childhood home that was no longer hers. Yet she'd done it for Tess.

The offer, he thought, was as big as her heart.

Faith needed to get some perspective and fast, which was why when Kate called and asked if she wanted to meet for a drink, Faith jumped at the chance. She left Ethan's and drove straight to Joe's.

The bar was crowded for a weeknight, but it was summertime and people enjoyed going out.

Faith was numb. "I've lost my mind."

What else could explain her willingness to uproot herself for a teenager she'd just met and a man she barely knew. Okay, that was wrong on so many levels she couldn't believe the thought had even passed through her mind.

She knew him. Intimately.

Kate raised her glass and touched it to Faith's. "To insanity. You first."

Faith drew a deep breath. "Ethan has to go out of town on business and I said I'd stay with Tess." When Kate didn't reply, Faith added, "At the mansion."

Kate's eyes opened wide. "You're right, you're insane." Kate drew a long sip of her wine spritzer.

Faith did the same.

"Will you be okay in that house?" Kate asked.

Which was why they were best friends, Faith thought. Kate understood the problems inherent in her offer without Faith having to explain.

"I'm a big girl. I can handle it." She swirled the champagne-colored liquid in her glass.

"Can you handle sleeping in Ethan's bed?"

Faith raised her gaze.

"Unless there's more than the two beds you once mentioned?" Kate wiggled her eyebrows and took another, longer sip of wine.

Faith tried to swallow, but her mouth was too dry and she drew a long gulp from her glass. "I hadn't thought about that."

"That's what best friends are for!" Kate said too cheerfully.

Faith pressed the cold glass to her forehead. "Okay, your turn. What did you do?"

"Nick asked me out and I said no." This time Kate stared into her glass, looking for answers.

"Why?"

"Because no man goes from head over heels for one woman, then decides to go after her best friend unless it's rebound. And I'm many things, but I'm nobody's second choice." Kate tipped her glass and Faith toasted with her once more.

"But I have to interrupt. Nick wasn't head over heels for me. He was curious, we had unresolved issues, and one kiss later and we both realized there was no chemistry. None. Nada. Zilch." She curled her thumb and forefinger into a zero. "Which makes his interest in you genuine, not rebound."

Kate frowned. "I didn't know about the kiss."

"Because there was nothing to know! You know I'm not interested in Nick."

"Because you're interested in Ethan."

"Yes. No. Argh!" Faith glanced at her best friend and

together they lifted their glasses and finished their drinks in silence.

After which Faith headed upstairs to pack so she could head over to Ethan's the next morning to stay with Tess. And sleep in Ethan's bed.

Hard rock music blasted from Tess's room. Ethan drew a deep breath—who'd have believed he was afraid to face one tiny teenage girl—and knocked on her door.

No answer.

She probably couldn't hear him over the music, so he turned the handle and walked inside. Tess lay on her bed wrapped in the army jacket he'd coaxed her out of earlier, sketching. He knew she saw him, but she didn't say a word, not even when he walked over to her nightstand and shut off the iPod.

"Hey," he said.

Silence.

He sat down on the side of her bed. His hip touched her pant leg, but she didn't move or make more room for him to get comfortable. She'd removed her makeup and looked very, very young.

His heart was in his throat. A few weeks ago, he hadn't known she existed. How had she come to mean so much to him in such a short time?

He knew he'd hurt her and even understood why, but it wasn't enough. There was more. He wanted to comprehend the anger beneath the surface and he sensed it was all tied to how she'd been raised—how her mother had treated her and later her sister.

"Tell me about your life before you came here," he urged.

Silence.

If she wouldn't talk, then he would. "We share the same father. You wouldn't remember him because you were young when he died, but I do. His name was Mark. You have his eyes," Ethan told her.

She blinked and raised her gaze to his, obviously interested. Still silent, she watched him from beneath her lashes. But she was listening.

"Since you showed up on my doorstep, I've thought a lot about what I was like at your age. I hung out with the same kinds of kids you did and I was arrested like you were too." He shifted to get more comfortable.

This time she rearranged herself, giving him more room.

"And you obviously heard everything my brothers said about me. And that's when you started to come around, when you realized we were kind of alike, right?"

When she didn't answer, he nudged her leg and she finally nodded. Her pad fell to the side on the bed and she picked at a nonexistent thread on her purple and black zebra comforter.

"Then today, while we were shopping for the television and playing Wii, I realized that I never went shopping with my mother or father for the games we had in the house. The only times my father brought something home was after a long trip. Want to know why?"

Tess studied the bed, but her hand had stilled.

If he had to slice a vein, at least he was reaching her, Ethan thought. "My father felt guilty because he'd been with your mother, so he'd bring home stuff to make up for it. And guess what? I knew he was fooling around. I heard my parents arguing about it. I figured, I was the oldest, I had to do something. So I went out looking for trouble, hoping my father would have to pay attention and stay home more." He paused, letting his words sink in. "Is that what it was like for you? Are you running from something there?"

He studied her, patiently waiting her out. He had all night.

Tess began to bite her nails, twisting one cuticle between her teeth. "Hey, you're gonna hurt yourself. Talk to me," he said.

She expelled a long breath of air. "When I was little, my mom used to go out at night. She said she had to work and she'd leave me with Kelly." Tess pulled her knees up to her chest.

Ethan clenched his hands into fists. "Was Kelly good to you?"

"Real good." Tess nodded, her eyes brightening when she spoke of her sister.

"Have you spoken to her since you've been here?" he asked for the first time.

"She calls every night."

"Let me guess. She talks, you grunt?"

Tess gave him a reluctant smile. "Kelly's twelve years older than me, so even after she graduated high school and went to college, she helped Mom watch me."

Ethan's admiration for Kelly Moss rose.

"But then she moved in with a friend. Mom said I was old enough to stay by myself at night. She said she had to work." Tess's voice cracked.

Ethan put a hand on the bottom of her leg for support. "What did she do during the day when you were in school?"

Tess sniffed. "I thought she worked two jobs."

Ethan caught the terminology. *Thought.* "What was she really doing?"

"Men," Tess said, her disgust plain. "One after another."

Ethan curled his hand into a fist around the comforter.

"One night," Tess continued, "it was dark and raining. I was really scared, so when I heard her in the hall, I ran out to meet her and she was with this guy. He had his tongue down her throat and then he promised he'd pick her up again tomorrow night. She wasn't out working hard for us—she was going out." Tess studied a point on the wall, holding her emotions tightly inside.

No wonder she was so angry, so troubled. Her mother had basically abandoned her, he thought. "Did Kelly know?"

Tess shook her head. "And when I threatened to tell her, Mom said that if Kelly knew, she'd give up school and her job. She said I'd ruin Kelly's life." Finally real tears dripped down Tess's face.

So much for such a young kid to handle, he thought, wishing he could throttle her mother. Ethan reached for a tissue from her nightstand and handed it to Tess.

Embarrassed, she ducked her head and wiped the tears.

"And that's when you started running wild," he guessed.

She nodded. "I guess I thought kinda like you did. That if I got in enough trouble, Mom would have to come home and pay more attention to me." She cleared her throat. "But nobody cared where I was or what I did."

Ethan knew better and Tess needed to as well. "Kelly would have cared, but your mom talked you out of going to her for help. You know that, right?" Because it was obvious to him that Kelly loved her sister.

Tess laid her head on her knees and stared back at him with big eyes. "She oughta hate me."

"Why would you think that?" he asked, stunned.

"Because I was so bad, it's no wonder my mom left me and took off for a fresh start."

Ethan pulled in a deep breath, horrified she'd blame herself. "Is that what your mother told you?"

"I came home to a note that said I was on my own. That she needed to get away and this guy could give her the life she deserved. It doesn't take a genius to figure out she wanted to get the hell away from me." Tess bit down on her lower lip to keep the tears from flowing.

Ethan had a lump in his throat, thinking that Leah Moss had let Tess believe she wasn't enough, wasn't worth sticking around for.

Acid burned in Ethan's chest. "Did you ever tell your sister the truth?" he asked.

Tess shook her head. "Things were already a mess. And Mom had said if Kelly moved in to watch me, it'd ruin her life. Then she up and left, and Kelly got stuck with me anyway. I ruined her life just like Mom said." More tears dripped down Tess's cheek and he silently handed her another tissue.

He wished like hell he could make her past go away. But he knew better than anyone that was impossible. "You didn't ruin Kelly's life. Would she be calling you every night if you had?"

Tess sniffed and paused for way too long. "I guess not," she finally said.

"You just made it more challenging, but that's not necessarily a bad thing." He grinned.

To his surprise, Tess smiled back.

"Look, I have to go to D.C. tomorrow, but I want you to understand that *I'm not leaving you*, I'm not abandoning you, and Faith will be here until I get back. Got it?"

"Yeah," Tess said in a soft voice. Her eyes still shimmered, but he saw the gratitude in her expression too.

He wanted to pull her into a hug but she was still withdrawn into herself and he figured he'd pushed enough for one night.

"I'll see you in the morning?" she asked.

"You bet." He rose to his feet.

"Ethan?"

"Yeah?"

Tess held out her sketch pad. "Here. I want you to see."

Stunned, he accepted the pad. "I'm honored."

"Don't look at my drawings in front of me, okay?" For the first time, he caught sight of a real blush on her cheeks.

"No problem." He paused. "Thanks for trusting me." He winked at her and let himself out, shutting her door behind him.

At least now he understood why she acted out, and he couldn't blame her. Nor did he kid himself that things with Tess would change overnight, but at least now they had an understanding.

A starting point.

He sat down on his bed and opened the sketch pad. Dragon warriors stared back at him. At least that's what he thought they were. But even to his untrained eye, they were damned good. She had talent and deserved to have it nurtured.

He glanced at his watch. It was late but not obnoxiously so. He dialed Kate Andrews to find out about the best local art programs and teachers. She gave him the name of a colleague at the local college the next town over, as well as the dean of Birchwood Academy, a private school that specialized in the arts.

He'd make inquiries in between his business dealings tomorrow. He also planned to put his PI on locating Leah Moss. If Ethan and/or Kelly were going to be her guardians, Ethan wanted it to be legal, so they could make all the right decisions for Tess from now on.

Fifteen

Ethan left to catch his flight before Faith arrived at his house the following morning. Faith admitted to herself that she'd stalled on purpose, not wanting to add to the overwhelming idea of staying in his house by seeing him too.

Rosalita let her in and Tess was waiting for her in the family room. To Faith's surprise, the teen had lightened her makeup (which was still too dark), but she'd made the effort at change. She also wore a pair of normal jeans, a black T-shirt, and flip-flops. No cargo pants or jacket to be found.

Interesting.

"Good morning!" Faith greeted the teen.

"Hey." Tess looked at Faith and narrowed her gaze. "Where's your suitcase? Did you change your mind?"

Faith's heart squeezed at the distrust that came so naturally to the girl. "Rosalita took my bag upstairs for me."

A flash of relief crossed Tess's face. "Do I have to go to the community center today?"

"What would you rather do?" Faith asked. Ethan hadn't left a specific schedule so Faith figured it was up to her.

The teenager glanced up from beneath her lashes. "Hang out with you," she said softly, as if unsure of how her request would be received.

Faith smiled in reassurance. "I'd like that. But I have to be in the shop this morning. My mother's stopping by. After that, we can figure out what you want to do. Sound good?"

Tess shrugged. "Yeah. That sounds okay."

"Are you ready?" Faith asked.

The teen nodded.

A few minutes later, they were in Faith's car, on the way to town. "It smells new." Tess wrinkled her nose.

"It's my baby," Faith said proudly, patting the steering wheel.

"So what's your mother like?" Tess asked, more curious and chatty than Faith had ever seen her.

Clearly something had changed between last night and this morning, but Tess was watching her and waiting for an answer. Her own questions would have to wait.

"My mother." How to describe Lanie Harrington, Faith wondered. But she knew she'd better come up with something that would prepare Tess for the difficult woman she was about to meet. "She's spoiled and a lot selfish. She wants what she thinks she's entitled to and who cares what the rest of the world thinks."

Faith wanted to wince at the awful description, but the problem was, every ounce of it was true.

"Sounds like my mom."

Stunned by Tess's sudden willingness to open up, Faith's hand jerked on the wheel. "I didn't know that."

"Yeah. Well, Ethan got me talking last night. Now I can't seem to stop," Tess said, curling one leg beneath her.

He was full of surprises, Faith thought. But he was also clearly good for his sister, and for that Faith was glad.

Faith forced herself to focus on the morning ahead. "Tess, my mother can be . . . rude," Faith said as she pulled into a parking space behind the store. "In other words, don't take anything she says personally."

Faith put the car in park and shut off the engine before turning to face her passenger. "The thing is, my mother doesn't like many people. Mostly because she's bitter and angry. I'm not excusing her, but I'd appreciate it if you didn't let her . . . bait you."

"So watch my mouth?" Tess asked, a devilish grin on her face.

Faith had never seen this side of the girl, and warm protective instincts flooded through her. She wouldn't let her mother hurt this child who'd obviously had enough pain for one lifetime.

"That would help. And let me handle her, okay?"

Tess blew out a long breath of air. "You're no fun."

Faith laughed. "Speaking of fun, what do you want to do this afternoon?" She deliberately changed the subject.

Tess stared out the window, suddenly silent.

"What is it?" Faith asked.

"You'll laugh." Tess folded her arms across her chest, in a familiar gesture.

Unwilling to let her withdraw, Faith decided to take a page from Ethan's playbook. "You tell me what you want to do and I'll tell you how I'd like to spend the afternoon. Seems like a fair trade to me."

Tess turned her head and met Faith's gaze. "I want you to show me how to do makeup," the teen rattled off, at close to one hundred miles an hour. She'd obviously wanted to get the words out before she could change her mind.

At the simple yet endearing request, Faith practically melted. "Well, that goes along with what I was going to say. How about we have lunch, do some clothes shopping for you, and then head home for a makeup lesson?"

Tess blinked. "You really want to do all that with me?" The insecurity spoke to the girl who'd been left on Ethan's doorstep.

And Faith, who felt betrayed by her father and used by

her ex-husband, understood that insecurity very well. "Of course I want do all that with you!"

They just had to survive Faith's mother first.

Faith settled Tess at the corner of her desk. Tess seemed happy to stick her iPod ear buds on, sketch pad in front of her, and tune out the world, so Faith let her. She made a few calls to vendors and discovered she'd been able to push up shipment of both Tess's and Ethan's bedroom furniture, along with the family room sofa, recliner, and other pieces. Although she'd have preferred to do a full installation, giving him completed rooms at one time, the way she planned to do for Caroline Bretton, Ethan needed the items as they came in. She was pulling in every string she and Joel had to make sure the two people she cared about had what they needed.

She was deep in thought, planning Caroline's room, when the chimes she'd put on the door rang out. Faith glanced up to see her mother stride through the doors. A quick glance told her Tess hadn't yet noticed.

Faith rose to her feet and headed to greet Lanie in the center of the room. "Mom! Welcome to my place of business," she said with a grin, hoping to start this meeting off on the right foot.

"This is . . . interesting," her mother said, taking in the pieces Faith had started to accumulate.

There were show items like floral centerpieces, an antique desk, and a marble pedestal, all meant to lure pedestrians into the shop. She would sell them or use them as part of a decorating project, replacing them as she came across unique items online, in catalogs, and courtesy of Joel.

"Thank you. That large leopard reminds me of something we used to have when I was growing up." Faith pointed to a large ceramic cat in the corner.

"Your father's favorite," Lanie murmured, her voice soft and unguarded.

"Have you spoken to him?" Faith managed to ask.

"No. He asked that I keep my distance. He thought it would protect me, you know?"

Faith shook her head. "And you think that makes him admirable?"

"He's looking out for me."

Faith swallowed hard, determined not to argue with her. "Well, come in and have a seat."

Her mother started toward the desk and came to a halt. "Who is *that*?" She pointed her long, painted nails toward Tess, who sat, head back, iPod on, pretending to play the drums with her hands. "Or should I say, what is that? She has purple in her hair." Lanie shuddered.

Faith straightened her shoulders, an overwhelming feeling of protectiveness sweeping through her. "That is Ethan's sister, Tess. I'm watching her for a few days. And let me be clear, Mother. If you can't be nice to Tess, turn around and walk out that door right now. We have nothing further to discuss."

Nobody would hurt Tess on her watch. Not even the one person who'd managed to damage her own self-esteem, Faith thought, the realization stunning and painful. She hadn't been a rebel like Ethan, but maybe if her own mother had loved her, protected her, been proud of who she was and who she wanted to be, she never would have married a self-serving bastard like Carter Moreland.

"Well?" Faith asked her shell-shocked mother. "What's it going to be?"

"Hey, is this your mother?" Tess let her feet hit the floor with a thud.

Faith closed her eyes and said a silent prayer. Then she faced the two people in the room. "Yes, this is my mother, Lanie Harrington. Mom, this is Tess Moss."

"Ma'am." Tess nodded her head, on her best behavior, as if she were meeting the queen of England.

Faith shot her a warning glare and hoped the kid didn't take it too far and curtsy.

"Moss," Lanie repeated. "I thought you said she was a Barron." She said the name with all the disdain she could muster.

"Half Barron," Faith said through gritted teeth.

"Ahh. Why didn't you say so? That's much better," Lanie said.

Most people might take Lanie's words for sarcasm. Faith knew her mother merely spoke her own truth. Better half than all Barron blood.

"Hello, Tess. And what is Tess short for, may I ask?" Lanie continued.

The teenager shrugged. "Just Tess."

"Interesting hair color, Tess."

"Mother . . ."

Tess reached a hand to her purple strands. "Yeah, well, that's another thing I thought we could talk about?" She looked up at Faith hopefully.

Faith couldn't stand it another minute. She walked up to the girl and placed her arm around her shoulders, pulling her close in a way her own mother had never done for her. Instead of pulling away as Faith expected, Tess stiffened in surprise but remained in Faith's protective grasp.

Suddenly Faith's cell chimed at the same time the phone rang on her desk. She reached for her cell and did the only other thing she could. "Mother, could you possibly get that?" Faith asked.

Faith took a call from Ethan. He was rushed and in between meetings, but he needed to talk to her about Tess and a potential art class opportunity, so she headed to a private corner for the conversation.

When she returned, her mother was sitting at her desk, Tess in her chair across the way.

"How old are you, Tess?" Lanie asked.

"Fourteen."

"And how are you related to Ethan Barron?"

"I think that's enough of that!" Faith inserted herself back into the conversation. "So, who called earlier?" she asked her mother.

"Ahh. That was Caroline Brennan. She changed your appointment by a day." Lanie scowled at the mention of her friend. "Since your calendar was open on your desk, I took the liberty of scheduling her."

"Thank you." Faith had no idea why her mother seemed to be behaving, but she was grateful.

"A trucking company called too. I scheduled them also. Here." Her mother pointed to the same day next week she had other deliveries at Ethan's. "Make no mistake. I don't approve of this venture."

Here we go, Faith thought. *The long-awaited conversation.* "Why not? Don't I need to make a living?"

"I thought you received a nice settlement from Carter?" her mother asked pointedly.

From the corner of her eye, Faith saw Tess listening to them, her eyes wide in fascination.

Faith bit the inside of her cheek. "I received enough to start the business and to know I have a cushion," she said carefully.

Lanie shook her head. "You should have invested well and lived off the interest. Working like a common person is so . . . beneath you."

Faith drew herself up straighter. "I'm proud of this place and I like what I'm doing. Of course I'd like it better if I could get more clients, but thanks to Dad's illegal dealings, no one wants to do business with me." Faith met her mother's gaze.

Lanie opened her mouth to reply, and Faith jumped back in before she could. "And don't give me that nonsense about him being misunderstood. He pleaded guilty. The feds took everything and sold it at auction. He knew what he was doing."

Her mother pursed her lips together. Lanie's version of *I don't like this conversation; therefore, I'm not having it.*

Everything in Faith wanted to reach out and touch her mother on the shoulder. She didn't, unsure of what she was more afraid of—Lanie shattering or rejecting her daughter's offer of comfort.

"Look, Mom, can't you understand that our lives have changed?" she asked, her tone more gentle. "That times have changed? And we need to change with it. Both of us."

When her mother didn't reply, Faith backed off. "Well, I appreciate you answering the phones and figuring out when the delivery would work."

Her mother's posture relaxed at the change of subject. "Yes, well, you might not remember, but I held quite a few dinner parties in my day and I became a pro at scheduling."

Faith smiled. "I remember."

Lanie rose from her seat and walked around the store, her fingers trailing over things as she moved, her walk graceful, serene. Still very much the lady of the nonexistent manor, but Faith knew now there were chinks in her armor. Lanie Harrington was more fragile than she wanted to admit. She was holding on to the illusion of grandeur so tightly that with only a little push she'd fall apart.

"Would you mind if I rearranged some things?" Her mother surprised Faith by asking.

"Suit yourself."

Tess, noting the fun conversation was over, had plugged back into her iPod.

Faith settled back into her desk while her mother seemed content to shift things around. "Mom, Caroline tells me she's tried to reach out to you, but you're shutting yourself up in your own house."

"Shh." Lanie pointed to Tess. "Little ears," she said.

"I'm not little. And I don't know anyone in town to repeat shit—" Her mouth opened in horror and she said a silent

I'm sorry to Faith. "I mean . . . I don't know anyone in town to repeat stuff to. You can talk in front of me."

Faith laughed. Apparently the kid had turned down the volume just in case.

"Yes, you can speak in front of Tess," Faith agreed. "Everyone in this small town knows what Dad did. You didn't know while it was happening. There's no shame in starting over."

Lanie kept her back to Faith.

"And there's no reason to turn your back on the one person who has been a real friend to you, or tried to," Faith said.

Just like there was no reason to turn her back on her own daughter. But *that* wasn't a conversation Faith wanted to have in front of Tess . . . Maybe not ever. It was too painful to think about how her mother had treated her with disdain over the years, angry with her for the sole reason that her father paid attention to his daughter.

She'd told Tess that Lanie was selfish. *Narcissistic* was probably a better word.

"Did you know that Caroline's husband lost his job?" her mother finally asked with an exaggerated shudder. "True, they have her family's money, but how humiliating!"

"And this affects you or your friendship how?" Faith asked. "Your husband bilked people for millions. Caroline could probably use a friend who understands what it's like to have problems. I'd think you could use the same thing," Faith pointed out.

"I don't need anyone!" Lanie's voice was shrill.

"Well, then that's your loss." Faith turned to a now wide-eyed Tess. "Come on. It's time to go shopping."

She glanced at her mother, hoping to see a flicker of emotion in her expression. Anger, frustration, sadness, *something*.

Her face was a frozen mask.

But Faith knew enough had been said here today to make an impact—should her mother choose to listen.

"I'll see myself out," Lanie said frostily. She rose and headed for the door and walked out without another word.

"Chilly!" Tess said. "Like, brrr."

"Yeah. Try growing up with that." Needing a minute, Faith lowered herself into the chair her mother had just occupied.

She glanced down and noticed her mother had rearranged her desk, making it more organized. A glance out at her shop told her Lanie's touches had actually improved the display and appearance. Her mother had the ability to do more with her life than judge others, Faith thought. It was a pity she lacked the desire.

Faith spent the entire day with Tess, who was on her best behavior. Faith thought she might actually be seeing who the teenager really was. Faith wondered if her own life might have turned out differently if *she'd* had a sister, someone to share her thoughts and feelings with instead of always feeling as if she were treading water alone. She'd definitely enjoyed the day, and Tess had made out like a bandit. Faith had bought her an entire new end-of-summer–into-fall wardrobe, knowing Ethan wouldn't care one bit.

After a delicious dinner cooked by Rosalita, they sat together on Tess's bed, exhausted from a girl day of shopping and makeup. Using her own makeup, Faith had taught Tess the fine points of using a light touch when applying eye shadow and liner. She promised to take the teen to buy her own supplies one day soon.

Right now, they'd both collapsed on Tess's mattress, full and tired.

"Have you heard from Ethan?" Tess asked.

"As a matter of fact, I have." And she'd been waiting for the right time to talk to Tess. "He was busy in and out of meetings all day, but he called to tell me something."

"Yeah, what's that?"

"He's been looking into special art classes for you." She eyed the teenager, gauging her reaction.

"Already? I just showed him my stuff last night!" She sounded pleased, not pissed off.

"He liked what he saw." Enough that he had already called Kate and asked her about classes.

Kate had done some research and made a few phone calls. There was an opportunity for Tess at the Birchwood Academy private school, but Ethan would have to move fast because the deadline for admission had passed. Kate had also heard whispers of financial troubles, so maybe a hefty donation would help get Tess into the school. But before they moved forward with their plan, they needed Tess on board.

"So you'd be interested?" Faith asked.

Twenty-four hours ago, she would have laid odds Tess would have made light of the idea, using a few choice words to boot. But now . . .

"Yeah, I'd like that." She scooted back against the pillows, eyes wide. "I can't believe he looked into that for me. So fast and everything."

"He's a great guy." Faith smiled.

"Who knew?" Tess asked, grinning.

Faith propped herself up on her elbow. "You miss him, don't you?"

"Nah. He's a pain in the butt." But the young girl's widening grin belied her words.

There was no doubt she'd hit the jackpot in brothers, Faith thought. She was even determined to find some good in Nash, the brother she found the most difficult.

The ringing doorbell interrupted her thoughts. "Who could that be?"

Tess shrugged.

"Rosalita left, so I'll go see." Faith rose to her feet and headed downstairs.

Tess padded along behind her.

Faith glanced out the side window and saw Nash standing at the door. Not the brother she'd choose to deal with, Faith drew a deep breath and swung the front door wide.

"Hi," she said in greeting.

He seemed surprised to see her and didn't reply right away. Nothing like Ethan in appearance, Nash, with his lighter hair and carefully matched khaki pants and polo shirt, reminded her too much of her ex-husband.

"Would you like to come in?" she invited.

He stepped inside. "Hi, Tess."

Faith wasn't sure if he was ignoring her on purpose or just focused on his new sister and reserved judgment.

"Hey," Tess said, in a stiff, wary tone Faith hadn't heard her use all day. But she sure recognized it now.

"You ready to go?" Nash asked the teen.

Faith's guard went up. "Go where?"

Nash met her gaze with a cool one of his own. "Tess and I have plans to go to the sidewalk fair in town tonight." *Not that it's your business.*

Faith heard the words Nash didn't say. His expression made it clear what he thought of her interference.

"The hell we do," Tess said, her angry belligerence back.

Apparently the thaw didn't extend to Nash just yet. And though Faith didn't blame the teenager for her distrust of a man she didn't yet know, he was the girl's brother.

"Tess, do me a favor? Go upstairs and start putting away the clothes you bought today, okay?"

She narrowed her gaze. "Rosalita said she'd do it tomorrow."

"Well, it won't hurt you to do it yourself. That way you know where your own things are." Faith caught Tess's gaze. "Go. Your brother and I need to talk."

"Where's Ethan?" Nash asked.

"He had to go to Washington, D.C., on business," Tess said.

"Upstairs!" Faith pointed to the long circular staircase.

Tess let out a put-upon sigh. "I'm going," she muttered, and stomped to the stairs, proceeding to take the steps slowly, one at a time, a loud thud accompanying each one.

Faith waited until she was alone with Nash, though she was sure Tess was doing her best to listen.

"What the hell did she mean, he went to D.C.?" Nash asked.

"I think it's self-explanatory. He had a business emergency."

"And of course it was more important than Tess, so he up and abandoned her. It's what he does best." Nash came to his own biased conclusion.

"That's not how it was." Faith set her jaw.

He folded his arms across his chest. "No? Who's watching Tess?"

Faith straightened her shoulders, and though the answer was obvious, she replied anyway. "That would be me."

The other man let out a harsh laugh. "He left her with a stranger instead of calling me or Dare? Why am I not surprised?"

Faith placed a hand on the wall beside her for support. "Excuse me for pointing this out, but I'm less of a stranger to her than you are."

He narrowed his gaze. "Let me guess. Ethan didn't remember to tell you Tess and I had plans."

Faith shook her head. "Like I said, he had a business emergency and left in a hurry."

"Well, it's only seven and the fair goes until ten, so I'll take her into town."

That will be Tess's choice, Faith thought, though she'd try to encourage the teenager to go with her brother. But before she could voice her thoughts, Tess's voice rang from the top of the stairs. "I'm not going with him!"

Faith met Nash's frustrated glare. "I'm going to give you some unsolicited advice. That girl upstairs is sensitive. She knows exactly how you feel about your brother."

"Your point?"

"Like it or not, she's bonded with Ethan. Unless you soften up a bit, you won't make any headway with her."

Nash bristled at her words, his posture becoming impossibly straighter, his glare more angry. "Not only is this none of your business, but you can't possibly understand what *he* did to our family."

Faith walked up to Nash, standing toe-to-toe with him. "It must be nice."

"What is?"

She tipped her head to one side, appraising him and definitely finding him lacking. "Being such a perfect human being that you never need anyone else's forgiveness or understanding." She clenched and unclenched her fists at her side.

A muscle ticked in his jaw. "Are you telling me you've forgiven your old man?"

Bull's-eye, Faith thought, but she refused to let him get to her. "Are you telling me you're finally separating me from what my father did? Because if so, there's no reason for you to be so damned hostile!" she yelled at him, losing her temper for the first time.

"I think the lady has a point." Ethan appeared out of nowhere, walking into the house and joining them in the entryway.

His entrance surprised everyone. He placed his suitcase down on the marble floor and folded his arms across his chest, looking from Nash to Faith. It didn't matter that his brother thought he was dirt, Ethan looked like the imposing, impressive man Faith knew him to be.

And she was, despite herself, so happy to see him. "What are you doing back?"

"I wrapped things up as quickly as I could." *And from the looks of things, not a minute too soon.* "What's going on?" he asked.

"You took off, left Tess with her instead of one of her

brothers, and oh yeah—you forgot to tell her I was supposed to take Tess into town tonight." Nash pointed a finger at Faith.

Ethan winced. "Yeah, I forgot. And I'm sorry. Tess!" he called out.

"I'm right here!"

He looked up at the top of the steps, where Tess sat watching the adults below her. "I screwed up, but you're supposed to go with Nash overnight," he said to her.

"No!"

Ethan rolled his eyes. "Yes. He's your brother and you two need to get to know each other. Go get ready," he directed her. "Unless you don't want to go to the beach when I pick you up tomorrow!"

Tess paused and Faith wondered if Ethan was in for an argument. Even Nash seemed to hold his breath.

"Fine," she said, not hiding her displeasure, but she ran for her room anyway.

"She'll warm up to you," Ethan said to his brother.

Nash narrowed his gaze. "I appreciate you pushing her."

Faith blinked, surprised Nash had conceded even that much.

"Tess needs family. Just go slow with her."

Nash nodded. "We'll go to dinner and the festival first."

"She already ate," Faith said.

"Fantastic," Nash muttered.

"I'm ready!" Tess bounded down the stairs, dressed in a pair of denim shorts Faith had bought her, a black T-shirt with a huge sunglass decal on the front, flip-flops, and very little makeup. She also had a large bag she'd obviously put her overnight things in.

She looked like the quintessential teenager, and pride blossomed in Faith's chest.

Ethan stared at her. "Who are you?" he asked, grinning.

Nash merely blinked.

"Thank Faith!" Tess said, and headed for the door.

Ethan stared at the woman he had come to care so much about, the woman he couldn't wait to come back home to. "I don't know what to say."

She treated him to a soft, private smile.

"I'm holding you to the beach," Tess yelled at Ethan.

"I'll pick her up early tomorrow morning. Eight thirty, okay?" Ethan asked.

"Yeah. I'll go to work right after." Nash pulled his car keys from his pocket and started for the door.

"Remember my advice," Faith called out to him just before he slammed the door shut behind him.

"What advice?" Ethan asked.

Faith rocked back on her heels. "Oh, I just told him Tess had bonded with you and he wouldn't make headway with her unless he learned not to be such a condescending, pompous ass. Not in those exact words. I was much nicer." She grinned.

And Ethan pulled her into a kiss.

Sixteen

Ethan had been gone twelve hours max. Not long in the scheme of things but long enough to know he couldn't wait to get back to the two most important women in his life. He understood his feelings for Tess. He already loved the little stinker. Faith was more frightening because he loved her too.

The revelation came to him at thirty thousand feet, while he was staring out the plane window at the peaceful, beautiful clouds and realized Faith brought that same peace and beauty into his life. Things he'd given up on and thought he didn't deserve. It had taken Tess and her fragile honesty to convince him otherwise because she didn't believe she deserved good things either. He knew better.

As for himself, maybe he didn't deserve Faith, but he'd fallen hard and fast. And deserving or not, he wasn't giving her up. Ethan put his heart and soul into the kiss, breathing her in. He hoped she understood everything he was showing her because he knew telling her would scare her away. When she wound her arms around his neck and pulled him close, aligning her body with his, he realized she wasn't frightened by the intensity of his feelings—as long as he didn't verbally express them.

She tipped her head back and met his gaze, her eyes heavy lidded and sensual. "What was that for?"

"I missed you."

He eyed her warily, but her lips turned upward in a smile.

"Gotta say, I missed you too. But you've got to know, I'm fighting myself here, Ethan."

Her honesty was more than he'd expected. "Why?"

She bit down on her lower lip. "When I was married to Carter, I gave up so much of myself to be his wife. It was as if Faith Harrington and what she liked and cared about no longer mattered. I came back to start over and be independent, but I can't seem to stay away from you."

Instead of frustrating him, her words soothed his concerns. "Am I asking you to be anything other than what—and who—you are?"

"No, and that's why I keep coming back."

"Smart girl." He placed his hand behind her back, lowered his head, and slid his tongue across her lips.

She trembled in his arms. "We have this entire house to ourselves," she murmured.

And he wanted to make use of it. Later. "I thought we'd go out first."

Her eyes opened wide in surprise. "Seriously?"

As much as it pained him not to get into bed with her immediately, he was looking at his long-term goal. He wanted her in his bed and his house for much longer than one night. "I haven't eaten all day. I thought we could grab a bite in town."

"And keep an eye on Tess and Nash?" she asked.

Ethan actually trusted Nash with their sister. It was Tess he had his doubts about but not enough to follow after them. He just wanted to go out with Faith. Stake his claim publicly. Make a statement about them as a couple, something she might not be so quick to go along with.

So, if assuming he had an ulterior motive helped convince her . . . "I wouldn't mind checking up on Tess," he agreed.

"I can understand that."

"Then we can come back here and be alone." He grinned, knowing that for this one night, he had everything he wanted and more.

Faith hadn't been to a Wednesday night in Serendipity since she was a teenager hanging out with her friends. Holding with town tradition, every Wednesday of the summer meant a different local band, Italian ices, cotton candy, and *zeppoli*. Apparently Ethan had a sweet tooth she didn't know about because he'd decided dinner wasn't as important as sampling the various treats.

"Look, there's Tess." Faith pointed to where Tess and Nash stood beneath an awning on Main Street, where the Guiding Eyes, with its Seeing Eye puppies, was located, raising money for its cause. The teenager knelt down and was playing with the puppies.

"You know they loan them out to families to help socialize them before they're fully trained and given to their person." Faith nudged Ethan in the side. "And she looks really attached to them."

He shuddered at the thought. "Maybe she'll talk Nash into an overnight visit."

"Are you telling me you're not a dog person?" she asked, disappointed. "Because they say people who don't like dogs aren't really good people."

"I like dogs just fine. But Tess and a dog might be a bit much right now."

She laughed at the exaggerated fear in his voice. "Okay, good point." Faith glanced across the street only to see Nash coming their way. "Uh-oh. Company."

Ethan looked over, caught sight of his brother, and

immediately wrapped a protective arm around her waist. She didn't need him to look out for her but liked the fact that he did it anyway.

"How's it going?" Ethan asked as Nash strode up to them.

"She's begging me to take home a puppy." Nash's grimace was priceless.

"I take it you don't like dogs?" Faith asked. A silent understanding passed between her and Ethan and he lightly squeezed her hip, causing her to chuckle.

"I like dogs," Nash said defensively. "I just happen to think Tess is enough of a handful for one night."

Faith raised her eyebrows, surprised Ethan and Nash would have such similar reactions. To anything.

"I hear you," Ethan said.

"She told me you're thinking of enrolling her at Birchwood."

"I am."

Faith stiffened, waiting for the inevitable criticism. Though she couldn't imagine what Nash could find objectionable, she figured if Ethan's brother had crossed the street to discuss it, he had issues. If only because Ethan had suggested it.

"Do you have something to say about it?" Ethan asked.

"As a matter of fact, I do." Nash's blue eyes bored into Ethan's.

Ethan's grip on her waist tightened. "Well? What is it?"

Nash's jaw tightened. "I think it will be good for her." The words sounded torn from him. Obviously giving Ethan credit for anything was painful in the extreme.

Faith exhaled a breath she hadn't been aware of holding.

"I agree," Ethan said.

"She looks up to you," Nash said.

Ethan shrugged. "I wouldn't go that far."

"She's protective of you." Nash's gaze darted to Faith, acknowledging her earlier point. "I'm not sure what you did to deserve it, but don't let her down."

"I don't intend to," Ethan said, annoyance clearly simmering below the surface.

"Good." Nash's eyes flared a darker hue, the message to his older brother clear. Nothing between *them* had changed.

"I have to get back and make sure the little tyrant hasn't forged my name on the permission slip for the dogs." Nash turned and headed back across the street.

"It's enough already!" Faith exploded when Nash was out of earshot. "The man acts as if he's never made a mistake in his entire life."

Ethan's mouth curved upward.

"What's so funny?"

"It's not funny. It's sweet." He caressed her cheek with his knuckles. "How you stick up for me."

"It's second nature," she admitted. He dipped his head for a long, thorough kiss, his tongue teasing and tangling with hers. "Mmm. You taste like sugar."

Her stomach curled deliciously. "Want some more?"

His gaze burned into hers, making her yearn to have him, skin against skin, his body hard inside hers. "You bet I do."

She shuddered in anticipation of heading home to his bed. Instead, he turned and walked away.

She caught up with him at the *zeppoli* stand, where he bought her another piece of fried dough, laden with powdered sugar, then watched as she tortured him in return. She slowly ate the treat, deliberately savoring the warm dough, licking the sugar thoroughly with her tongue. She hoped she was stoking his flames because she was already completely aroused and couldn't wait to end the evening in his bed and his arms.

But he evidently intended to make her wait, because first they walked hand in hand through town. Faith felt people staring. At her? At him? Them as a couple? She didn't know nor did she care, because as the music played around them and Faith strode through the town she called home, Ethan by her side, an odd sense of peace filled her.

Odd because she was finally feeling like she just might fit in. Back when she was a teenager, she had her group of friends and thought her life was amazing, but she hadn't a clue about the real world. Now she had a business she was building, friendships she was renewing, and a man who represented all sorts of possibilities if she was willing to explore them. And hadn't he given her every reason to believe in him? Didn't he admit he liked her just the way she was?

"What?" he asked, breaking into her thoughts.

"What what?"

He laughed. "You're smiling, so I wondered what you were thinking about."

"That's an easy question to answer. You."

He grinned. "Now that I like to hear." He reached out and brushed his finger over her lips. "Powdered sugar," he explained before she could ask.

Her skin tingled from his heated touch, a flame she felt all the way to her core. But they were still in town, in public. "So how did your business go in D.C.?" she asked, trying to keep things between them proper and acceptable. Otherwise she'd wrap her body around his and try to crawl right into him.

"Actually, it went well," he said, unaware of her building desire. "It seems that Dale is still his own worst enemy. Yes, he'd been sleeping with my executive assistant so he could steal information—"

"You mean she wasn't just handing it over?"

He nodded. "That was another plus. She was gullible but not guilty. He used her. Unfortunately for him, he's still the most arrogant SOB I've ever come across and he thought her feelings would counteract her common sense."

Faith raised an eyebrow. "One of those men, huh?"

"Yep. When my PI told me about their relationship, my hunch told me Amelia wouldn't deliberately sabotage my business. She's just not the type. I was right. When I showed her the evidence that Dale used my specs on his own bid, she broke down. She was devastated. Even quit."

"You *let* her?"

"Of course not. I told her to take a paid vacation and get herself together. She agreed to testify in my lawsuit against Dale for stealing proprietary business information. And I grabbed the next flight home. To you."

Okay, so maybe he wasn't as unaware of her needs as she'd thought.

She couldn't stand another minute of small talk on the street. "And I couldn't be happier that you did."

"Same here," he said in a husky voice that reassured her he wanted her every bit as much as she needed him.

Faith leaned in close, inhaling his sexy masculine scent. "So . . . when are you going to take me home?"

Ethan wouldn't call himself a romantic, not by a long shot, but even he knew when he was about to get lucky—and he didn't mean it in the obvious sense. Having the entire house to himself wasn't something that would happen often. Especially not an entire night alone with Faith on the same day he'd accepted his feelings for her.

The drive home was comfortably silent yet sexually charged. Two things he appreciated about Faith: her ability to ease away the tension in his life and keep him in a constant state of arousal. Not a bad combination and one he looked forward to remaining in for a good long time.

Hand in hand, they walked from the garage through the house. She automatically kicked off her sandals by the door and he ditched his sneakers. She was dressed in white jeans and a purple asymmetrical flowing tank top, the same color as Tess's streak of hair, he noted, amused. But there was nothing funny about how she looked, casual and relaxed, and so sexy she took his breath away with her bare feet and light pink polish peeking out from beneath the bottom of her white jeans.

His body felt primed and ready as they walked up the circular stairs toward his bedroom.

"I can't wait to get this place finished," she said, unaware of his thoughts. "The painters are coming in next week to strip all the wallpaper, prime, and paint. Then Nick will come in and put up the molding and chair rail."

"Sounds great." He was barely listening. He tugged her hand, pulling her down the hall and into his bedroom, kicking the door shut behind him with his foot. Just in case Tess decided to make an unplanned return home.

"You're not paying attention, are you?" Faith asked, sounding upset.

"Hell, no." He swung her into his arms and dropped her onto the mattress. "Do you really think I can concentrate on home decorating?" he asked, pinning her to the mattress with his body, letting her feel the hard ridge of his arousal flush against her.

"I guess not," she said on a dreamy sigh, no longer caring about his lack of attention to her house plans.

He held her wrists in his hands and lowered his head for a kiss, sweeping his tongue inside her mouth at the same time he rolled his hips against her waist.

"Oh God." Her entire being shook in reaction.

He could barely hold himself in check. "Feels good?"

"Mmm-hmm." She met his gaze, but another shift of his hips had her eyes rolling back in her head.

He grinned. He liked giving her this kind of pleasure. While her eyes were closed, he released her wrists and slid his hand beneath her shirt, pulling it up and over her head, revealing a white bra edged in pink lace. A flick of his finger released the front hook, exposing her breasts, full, ripe, and ready, not just for his gaze either. He dipped his head and pulled one already rigid nipple into his mouth.

She groaned and threaded her fingers into his hair, holding him in place. Time was a luxury and he took his, lavishing all his attention on the soft mound of flesh. Only when he was finished with one did he move to the other breast, keeping her writhing beneath him. Every shift of her hips caused him a mix of pleasure and pain, but he wasn't finished enjoying her yet. He trailed his lips down the center of her stomach, her flesh quivering beneath his mouth, until he reached the waistband of her jeans. With her help, they got rid of her clothing and his followed, after which he picked up where he'd left off, tasting her soft flesh. He was relentless, arousing her with long, damp strokes of his tongue until he came to her center.

She was already wet and damp and when he licked her there, her hips rose off the bed. He held her in place and continued a gentle assault, until she was shaking and begging for relief. One touch at exactly the right spot and she came apart, her climax more gratifying than any of his own. Though right now his body was aching for release, he still took pleasure in hers.

Because he loved her.

Rising up, he settled his hips over hers, and then, holding on to her gaze, he thrust deep inside. His entire body registered the moment, every nerve ending, every part of him joined with Faith.

He belonged to her. And she to him.

Awareness lit her gaze. She felt it too. Whether she accepted it or not was another story.

She shifted beneath him, the shock waves echoing everywhere, and he began to match her rhythm, his hips pumping in conjunction with hers, their pace and tempo perfection. Next thing he knew, he was spinning out of control, losing himself inside her.

Later, spent, he knew he'd given her everything he had. He could only hope she'd find the strength within herself to give back.

* * *

Faith awoke cushioned in heavy, delicious, body-hugging warmth. As awareness came to her, she realized where she was, who she was with, and she never wanted to leave. Of course, the notion ran contrary to every thought she'd had since she and Ethan had . . . renewed their acquaintance. She couldn't stop the smile that curved her lips. They'd done so much more than become reacquainted. And she could no longer deny her growing feelings for this man or the obvious truth.

She loved him.

Faith didn't know how it had happened or when. She only knew she couldn't picture her life without him in it. All her reasons for steering clear, the ones that revolved around her being independent, fell apart when it came to Ethan. He wouldn't stand in the way of her growing into the woman or the interior designer she wanted to be. Nor would she allow such a thing to happen to her ever again. So maybe, just maybe, she could allow a little bit of hope to enter her life and believe the pain and the past were behind her.

She rolled over and found her face buried in Ethan's broad chest and she took a moment to inhale deeply and snuggle closer into his embrace. "I like waking up like this," she said, her voice muffled and lost.

"I can't hear you," he said, laughing.

She tipped her head back and looked into his eyes. "Good morning."

"Morning," he said in a sleep-roughened voice she found incredibly sexy.

As she stared into his handsome face, suddenly and without warning, nerves kicked in. True, they had a deep connection and he seemed to want more from her than a casual fling. But the fact remained, she'd stayed the night without discussion and without asking. She'd never been a big one-night-stand girl, and though her heart told her this was anything but, her mind had her wanting to run. Especially since he just stared at her with those fathomless eyes. *Talk about awkward,* she thought as the silence stretched endlessly between them.

Ethan stared into Faith's gorgeous eyes, feeling like he could wake like this every morning for the rest of his life. Suddenly her happy, serene, *satisfied* morning-after expression vanished, replaced by wide, anxiety-filled eyes and a distinct stiffening of her body. He recognized her panic for what it was, and when she tried to pull away he was mentally prepared and grasped her arms before she could roll over.

"Going somewhere?" he asked.

She blinked, startled. "I don't know. I thought . . ."

He knew what she thought, his heart clenching in his chest. "You were going to run away like a one-night stand who'd suddenly overstayed her welcome." His voice sounded harsher than he'd meant to, but he'd never held back with her when it mattered and wasn't about to now. Not about anything, he decided.

She inclined her head. "I don't remember falling asleep and I thought maybe you never wanted—"

He cut her off, closing his mouth over hers, showing her just how wrong she was about what he did and didn't want. She got the message immediately. Her lips softened and soon she wasn't just kissing him back—she was climbing on top of him.

They'd slept naked and he slid his hand between them to find her already wet and, seconds later, she straddled him, enclosing him in her damp heat. She ground her hips against him and his climax immediately beckoned. Good thing hers did too, and his world exploded at the same moment she cried out his name.

A few minutes later, his breathing slowly returned to normal. "Do we understand each other now?" he asked, stroking the back of her hair with his hand.

"Mmm-hmm. I'm not a one-night stand who overstayed

her welcome." She snuggled backward into his arms. "And I'm allowed to sleep over when Tess isn't home," she murmured sleepily.

Not quite what he had in mind and he rolled her over until she faced him. "No, you're not a one-night stand. You're so much more." She'd distracted him when she'd climbed on top, but he had his mind back where it belonged now.

He saw the questions in her eyes. "Go ahead, ask me."

She swallowed hard. Ran her tongue over her lips. "How much more?"

"You're everything," he said simply. "I love you."

Her mouth opened and closed again. "You love me? I—"

A cell phone rang somewhere in the pile of clothes on the floor. Not his ring tone.

Her gaze darted toward the sound. "That's mine."

"Let it wait."

"Okay." She drew a shaky breath.

The phone continued to ring and the moment between them was gone, lost in the distracting sound.

"Get it."

She nodded and rolled over, climbing out of bed, but by the time she found the cell, the ringing had stopped. She checked the phone. "My mother," she said.

"You sound surprised."

"She rarely calls me." Faith rose and climbed back into bed, pulling the covers over her naked body before redialing the number.

Her mother answered on the first ring. "Mom?"

"Have you seen it?" From right beside Faith, Ethan could hear Lanie's voice loud and clear.

"Seen what?" Faith asked.

"It's your father. He's destroyed my life all over again!" Lanie Harrington cried into the phone.

"Calm down and explain," Faith ordered her mother in a composed voice, but at the mention of her father, her hand began to tremble.

Faith's mother was obviously incapable of coherent conversation, so Faith ended the call, promising to come right over.

Their morning, their moment had passed. They wouldn't be discussing the three words Ethan had spoken, and whatever she'd wanted to say in return would have to wait. His heart pounded hard in his chest, making him painfully aware of what he'd put out there, left unanswered.

Seventeen

Faith arrived at her mother's small house and found Lanie still wearing her nightgown, in bed crying hysterically.

"Mom?"

"How could he?" Lanie pointed to the magazine on her lap with a shaking hand.

Faith's legs felt wooden as she crossed the bedroom floor. "What is it?"

"An interview."

Faith picked up the copy of the *News Journal* magazine and stared at her father's familiar face. His hair was grayer and a few more lines creased his skin, but his expression hadn't changed. What a younger, more naive Faith hadn't noticed was the arrogance in his eyes and posture. Prison hadn't diminished either of those traits.

With dread, Faith flipped to the beginning of the article.

"You might want to sit down. It's long," her mother suggested.

Faith turned and faced the parent who'd never acted like one. "Did you know about this before it hit the stands?"

Lanie glanced down at her hands. "The reporter called and asked if he could interview me."

"Of course you agreed." Her mother would grasp at any chance at fame or publicity, never bothering to think about the repercussions. "What did you tell them?"

"The truth as I saw it. Among other things, that your father was either misunderstood or misguided but not an evil man at heart. Unfortunately, they printed selectively."

Faith swallowed hard. "What quotes did they use?"

"Ones about my old life. What things I miss most now." Lanie didn't glance up or meet Faith's gaze.

"In other words, you came off sounding like an unrepentant spoiled brat?"

Now her mother glanced up, startled. "Don't speak to me that way!"

Faith sighed and lowered herself into a Queen Anne–style chair in the corner, magazine still in her hand. "Don't you think the time for cushioning our words and pretending are over?"

Lanie waved her hand at Faith. "Just read it."

Faith settled in to pore over her father's words. At the headline on the cover, "Anatomy of a Scam," any hope that her mother was overreacting died a quick death. Faith read the article, her stomach in knots and cramping, her head pounding. Because for once in her life, Lanie Harrington hadn't exaggerated.

Martin Harrington had bared his soul and, in doing so, revealed he had none. Her once beloved father didn't deny any of his wrongdoing. He'd known from the beginning that what he was doing was both illegal and immoral, but when the money started pouring in he couldn't bring himself to care. Not when he and his family had lived a lifestyle of opulence and luxury.

Did he feel guilt? he was asked. For the people whose

life savings he'd lost? No, he did not. Those same people who complained now hadn't batted an eyelash when he'd made them profits beyond their wildest dreams. If they'd enjoyed the fruits of his labors then, who were they to find fault now? To Martin Harrington, it hardly seemed fair that he was in jail, estranged from his wife and only child.

At the mention of her name, nausea rose in Faith's throat. Because her father didn't stop there. He went on to elaborate on how Faith's marriage to Carter Moreland had united two powerhouses—Martin in business, Carter in the legal arena—bringing more clients to Harrington Investment Securities—and more money to the associates whom Carter Moreland had introduced to Martin Harrington. He'd incriminated Carter by implication and dirtied Faith by extension.

Faith had believed that by distancing herself from her father, she had nothing to be ashamed of. In fact, she'd thought of herself as another one of Martin Harrington's victims. No way in hell would she or anyone else ever see her that way again. She'd lived off her father's money, then Carter's. And if the article implied his guilt, Faith had both *known* and had benefited from her ex-husband's guilt to gain what she believed to be a fair divorce settlement. But there was nothing fair about anything or anyone who'd been in Martin Harrington's life. This article made her seem guilty by association. And she was.

Faith looked up at her mother through tear-filled eyes.

"I was so wrong about him," Lanie admitted at last.

Faith licked her dry lips. "We both were."

"But you accepted it long before me. How could he do this to us? How could he allow this magazine to show us in this light?" her mother asked, her voice cracking.

Faith rose and crossed the room, seating herself on the edge of the mattress. She didn't recall ever cuddling with her mother on her bed. But the past didn't matter. The present did.

"The magazine isn't at fault, Mom. Dad is. He did these

things. He admitted them. And he had no problem throwing us under the bus along with him." It hurt Faith to verbalize the painful truth to her mother.

The woman beside her had been beaten down and broken. Whether or not the outside world thought Lanie Harrington deserved sympathy, Faith understood how important her status in life was to her mother. After her father's guilty plea, Faith knew just how far her mother had fallen.

For the first time, Lanie Harrington knew it too. And Faith pitied her.

"What am I going to do?" Lanie asked, childlike as she sought advice from her daughter.

Faith forced a grim smile. "Exactly what I'm doing. Rebuild your life from the bottom up with a new awareness of who you are and who you want to be."

The only problem was that Faith's perspective on those things had just undergone a drastic one eighty.

"Do you think I can do that?" her mother asked.

Faith nodded. "Of course you can. I'm more than willing to help—but you have to be willing to meet me halfway."

Faith laid out rules for her mother to follow. Lanie's answer would tell Faith whether or not she had a chance at a real mother–daughter relationship.

"I'm not sure I know what you want from me," her mother said honestly.

For Faith, that was a start. "It means calling me to talk, being honest about your feelings and what's going on in your life. And most important, it means accepting that you aren't the lady of the manor anymore. You aren't any better than anyone else in Serendipity and you need to start acting more humble."

Lanie wrapped her arms around herself, rocking back and forth like a little girl. "You don't ask for much," her mother said, sarcastically but without bite.

"No, not much. I'm just asking you to be human," Faith said wryly.

A genuine, somewhat pained smile touched her mother's face. Without makeup, her age lines were more apparent, the real person more evident without the mask of wealth and haughtiness she normally wore.

Faith wondered if it would last. "I could use some help at the shop," she said, venturing another step toward forging a relationship. "It would mean answering the phones, maybe making some cold calls, helping me drum up business. I couldn't afford to pay you much, but over time I hope that would change." She waited while her mother processed what Faith was asking.

"You want me to work for you?" Lanie sounded surprised.

Faith nodded. What she really wanted was to give her mother an excuse to leave the house and face people—before hiding out became permanent.

"Can I think about it?" Lanie asked.

"Just don't take too long. After this article, I may have a ton of applicants banging down the door." Faith winced at the bad joke.

For the first time in a long time, her mother laughed.

Ethan showered and rushed downstairs. He didn't want to be late to pick up Tess and face his brother's wrath. Better to be early and get his sister out of there without giving Nash added ammunition for an argument.

Grabbing his car keys from the kitchen counter, he was about to head to the garage when Rosalita cornered him.

"Oh, Mr. Ethan, bad news." She muttered something unintelligible in Spanish.

"What's wrong?" he asked.

"Oh, that Mr. Harrington, he's a very bad man." She crossed herself as if to ward away evil spirits.

At the mention of Faith's father, Ethan grew wary, but it was the last part of the dismayed woman's statement that caught his attention. "Rosalita, I'm hurt. I thought I was the only very bad man in your life," he said, unable to resist the opportunity to goad his housekeeper the way she goaded him.

"Oh, no." Rosalita shook her head. "Compared to him you're a saint!"

If Rosalita was complimenting Ethan, something was very wrong. "What is it?" he asked the other woman. "What's going on?"

"Your mail came too late yesterday, so I get it from the box this morning. I put everything on your desk like always, except this. Look!" She shoved his subscription copy of the *News Journal* magazine into his hand.

The *News Journal* covered the latest in business and important world news. And from the cover, a smug Martin Harrington, Faith's father, smiled up at him.

"'Anatomy of a Scam,'" Ethan read aloud. "Son of a bitch." Just what Faith didn't need, Ethan thought.

Rosalita nodded and crossed herself once more.

No wonder Faith had gotten a panicked phone call from her mother. He had to go pick up Tess, but he was worried about Faith. So was Rosalita, and after promising Rosalita he'd take care of the woman she considered like a daughter, Ethan left for his brother's place across town.

While driving, he called Faith on her cell phone more than once, but he kept getting her voice mail. He finally gave up and left her a message asking her to call him as soon as possible.

Nash lived in a new condo development on the outskirts of town. Ethan pulled into a parking spot and discovered Dare's police car already there.

Already tense, Ethan rang his brother's doorbell and the door opened immediately, Tess greeting him on the other side. "Thank God, you're here to rescue me!"

Relieved by her greeting when he didn't know what the dynamic duo had in store for him, he grinned. "Hey, kid. Miss me?"

She rolled her eyes, her way of letting him know he was a dork. At least she wasn't cursing at him, he thought.

"Want breakfast? There's extra bagels," she said, pulling him inside.

In the kitchen, Nash, Dare, and Tess had already shared a cozy breakfast, which had clearly deliberately excluded him.

Ethan drew a deep breath, forced the hurt down into a place he'd created years ago, and stepped into the room. "Morning," Ethan said.

"Want a bagel?" Tess asked.

"No thanks." Ethan set his jaw. "You ready?" he asked her.

"I just have to get my things." She bounced out of the room.

"Seems like she had a good time," he said, hoping like hell the kid moved fast. He didn't want to be stuck here too long.

"She did." Dare rose to his feet and, to Ethan's surprise, reached out a hand for Ethan to shake. "So I hear you want to put her in private school."

Ethan didn't know his youngest brother well enough to gauge his feelings on the matter. He'd already gotten Nash's grudging okay and wondered if that automatically meant Dare would feel the same way.

"I want her to have access to one of the best art teachers in the country. After that, we can discuss where she wants to enroll in school permanently." Ethan shoved his hands into his pockets.

Dare nodded. "I think it's a good idea. She's obviously got an interest since she drags that sketch pad everywhere."

"Did she show you her work?" Ethan asked.

"No. She's pretty protective of that pad." Dare laughed.

"How about you?" Ethan asked Nash, who until now remained silent. No big surprise there, since he clearly held more of a grudge than Dare.

"Nope," Nash said. "Haven't seen it."

A unbrotherly-like feeling of relief settled in Ethan's chest. As much as he wanted Tess to have a relationship with her other siblings, the fact that she trusted Ethan with her artwork and not them gave him a feeling of satisfaction he wasn't proud of but couldn't control.

It was because of the way Nash treated him, like he wasn't worth the dirt beneath his shoe, that got to Ethan. He wasn't that same selfish, mixed-up eighteen-year-old who'd abandoned his brothers, and though it had taken him too many years to grow up, he finally had. Ethan was finished apologizing for a past he couldn't change. He could only control the future and he knew who and what mattered to him now.

"Well, when you do see Tess's work, you'll understand why I want her to have this opportunity," Ethan said.

"She hasn't warmed up to me that way yet," Nash admitted.

No big shock there, Ethan thought. Though his middle brother had ended up with the better foster care arrangement, his attitude toward people and life was obviously darker.

Tess was a great judge of character.

"I take it you've seen the interview with Martin Harrington?" Nash asked, leaning back in his seat, taking pleasure in the question Ethan knew he'd inevitably ask.

"I thought we agreed not to bring that up this morning." Dare glared at Nash, annoyance in his tone and tight body language.

Nash shrugged. "What can I tell you? I just look at him and all my anger comes back." He rocked his chair forward and planted his feet back on the ground.

"Well, back off," Dare said. "Tess is in the other room and—"

"Thanks, but I don't need you fighting my battles," Ethan told his youngest brother. "I know how he feels about me and about Faith." Ethan gestured to Nash. "As soon as Tess is ready I'll leave and you two can get back to your *family* breakfast." Ethan hadn't meant to show them that excluding him hurt, but the truth slipped out anyway.

Of both men, only Dare looked uncomfortable, confirming Ethan's notion that maybe he had a shot of making peace with his youngest sibling.

"I'm ready!" Tess said, bounding back into the room, full of energy and oblivious to the undercurrents in the room. "I have to stop home and change before we go to the beach. And so do you," she said, looking Ethan up and down, taking in his black jeans and T-shirt.

"Before we get near the beach, I got a call on the way over here. You and I have an interview at Birchwood today at eleven. We need to go home and change for that. Did Faith buy you something suitable?" he asked hopefully.

He reminded himself to find out how much Faith had spent so he could pay her back for Tess's new wardrobe. When he finally heard from her, he thought, realizing his phone hadn't yet rung.

"I guess there's one dress," Tess said, sounding pained at the thought. "Can we go to the beach afterward?"

Ethan nodded. "If it doesn't rain. The sky was cloudy this morning."

She frowned but nodded in understanding. At least there was something Ethan couldn't be blamed for today.

Tess dressed up nicely, Ethan thought, unsure of whether or not to tell her and risk embarrassing her before their interview.

What the hell. "You look good," he said, watching her come down the stairs in a feminine dress, light lavender and white, with a pair of silver sandals.

She blushed and ducked her head. "I look like a dork."

"Do not."

"I do too. And so do you, in that suit."

He shook his head and laughed, but Tess didn't join him. "What's wrong?"

She hesitated.

"Come on, spill."

Tess blew out a long breath of air. "Fine. Faith was supposed to fix my hair this weekend, but now—" She fingered the purple streak, her uncertainty showing through.

"I thought you liked purple," he responded, deliberately playing dumb. He understood she didn't want to show up at a private school meeting with the rebellious hair.

"You know what I mean."

She picked at her nails and he smacked her hand. "Yeah, I do. But you know what? You look cool." He held up a hand before she could reply. "I know, I know, nobody says 'cool' anymore. But there's nothing wrong with showing your individuality." Minus the attitude, the hair wasn't as objectionable, but if she wanted to let Faith soften it, Ethan was all for it.

Assuming he could get in touch with Faith. So far she still wasn't answering her phone or calling him back.

"Are you ready?" he asked.

"Yep. I'm gonna kick some butt," she said, back to her old self.

He grinned. "Good. Just watch the mouth when we get there and you're all set."

A half hour later, one of the female administrators took Tess for a tour around the school while Ethan met with the head director in his office.

Once they were seated, Dr. Spellman, a balding, sixty-something-year-old man got right to the point. "You'd like to enroll your sister in our school, specifically our art department?"

Ethan nodded. "She's new in town, so wherever she starts school will be a transition for her."

"It's a new world for us here at Birchwood. Normally I'd have to turn you down and put your sister on a waiting list, but things have changed. Thanks to the recent economic downturn and some unsuccessful investment choices, we find ourselves in need of an influx of funds," the other man said bluntly.

Ethan leaned back in his chair, seeing the other man as a businessman rather than an academic. "In other words, it's about how much I'm willing to invest in your school?"

"In a word, yes. In addition, we'd like you to sit on the board. Your business acumen would also be an asset for us going forward."

Ethan understood the compliment was more about his success than who he was, but that was the way of the world. If it got Tess in, he'd suffer through being on the board. "It's tough economic times all around," Ethan said.

"For some more than others. You see, our school invested funds with Martin Harrington, as did many of our largest benefactors."

"I see," Ethan said, not happy with the turn this conversation had taken.

The director picked up a letter opener and rubbed it between the palms of his hands. "Not only did we lose funding, but we lost students whose parents could no longer afford to enroll them in our school. As a result, we've had to cut many beloved teachers and programs that our school is known for. The only reason we are able to offer the visiting professor program you want to enroll your sister in is because of one very generous patron whose daughter loves art. But that doesn't help the other lost programs, the fired teachers, or the students who have suffered greatly all because of Martin Harrington's greed."

"I understand the school has suffered," Ethan said, treading carefully for myriad reasons.

Adam Spellman nodded his head. "Now this." He pulled the *News Journal* magazine from the inbox on his desk. "Rubbing our noses in fresh wounds. A reminder is the last thing this school needs going into a new year."

"I agree," Ethan said. And a school board with an inherent bias against a Harrington was the last thing Ethan needed.

Not when he intended for Faith Harrington to be a part of both his and Tess's life in every way possible—including attending any events at this school by his side or with his sister. But Ethan recognized the value of silence, and he would only be revealing information to Dr. Adam Spellman on an as-needed basis. Until Ethan had written a substantial check to this institution, nobody here needed to know his relationship to Faith Harrington. After all, money could buy acceptance of many things and people. Martin Harrington's daughter included.

But how fair would it be for Ethan to ask Faith to deal with people who blatantly hated her father? And how difficult would it be for Tess and Faith to deal with the parents and kids, who'd lost programs and favorite teachers? Faith already had his brother Nash to contend with.

"Mr. Barron?"

Ethan snapped back to the present. "Sorry. Yes, I can assure you my donation will help the school get back on its feet. In return, I would appreciate it if you'd make my family feel welcome here."

Adam Spellman rose to his feet, a smile on his face. "That is an easy promise to make. There's just one more thing."

"Yes?"

"This is a bit awkward, but we're a conservative school. It would help if your sister . . . modified her look? The purple hair? The piercing?"

Ethan bit the inside of his cheek. No matter how he felt about Tess's *accessorizing*, he disliked anyone else criticizing her. "My sister is entitled to a little individuality. But I will talk to her," he said, knowing Tess already planned to change her hair. Maybe the piercing would follow. Maybe not. He could live with that, he realized, knowing how far she'd already come.

Spellman held out his hand and Ethan shook on the deal. "I'll have a check in the mail by the end of business today."

Wasn't it ironic, Ethan thought. Ten years ago, he hadn't been good enough for Faith Harrington. Hell, he still wasn't. But in the eyes of the town, their situations were now reversed. Money truly could buy just about anything, including acceptance.

But would Faith allow herself, her acceptance, to be bought, no matter how good the reason?

Later that evening, after spending the day at work and avoiding any and all talk about Martin Harrington, a part of Faith wished she could continue the pattern and evade Ethan and the inevitable conversation about her father's interview. She was used to dealing with her troubles alone, and burying herself under the covers for at least one night sounded good to her right now. But another part of Faith had gotten used to having Ethan Barron in her life and desperately wanted to feel his arms around her and let him chase away the demon that was her father.

So Faith found herself driving to Ethan's and pulling her car up the long driveway. Funny, but she no longer thought of this as her old house. Sometime in the last few weeks, she'd not just accepted the change she'd had no control over but also had come to feel his living here just felt right.

Ethan greeted her on the front porch before she could even think of ringing the bell. He pulled her into his arms and settled his lips over hers.

His big hands clasped around her waist and he kissed her senseless, chasing away all the bad things in her life, just as she'd wanted.

"Thank you," she said, tilting her head back and looking into his eyes.

"For what?"

"For being you. And for knowing exactly what I need."

She only hoped she gave back to him in equal measure. "I'm sorry I didn't call you back today. I knew you'd hear about the article anyway and I needed time to process that interview."

"Understandable." He slipped his hand into hers, led her into the house and straight to the kitchen. "And have you processed it?" he asked once they'd settled into the folding chairs.

"As much as I'm going to. I just feel so . . . betrayed." She leaned her chin on her hands, trying to sum up her feelings, which were still raw. "It was bad enough when I found out who my father was and what he did. But despite all my denials, I wanted to believe he still loved me. That because I was his daughter, that meant something to him."

She pulled in a ragged breath, the words she'd refused to let herself think or express, escaping at last. "In that way, I was no better than my mother, still in denial. I just put on a better face to the outside world. But this interview shattered every illusion I'd been holding on to—no matter how deep inside me. He told the world he'd used my marriage as a stepping-stone in his scam, and if that wasn't bad enough, he implied that my ex-husband knew all about his dirty dealings. He destroyed any bit of reputation I'd held on to and most of my self-respect."

Ethan rose and wrapped her in his arms, in his warmth. "You aren't a reflection of your father or his actions."

"What if I knew that Carter had more than an inkling of his dirty deals? I threatened to expose him if he didn't give me a fair alimony settlement. What does that say about me?"

Ethan stroked the back of her hair. "It says you're smart. But it doesn't say you're just like him."

"How could my own father use me that way?" she asked, tears escaping despite her attempts to hold them back.

"He used everyone."

Ethan held her in his arms, comforting her and letting her gather his strength until she pulled herself together.

"Enough about me." Faith grabbed a napkin from the holder in the center of the table and wiped her eyes. "You said in your voice message that you had a meeting with the head of Birchwood. How did things go? Is Tess in, no problem?"

Eighteen

Ethan did not want to have this conversation. In fact, he'd give up everything he owned to make the subject disappear. Instead, he faced the woman he loved and prepared to hurt her even more.

He pulled out the chair and pulled it closer to Faith's.

"Tess had a great day. She toured the school and saw the amazing art supplies she'd be using. I already know what I'm going to get her for Christmas," he said, laughing.

Avoiding.

Faith smiled. "You know, I think that Kelly's dropping Tess on your doorstep was the best thing that ever happened to either one of you?"

He reached out and stroked her soft cheek. "No, I think that would be you."

She shook her head, but her feelings were evident in her eyes, all the love he felt for her reciprocated, and his heart swelled with hope.

"While Tess took her tour, I met with the head of the school," he continued.

Though he was painfully aware of this morning's open-ended "I love you" conversation, he couldn't bring himself to hear her say it back and then break her heart. And he had no doubt she loved him too.

"Will Birchwood take her?" Faith asked.

He nodded. "As long as I write a big fat check and agree to sit on their board, she's in. Of course, the dean mentioned that the school is a little conservative and Tess could help herself fit in better by changing her hair, to start. I haven't broken the news to her yet."

Faith laughed. "Something tells me she's ready for that. She must be over the moon!" Faith's smile lit her face, those expressive eyes filled with joy. "Where is she?"

"In her room. After she called her sister, Kelly, she headed upstairs. She's been blasting her music in celebration ever since." He couldn't help but grin.

"That's great! But you on the board of directors? Is that something you want to do?" Faith asked, all too perceptive when it came to him.

He shook his head. "Not really. But for Tess, I'll chew nails once a month or for however long those meetings take." He grasped her hand in his and began rubbing lazy circles over the sensitive pulse in her wrist.

She shivered and he appreciated how sensitive she was to his touch.

"What do they want from you?" she asked.

"According to Adam Spellman? My cash and my business expertise." He shrugged. "Personally, I also think he wants to know he has easy access to me and my funds should the need arise."

Faith glanced at him, questions in her eyes. "More than the money you're already giving?"

"Maybe. The school's been hit hard financially. They've had to cut teachers' jobs as well as extracurricular activities. Some of the kids who attended the school last year can't afford to come back."

Faith winced. "That's awful. I'm glad Tess can benefit, but I really feel for the school and the kids."

"Me too."

She glanced down at their still intertwined hands. "How'd they get into so much trouble?" she asked.

He met her gaze and held on to her hand. "Well, they've made some very damaging financial decisions," he said deliberately slow and pointed. He squeezed her hand tighter, pausing to let the truth come to her in her own time.

"Oh. *Oh*. No." Faith shook her head in denial. "My father?" she asked, her voice cracking.

He nodded. "I'm sorry. I didn't want to tell you but I couldn't not be honest either."

"God, will it never end?" Faith pulled her hand from his and buried her head in her hands.

"Faith?"

She raised her head, meeting his gaze with dead eyes.

"Your father's actions have nothing to do with us. Not if we don't let them," he said, wanting to believe his own words.

Ethan prayed she wouldn't come to the conclusions he'd already drawn today, about kids ostracizing Tess once they realized her connection to Faith, the woman whose father had caused the kids to lose teachers, classmates, and programs. And that was just the tip of the proverbial iceberg, he thought, disgusted with Martin Harrington.

"You're too smart to believe that." Faith yanked her hand from his and rose from her seat. "You love me. You said so yourself," she said, straightening her shoulders.

He stood up to face her, look into those beautiful eyes. "Damn straight I do."

"Well, I love you too." She blinked, and a tear dripped onto her cheek. She angrily wiped it with the back of her hand before turning away from him.

It wasn't the way he'd wanted to hear the declaration, but knowing it still filled the empty, lonely spaces inside him.

Now he had to convince her not to run, and he braced himself, already preparing counterarguments in his head.

When Faith faced him again, her face was pale, her jaw taut. "This morning, before my mother called, I'd convinced myself we could give this thing between us a shot. Because you're everything I always wanted."

Her sweet smile would have brought him to his knees, if he hadn't heard the *but* in her tone.

She gripped the chair with her hands until her knuckles turned white, her pain obviously as great as his.

"If it was just us, then yes, we could handle it together. But there's no way Tess deserves to be hurt because of your association with me."

Nausea filled him, followed by frustration. "What we share is not just some *association*," he said, hurt she'd use such a cold, generic word to describe what they shared.

"No, it's not," she agreed softly, tempering his anger. "But neither is what you share with Tess, and she's just getting comfortable with you. She's come out of her shell because she trusts you. And I won't be the person that shatters that trust or hurts her."

"Faith—"

She stepped out of reach. "You can't deny that Tess will suffer when people at that school find out about *us*."

He replied with silence. Of course he couldn't deny it. "But if we're a tight unit, if we back her up, she'll know she's loved, that she can trust us."

"Or maybe she'll blame you for sticking her in that school and that situation. Or she'll come to hate me for being the reason the kids exclude her, or you for bringing me into her life."

"That kid adores you," he argued back.

"And the feeling is mutual." Faith couldn't contain a smile. "But you do realize that if Tess becomes that emo-punk kid again, Birchwood will never accept her, no matter how much money you throw at them. And there's no way

I'll selfishly sit by and let her revert back to that angry kid. Not when I see how amazing she really is."

Faith was equally amazing, and Ethan loved her that much more for putting Tess's needs before her own. But he refused to let her go that easily.

"This isn't over. We aren't over."

She sighed and leaned against the counter, obviously exhausted and devastated, but the conviction in her eyes told him she wouldn't back down.

Good thing he was equally stubborn. "We *will* figure this out."

"I just did. Tess deserves to be in that school, to learn from that art teacher. She deserves to be happy."

"So do we." He grasped her shoulders but stopped short of shaking her in order to get her to see reason.

"Don't." Decision obviously made, she stepped back and straightened her shoulders. "You'll see I'm right. This is for the best." Faith pivoted and headed for the archway leading to the front of the house.

"The hell it is."

"Tess!" Faith said, obviously coming upon his sister as she left.

Son of a bitch, Ethan thought, rubbing his hands over his face.

Whether Tess had been deliberately eavesdropping or had stumbled upon the end of the discussion, there was nothing good about what she'd overheard.

Ethan walked out, planning to talk to Tess or stop Faith, but when he reached the hall outside of the kitchen, Tess was gone. A few seconds later, Tess's bedroom door slammed loudly and the front door beeped, signaling Faith had left.

"Damn it!" He stopped short of hitting his hand into the wall, knowing it wouldn't solve anything. "Could this day get any worse?"

He decided to let Faith leave and give her time alone to think. After all, she'd had one hit after another today and would have to process everything that happened, including acknowledging that they were in love.

And they were.

But she needed time to accept everything and come to the conclusion she couldn't live without him either. So for now he had to focus on Tess.

He ran up the stairs and paused outside her closed door. Loud music pounded from beneath the door, that hard rock music she used to tune him out.

He knocked on her door.

No answer.

So he banged louder.

"Go away!"

He ran his hand through his hair in frustration. "Fine," he muttered, though she couldn't hear.

With both Tess and Faith shutting him out, Ethan felt more alone than when he'd left home at eighteen. For the first time in his life, he knew what love felt like and he sure as hell didn't plan on letting Faith leave him any more than he'd let Tess withdraw back into that damn protective shell. Those two meant everything to him.

He knew now he'd probably been in love with Faith since she was sixteen and he'd idolized both Faith Harrington and that house on the hill. Except now he knew the woman was more substantial than some empty mansion, and this house would never be a home unless Faith moved in with him and Tess.

Faith walked into Cuppa Café, praying like hell Lissa had the day off. The last thing she needed after a sleepless night was Lissa's sarcasm and gloating over Faith's father's interview. Faith glanced behind the counter. So far so good. She ordered her favorite latte from the boy behind the counter, who thankfully had no idea who she was, and settled into the back table to wait for Kate.

A few minutes later, Kate strode in and walked straight back to Faith, not stopping to make small talk with anyone, for which Faith was grateful.

"You look like hell," Kate said as she slid into the seat beside Faith, only five minutes late.

"How can you see behind the sunglasses?" Faith asked.

"I said it because of the sunglasses. Now take 'em off and show me."

Faith frowned and slid the plastic frames off her face.

Kate let out a slow whistle. "Worse than I thought."

Faith had poured her heart out on the phone last night, telling Kate everything that had happened, including falling in love with Ethan, telling him so, and walking away from him all in one day.

Kate dragged her seat closer and pulled Faith into a hug. "You want to know the joke? Up until yesterday, I actually thought I'd suffered thanks to my father. Now I can really look at all those people he hurt and see how good I've had it. Lissa was right. Yes, I got divorced, but I managed a decent settlement. I opened a business. No wonder people believe I think I'm above it all." Her head pounded hard and she massaged her temples. "Now I'm suffering, but maybe I deserve it."

She'd spent the night alternating between anger and frustration, hurt and guilt, all different emotions she could barely separate or understand.

"Hey. You do not deserve to suffer. You just need to distinguish yourself from your father in the eyes of the good people of Serendipity."

"And how do you suggest I do that?" Faith asked.

"Beats me." Kate picked up her coffee cup. "Want another?"

"No. I want a new life," she muttered.

"Are you telling me you are going to let your old man ruin your future?"

"Do I have a choice?" Faith raised her hands and held them

palms up, like scales. "Let's see, *my happiness* on the left and *Tess's happiness* on the right." She weighed the choices and let her left hand sink to the table. "No contest."

Kate shook her head. "I applaud you putting the kid's needs before your own, but did it ever dawn on you that *you* make them happy?"

She glanced up. "They make me happy too."

Kate gave her such a knowing look, Faith figured she ought to know what her friend was thinking. But she waited for Kate's answer anyway.

"Then do something about it!" Kate's tone matched the fire in her eyes.

"Such as?" Because if there were something Faith thought would fix this, she would have come up with it sometime between 3:00 and 5:00 A.M.

Kate rolled her eyes. "Whoever said you were the smarter of the two of us?"

"Nobody as I recall." Faith grinned. "Come on. What are you thinking?"

"Same thing I thought the first day we met here when you'd just come back to town. If people knew the real you, none of this would be an issue." Kate rose to her feet. "I hate to leave you alone, but I have to get to the youth center."

Faith nodded. "I'm fine. Go. I'll figure out the answer to your riddle sooner or later." She waved as Kate turned and headed out the door.

"Let people know the real me," Faith mused out loud.

"Why would you want to do that?" Lissa asked, as she walked out of the employee entrance in the back.

Faith shook her head. "You shouldn't sneak up on people."

Lissa frowned. "You saw me coming."

"Yeah, I did," Faith conceded. She just wanted to take a shot before Lissa fired first.

The darked-haired woman paused by Faith's table. "So. I heard your life now sucks as much as mine."

Faith raised her eyebrows. "Don't tell me you read the *News Journal*," she said in mock horror.

To her credit and Faith's surprise, Lissa laughed. "Actually, I do. At the rate I'm going, it's the closest I'll get to real news reporting."

"Why are you being nice to me all of a sudden?" Faith asked warily.

Lissa shoved her hands into the front of her apron pocket and shrugged. "Maybe because I think you're getting a raw deal and I know what that's like. Shitty thing for your father to drag you down in the mud along with him."

Not trusting her nemesis's sudden one eighty, Faith remained wary.

"My shift doesn't start for another ten minutes. Mind if I join you?" Without waiting for permission, Lissa slid into Kate's old seat.

"Make yourself at home."

Lissa smiled. "Okay, here's the thing. I only hated you when your life was perfect. Now that it's not . . . I feel bad I was such a bitch."

"Great," Faith muttered. "Pity friendship."

"Beats me being a—"

"Bitch, I know." Faith laughed. "Still writing obits?" she asked Lissa, as an idea dawned in her mind. One that might accomplish Kate's goal of letting the world get to know her and rehabilitate her image at the same time.

With a dramatic sigh, Lissa leaned one elbow on the table. "Unfortunately, yes. 'She Writes about Dead People.' That's my byline."

Faith couldn't hold back a laugh. "Want to write my life story instead?"

Lissa cocked an eyebrow. "Think it will win me a Pulitzer?"

Apparently the woman was more perceptive than Faith had given her credit for. Just the right person for the job Faith had in mind.

She crooked a finger and Lissa pulled her chair over so they could whisper. "The idea came to me when you were suddenly nice to me. You see, I thought if I took the high road and never gave an interview, never discussed my childhood or my father, it would give me distance. People wouldn't look at me and automatically assume I'm just like him."

"Didn't work, huh?"

Faith shook her head at the rhetorical question.

"Because you grew up in that mansion, and even on your worst day you look like a million bucks," Lissa said, with less venom than ever before.

"Thank you. I think. My father's article linked my ex-husband to him, and by association, my reputation is now worse than it was before. Except, apparently, to you." Faith shook her head and laughed.

"What can I say? I'm unique. But go on. I'm listening." Lissa glanced at her watch. "Talk fast. My shift starts soon."

"The entire free world wants my story. They want to hear about Martin Harrington and his family, the early years through the present. What did we know, when did we know it, what was it like growing up the daughter of the biggest con artist of this century. It's a scoop the right reporter can parlay from barista and obit writer into a career."

Lissa's green eyes opened wide. "You'd give me your story?" Excitement tinged her voice. The woman knew a scoop when she heard one.

Faith shrugged. "Kate likes you, so I'm willing to give you a shot. All I ask is that you tell the unvarnished truth about me. No personal bias. If you do that, I'm hoping the rest of the world will finally separate me from my father."

Which would allow *her* to give a relationship with Ethan a fair chance.

With the two women in his life refusing to have anything to do with him, Ethan buried himself in work. His assistant, Amelia, was working overtime to make up for letting Dale seduce information out of her. Ethan's attorneys had already filed the lawsuit against his ex-partner, and Ethan's bid had been accepted by the government.

Back to business as usual.

Except that Ethan couldn't focus on work. Not when Faith wasn't returning his calls and Tess wouldn't come out of her room. By 10:00 A.M. Ethan was frustrated and convinced he'd have to tackle his problems with force.

"Tess!" he shouted up the stairs.

To his surprise, he heard her bedroom door open right away.

"Come on down. I want to go into town," he called to her.

"I'm coming!" She bounded down the stairs, her boots thudding hard with each step.

At the sound, Ethan turned and stared at her in shock. "What the hell are you wearing?" he asked, his stomach in knots at the familiar sight.

"What's it look like?" She pulled the army jacket tighter around her.

"I should have burned that thing when I had the chance." Ethan shook his head in disbelief.

Tess glared at him. "Don't fucking touch my things."

The black makeup was back, along with the foul attitude and bad language.

He leaned against the banister, eyeing her warily. He knew exactly what had caused the reversion. "You overheard the argument with Faith and you're mad at me for letting her go? News flash! I didn't want her to leave either."

Silence flooded the room, forcing him to wonder if he'd misjudged what had upset her. "Are you mad we never made it to the beach?" he asked.

She rolled her eyes, along with shooting him that *you're an idiot* look.

"What?" he yelled at her in frustration.

But Tess remained silent. Well, at least she had a therapy appointment this afternoon. Maybe the good doctor could get through to her since she'd decided to block Ethan out again.

He drove into town, Tess tense and clearly pissed off beside him. He planned to head directly to Faith's and see if the other female in his life could be reasoned with.

But as they drove past the main string of shops, Tess had other ideas. "Stop the car!"

He narrowed his gaze and slowed down, easing into an open spot. "What's wrong?"

"Let me out. I need something from the pharmacy."

"What?"

"None of your business." She folded her arms across her chest and turned to face the window.

He debated with himself. Turn her loose on Serendipity or take her with him to see if he could change Faith's mind about walking away from them.

"Be careful. If you finish first, you can walk around the corner and meet me at Faith's. If not, I'll come back for you here."

Without a word, Tess opened the door, climbed out of the car, and slammed it harder than necessary.

Letting her go had been a no-brainer. Tess was perfectly safe in town. Whether the town was safe from Tess was another story.

Faith walked through the pharmacy, picking up the items she needed on her list. She lingered in the aisles, in no rush to get to work. The phones had been silent since her father's magazine interview, but if someone were to call, her mother was now there to take a message. Lanie had shown up at the shop at 9:00 A.M., ready to work. Faith's heart squeezed tight, both proud and humbled by her mother's actions. She knew how much of an effort it had been for

Lanie to work in her daughter's place of business, let alone show her face in town.

The coming days wouldn't be easy. Faith had already heard the whispers at the coffee shop and had seen people point at her, but she refused to hide. Serendipity was her home.

She headed down the aisle, only to find herself looking at the magazines, staring at the man who'd ripped her life apart once more. This time, Faith hoped to fight fire with fire. Lissa had come over last evening. She'd interviewed Faith and they'd talked late into the night.

If her interview did its job, at least people would understand who Faith Harrington really was. She didn't know how others would respond, whether it would change their opinions, but at least she'd taken back control of her life. Sort of. If she had her way, she'd be with Ethan and Tess right now, but it was too soon. First her story had to be told. Lissa was already busy writing it and would decide where to pitch it for the most impact.

For Faith, the interview had been cathartic. She'd revealed what it was like to grow up in the house on the hill, with the man responsible for the largest Ponzi scheme in history. She admitted how it had felt to discover the father she'd idolized was really a man with no soul, who'd used her as a pawn. How her ex-husband had done the same. And how her own choices had brought her back to the town she'd left behind.

Lissa had been ruthless in her questions, and Faith had answered every one. No, she hadn't known about her father's scam. She'd found out when he was arrested, along with the rest of the world. No, to the best of her knowledge, her mother hadn't known either. Yes, she was very sorry that so many people had trusted her father and lost their life savings, and *of course* she was embarrassed to be related to a man who could do such immoral things.

Did she understand why the hardworking people in town

resented her? A lump rose in her throat again now, just thinking about how painful that question had been. But yes, she understood that the average person thought Faith Harrington had had it easy. And in comparison to those her father had hurt, she had. Maybe she hadn't realized it before, but she did now. Now she was one of those hardworking people, struggling to start over, to earn a living, to make friends and find a life.

If she could change the past she would, but all she could do was live by different rules and be proud of her own actions.

She wasn't part of her father's scheme and she shouldn't have to ask for absolution, but as his daughter, she understood she owed people an explanation and an apology. She offered both willingly. Serendipity was her home too and she hoped to one day be accepted.

Looking at her father's face on the magazine cover, Faith wondered if that day would ever come.

She turned away from the offending photo and immediately saw Tess at the end of the aisle. She couldn't mistake the army jacket, the boots, or the hair. *But why?* Why would Tess be dressed like that again when she'd come so far and had been so happy?

Before Faith could call her name and find out, she saw Tess pick up a small box, stuff it inside her jacket pocket, and turn to head not for the register but straight for the door.

Tess? Shoplifting?

Faith's heart lurched at the sight. She dropped her basket of items and bolted after the teen.

Nineteen

Faith wasn't home. Ethan left his car in the parking lot behind her apartment and walked to Main Street, figuring he'd pick up Tess and look for Faith at her shop. As he headed down the side street and approached Main, an ambulance siren grew louder and screeched to a stop in front of the row of stores that included the pharmacy. Where he'd left Tess alone.

A sick feeling settled in Ethan's gut and he ran toward the growing group of people.

Dare was already there, one of the cops on the scene. He held on to Tess, who seemed upset, while another cop spoke to a visibly shaken older man, and two ambulance workers knelt over someone in the street. Seeing Tess was okay, Ethan's heart rate slowed as he approached her.

As if she sensed him, she looked up and bolted straight into his arms. "I'm sorry," she cried, her black makeup already smeared all over her face. "I swear I'm sorry. I'm sorry." Her entire body trembled, her hysteria only increasing with every "I'm sorry" she continued to utter.

He wrapped his arms around Tess even tighter. "What the hell happened?" he asked Dare, knowing his sister was too incoherent to answer.

"Ethan . . ."

Dare appeared shaken and Ethan's entire body tensed once more. "What?"

Dare tipped his head toward the street and the ambulance he'd previously ignored.

Keeping Tess tucked into him, he walked toward the paramedics, heart in his throat. They slipped a neck brace onto a woman with blond hair. He couldn't see her face, but he already knew.

"I'm sorry, sir, but you'll have to step back," the other cop said.

"He's my brother. Let him through." At Dare's command, the officer moved away, giving Ethan access to the scene.

"Tess." Dare pulled a clinging Tess from Ethan so he could kneel down beside Faith.

"Sir." The paramedic took one look at Ethan's face and clearly changed whatever he'd been about to say. "We need to transport her to the hospital."

"Is she okay?" he asked, fighting back waves of nausea.

"No broken bones, but she's unconscious from her head colliding with the ground on contact," the man said.

"Ethan?"

Her voice was the sweetest thing he'd ever heard.

The paramedic pushed Ethan out of the way. He did a quick check of her pupils and asked her a few questions before turning to Ethan once more.

"Make it quick," he said before rising to talk to his partner.

Ethan knelt close, bringing his head down to hers. "Hey, princess."

"Hey." She winced, as if even that one word cost her.

"Shh. I'll do all the talking from now on."

"Don't you always?" she asked.

He grinned. A sense of humor had to be a good sign.

Afraid to touch her head, he stroked her arm with his hand. He didn't know what had happened and at the moment, he didn't care. As long as she was okay, that was all that mattered.

"Time to go." The paramedic's familiar voice broke through his thoughts.

He wanted to ride with her to the hospital, but from the corner of his eye, he saw Tess's makeup- and tear-stained face.

He rose, letting the paramedics move her from the ground to the stretcher.

Still torn, he leaned close and kissed Faith lightly on the lips. "I love you, princess."

She tried to smile. "Take care of Tess."

Was it any wonder he loved her? "I'll meet you at the hospital." He stepped back, letting the professionals take over, and within seconds, Faith was in the back of the ambulance and on the way to the hospital.

Ethan finally turned to Dare and Tess. "Someone want to fill me in?"

Tess started to cry again.

Dare wrapped an arm around her shoulder. "You need to explain," he said in a firm but kind voice, making Ethan proud of the man his youngest brother had become.

Tess wiped her eyes on her jacket. The sun and the heat beat down on his head and he couldn't understand how she could stand it underneath all that heavy material.

"I think you should start from the very beginning," Dare pushed, when she remained silent.

"I heard everything you and Faith said the other day in the kitchen about Birchwood. And how she wouldn't stay with you because it would mean I'd have problems there. I couldn't let you two break up because of me! I don't need that stupid art class or that school, especially if you have to buy my way in. And I didn't want to ruin your lives like I ruined Kelly's and my mom's." She sniffed but the tears still fell.

"Hey. Your mom ruined your life, not the other way around," Ethan reminded her. "But go on." Because he knew there was much more to come.

Tess shrugged, her shoulders drooping low. "I also heard you say I had to change my hair and ditch the piercing or the stupid school wouldn't take me. So I figured if I went back to the way I was, nobody would want me, and you'd be able to get back together with Faith."

Ethan blinked, stunned at the way her fourteen-year-old brain worked. "That explains the clothing and the attitude."

She nodded, her expression solemn.

"What happened today?" he asked her, in a rush to get to the hospital and check on Faith but knowing he'd get nowhere by pushing Tess faster than she was ready.

She looked down at the ground and mumbled something he couldn't hear.

"What?"

She repeated the same thing in the same low tone.

Ethan clenched and unclenched his fists. "Tess, I can't hear you."

"I said I got my period!" she yelled at him, her cheeks a bright red even beneath the awful streaks of makeup.

He met Dare's gaze over Tess's head, at a loss at how to handle this one. His younger brother merely grinned, and just like that, Ethan shared his first brotherly laugh with Dare in over ten years.

Still, he forced his focus back to Tess. "That's what you needed at the pharmacy?"

She inclined her head. "But I had no money."

"Why didn't you ask me for some?" he asked, kicking himself for not thinking to offer her cash.

She swallowed hard. "I wasn't talking to you for one thing. And I was embarrassed." She still was, and she shuffled her feet, her heavy boots scraping along the pavement.

"So . . . ?"

"I stole those and ran!" She pointed to a box on the sidewalk.

Ethan was stunned into silence.

But Tess kept explaining. "Faith was in the store. She saw what I did and followed me out. She yelled out my name. I kept running. I didn't even look to see if there were cars coming, but Faith did. And she pushed me out of the way." Tess's voice pitched higher and the waterworks started up again, tears flowing from her eyes, her nose running, her makeup everywhere.

"I didn't mean for her to get hurt. I didn't mean for anyone to get hurt." She looked up at Ethan with huge, wide eyes.

"I know you didn't." Her small shoulders shook and Ethan pulled her into his arms.

"Do you mean it? You believe me? You forgive me?"

"Yeah, I do." He braced his hands on her forearms and held her in front of him. "That doesn't mean we aren't going to have a long talk about shoplifting," he said as sternly as he could manage. "I don't care how uncomfortable the subject matter, you come to me no matter what you need. Understand?"

She bobbed her head up and down.

"As for the rest of it, same rules apply. We discuss things—we don't just react out of hurt, anger, or fear. We don't just take action. We talk about our feelings and we decide what to do *together*. As a family. Got it?" Ethan asked her.

She nodded and hugged him tighter once more.

Dare stepped closer. "Maybe if our parents had done more talking and less fighting, everything would have been different for us too."

Ethan stared at his sibling, stunned not just at his statement but at the obvious overture. The hint of understanding and maybe forgiveness underneath.

Even as he cautioned himself not to read too much into Dare's words, Ethan found himself opening up too. "I thought the same thing myself the first time I took Tess to her shrink. I acted out the same way. The smoking, the drinking . . . why the hell didn't they do more? Pay more attention?"

"I wish to hell I knew." Dare shook his head. "Look, you go to the hospital. I'll take Tess back inside to apologize and return the item she stole. I'm betting Mr. Finch won't press charges this time."

Ethan shot his brother a grateful look and Dare acknowledged it with a nod of his head. Then Dare placed a hand on his sister's back, taking over and freeing Ethan up to go check on Faith, like a brother who cared would do.

Faith's head pounded like it was going to explode. Maybe it already had. When she opened her eyes, a burning pain seared her skull and everything swam in front of her eyes. Nausea swept over her. She shut her eyes again quickly.

The next time she awoke, the pain was there but less severe.

"She's awake!"

A woman in a white coat, doctor or nurse, Faith didn't know, walked into the room. "How are you feeling?" the redhead asked in too cheery a voice.

"Like I smacked my head into a brick wall."

"Good analogy. I'm Dr. McCoy. Do you know your name?" she asked.

Faith licked her dry lips. "Faith Harrington."

"Next of kin?"

Faith shook her head and immediately regretted it. "Oh, no. You're not calling my mother!" she said in a sudden panic.

"She's fine." Faith recognized Ethan's relieved voice, followed by his rough laughter.

Dr. McCoy chuckled. "Okay. Ms. Harrington, you were in an accident. Do you remember?"

Faith closed her eyes and saw flashes of sunlight, a car coming at Tess too fast, Faith pushing her out of the way. "I remember."

"That's very good. The CAT scan showed no signs of internal bleeding or brain injury," the doctor said. "It looks like a mild concussion, but you'll be fine." She marked something down in her chart. "I'll send the nurse in with some ginger ale. Let's see what you can keep down."

"Thanks."

No sooner had the doctor walked out than Ethan settled himself on the corner of her bed. His hair was messy, as if he'd spent hours running his fingers through it, and his expression was tense and taut.

"You took at least ten years off my life." His words backed up her impression.

"Sorry. I can't say it was any fun for me either." She managed a smile. "How's Tess?"

"Guilt-ridden. Scared to death. Worried about you. Pick your poison."

He covered her hand with his and the warmth felt good against her skin.

"She swears she'll never shoplift again," he said.

"When I saw her put something in her pocket, I couldn't believe my eyes."

Ethan met her gaze. "Tampons."

"Excuse me?"

"That's what she put in her pocket. A small box of tampons. She was too embarrassed to ask me for money," he said, shaking his head in obvious disbelief.

Knowing it would be painful, Faith tried not to laugh, but the situation was too amusing. "You really do have your hands full with her."

"*We* have our hands full with her."

Did he really plan to have this argument again now? "I'm too tired to fight with you right now."

"Is that supposed to make me back off? Because it's not going to happen. I assume you noticed Tess was dressed in her emo-punk outfit again?"

"It's not like I could miss it," she said wryly.

He let out a groan. "She overheard our argument and took it upon herself to make sure Birchwood wouldn't take her."

"Why? She wants to take that art class!"

"Not at our expense. Not if I have to buy her way in—her words, not mine. Oh—and she definitely doesn't want to be responsible for ruining anyone else's life. In other words, you can't sacrifice us for Tess's benefit. She won't allow it. And for the record, neither will I." His eyes glittered with determination.

And love.

A love she walked away from once. Would she really be strong enough to do it again?

"Let me tell you how things are going to be from now on," he said, leaning closer.

"Oh, you're calling the shots now?" she asked lightly.

He nodded. "I am. First, you're going to admit you love me without planning to walk away the first chance you get."

She glanced up at the cracked hospital ceiling. "I don't think I'm walking anywhere at the moment."

"Funny." He leaned in and pressed his lips against hers.

She closed her eyes and savored the sensation. "What's next?" she asked him.

"Hmm?"

"You said first I'm going to admit I love you. What's next?" She knew she was teasing him, but she couldn't help it. She might not know how they were going to fix their future, but she understood now that they definitely had one.

"Next you're going to stand up for yourself against this

goddamn town, the uptight school, and anyone else who has something to say about you or your father. And I'll be right there by your side." He braced his arm on one side of her head and leaned his cheek against hers. "Understood?" he whispered in her ear.

"I'm way ahead of you." She snuggled into him, inhaling his sexy, familiar scent, letting his body heat cushion her in warmth.

She could lie this way for the next hundred years and never grow bored, never have any regrets, never fear she was giving up a part of herself or her independence by being with him.

"How so?" he asked, at the same time stretching out and pulling her into his arms, so they were sharing the twin-sized hospital bed.

Faith filled him in about the interview she'd given Lissa and how it had enabled her to take back control of both her life and how she was perceived by the rest of the world.

"Why am I just hearing about this now?" Ethan asked, hurt in his voice.

"Because I wanted to wait until Lissa freelanced the article and decided who she would sell it to. I wanted to make sure the interview did its job and Tess would be able to attend school without worrying about her relationship with me." But even as Faith explained, she already knew what a mistake it had been to walk away from them in the first place. "I was wrong not to stand up for us," she admitted.

He propped himself up on his elbow, his gaze never leaving hers. "But you did. You put Tess's needs before your own. Then you gave an interview you've avoided doing, putting your entire life out for public consumption because you believed that was the only way we could be together." He trailed his hand down her cheek, caressing her until she squirmed against him, despite her concussion. "Oh—and *then* you threw yourself in front of a speeding car to protect my sister. I think you stood up for us," he whispered. "The only question now is whether you're ready to follow through with what you started."

"What do you mean?"

"That house will never be my home unless you're in it. Come home with me," he said in a gruff voice.

She blinked, startled. She wondered if her concussion was causing hallucinations. "What are you saying?" she asked, needing to be sure.

Ethan looked into those surprised blue eyes. "I'm saying, marry me."

"Isn't that moving fast?" she asked.

He shook his head. For him it was long overdue. "When I was eighteen, I thought you were everything I ever wanted. Now I *know* you are."

The words, once said, were out there, unable to be recalled or changed, and he held his breath, waiting for her to answer.

"What about Tess?" Faith asked. "We still don't know if I'll ever be accepted or if who I am will cause trouble for her."

Ethan raised an eyebrow, knowing his sister was the least of his concerns. "Tess wants us together and I've already seen what she'll do if she doesn't get what she wants. The question is, what do *you* want, princess?"

"That's easy, Ethan Barron. I want you." Faith wound her arms around his neck and looked deep into his eyes. "So, yes. Yes. I'll marry you." Faith smiled wide.

Ethan grinned and lowered his head for a kiss that showed her just how very much he loved her. Which reminded him. "You still haven't told me—"

"I love you," she said, then kissed him again. "I love you."

Without warning, the door slammed into the far wall. "Eew! Get a room!" Tess said loudly.

"I believe we're in one," Ethan said, laughing.

Faith groaned as Dare ran into the room behind Tess.

"Sorry. The kid gave me the slip in the parking lot." Dare shot Ethan a grin, one that acknowledged they shared a bond when it came to dealing with one pain-in-the-ass teenage girl.

And another crack in Ethan's heart sealed shut.

A couple of weeks after Tess's shoplifting adventure, Nash Barron sat in his brother Ethan's newly decorated den for a family meeting. A command performance Nash took exception to. Ethan wasn't head of the family and hadn't been in over ten years, yet everyone showed up when he called.

Ethan and his *fiancée*, Faith Harrington, sat together on one side of an oversized couch, Dare on the other. Tess bounced between them as they waited for her half sister, Kelly, to arrive.

Nash took his seat on a club chair across the room.

"Faith, how are you feeling?" Dare asked.

"I'm still getting headaches and sleeping too much but, overall, a lot better, thanks."

"Well enough to have this place decorated. Fantastic job, by the way," Dare said.

Nash's gaze swept the room, taking in the warm, comfortable decor, chocolate brown and cream in color.

"The hard work was already completed. This was just execution. But thanks." She smiled at the compliment. "I just wish I had the energy to get up and out more, but the doctors say it's postconcussion syndrome and perfectly normal."

"I'm sure Ethan doesn't mind if you're spending more time in bed," Dare said with a grin.

"You just wish you were as lucky," Ethan shot back.

The banter between them was more proof that Dare's feelings toward Ethan had softened. Since Faith had pushed Tess out of the way of an oncoming car, something had changed between those two.

Once it had been Nash and Dare against the world, but Nash now felt like an outsider looking in. He envied Dare's easy acceptance of Ethan, when he, Nash, couldn't bring himself to forgive his older brother. Nash's entire life had been defined by before his parents' accident and after. For that he blamed Ethan.

As for Faith, Nash didn't care how much she'd revealed in that tell-all interview—he still couldn't separate her from her father. Not when his adopted father had had a heart attack not long after finding out how much money he'd lost thanks to Martin Harrington.

So yeah, this *family* business made him uncomfortable.

The doorbell rang and Tess bolted to answer it. Nash had only heard about Tess's older sister from Tess herself and from Ethan. He knew his preconceived notions weren't good ones. Kelly Moss had dropped Tess off on Ethan's doorstep. Strike one. Ethan sang her praises. Strike two. But Tess still adored her older sister. For Nash, that meant he'd have to judge for himself.

Tess came back into the room, pulling her sister along with her, and Nash's wariness turned to admiration as he rose to greet her. His brothers did the same.

Her light brown hair had bright blond highlights that accented her full face and distinct features. She wore a cropped top and tight jeans, ending with open-toed shoes and hot pink toenails. She was nothing like the girl next door and every bit a sexy, confident woman who commanded attention just by her mere presence.

Based on the kind of woman Nash had loved in the past, and the complicated connection he and Kelly Moss currently shared, she shouldn't interest him at all. Yet the attraction was there, and it was strong, and he silently thanked the fact that she was here visiting only. He sensed she'd offer all sorts of complications in his already complex life.

But he couldn't tear his gaze from hers and she didn't break eye contact either, until Ethan cleared his throat.

Cheeks flushed, Kelly turned to his brother and without warning pulled him into a hug—thoughts of Nash seemingly forgotten.

"I didn't know if you could pull it off, but look at her!" She gestured to Tess, her smile wide.

And damn, she had a gorgeous smile.

Ethan shook his head. "Like I told you on the phone, she came around all on her own."

"With a little help from you," Faith said, offering her support to her soon-to-be husband.

Nash couldn't deny that a part of him envied what his brother had found with Faith, even if Nash was wary of Ethan's choice of partners. He still had trouble separating her from her father's morality and actions.

"I like the hair," Kelly said, her fingers ruffling Tess's hair, which had begun to grow a little longer.

Tess beamed. "The color's lighter, more like yours now, huh?"

Kelly nodded, and again her smile lit up the room.

Nash understood Kelly's surprise and approval. Tess's eyebrow ring was also gone. All the changes had come courtesy of Tess's connection to Ethan and Faith. Even Dare had become more like a sibling Tess had grown up with than one she'd just met. Whereas Nash hadn't made any headway with her.

He spent time with his sister, took her to dinner, had her sleep over, but she kept her emotional distance. No matter how hard he tried, the teenager refused to warm up to him. One more way he was suddenly an outsider within his own family.

"Kelly, you already know Faith," Ethan said, interrupting Nash's thoughts with his introductions.

Ethan's fiancée waved hello and Kelly did the same.

"And I'd like you to meet my brothers. This is Dare," Ethan said, nodding toward their youngest sibling.

"The cop," Tess added helpfully.

Dare winked at Tess, then shook Kelly's hand.

"Nice to meet you," she said.

"Likewise," Dare offered.

Ethan then gestured to Nash. "And this is Nash."

"The ambulance chaser," Tess chimed in.

Nash shook his head and winced at the unflattering description. "Civil litigator. She just can't think of another slang word to call me." He was surprised to find himself amused despite the insult.

Was it his imagination or did Kelly take a fortifying breath before turning to face him?

"Hi," she said, hesitating before slipping her hand in his.

A searing jolt of awareness shot through him at her touch. Her eyes, which were an interesting shade of brown, widened at the stimulating contact.

So the attraction wasn't just on sight but on touch too. "A pleasure," he said, holding her gaze.

"Same."

Their hands still joined, they looked into each other's eyes.

"Come sit with me!" Tess said to her sister, shattering the unspoken link they shared.

"Sure." Obviously shaken, Kelly pulled her hand back and joined Tess in a love seat on Nash's side of the room.

Everyone else took their seats too.

"So, you're ready for this private school gig?" Kelly asked Tess.

The teenager nodded. "I can handle anything those snooty kids throw at me. My brother's got more money than—"

Ethan cleared his throat in obvious disapproval. Tess might have cleaned up her act, but she still needed guidance.

The teen let out an annoyed sigh at being reprimanded. "Yeah, I'm ready. Did I tell you about the art professor I'm gonna have?"

Kelly laughed. "Only every time we talk."

"So, I hear you got lucky with Faith's apartment," Dare commented, glancing at Kelly.

She nodded. "I did. Since Faith signed a two-year lease, she offered to sublet to me."

Nash narrowed his gaze. He thought she was a temporary visitor. "You're leasing Faith's apartment over Joe's?"

"Yes."

"To visit Tess when you're in town?" Nash asked, pushing for information.

She tipped her head back and laughed. "No, I couldn't afford that!"

"She's moving here," Faith clarified while Kelly was still busy laughing at his expense.

"Isn't that cool?" Tess asked.

Nash frowned at his sister. "I thought nobody said 'cool' anymore," he muttered.

She grinned. "Well, Ethan does. So now I do too."

Swell.

"You do realize the apartment's located over a bar?" Nash asked, unreasonably uncomfortable with the idea of Kelly moving here. Ridiculously bothered that all those single guys who visited Joe's would soon become acquainted with the new girl in town.

"So?" Kelly studied him, her confusion and continued amusement clear. "I'm a big girl. I think I can handle it."

"It just would have been nice if someone had filled me in," Nash muttered. He knew he was being an ass, but between *feeling* left out and now *being* left out, Nash couldn't help his foul mood.

"Maybe we would have told you if you showed your face around here more often," Ethan said, pointedly. "The only time I get to talk to you is when we have a family meeting."

Yet Dare had known about Kelly moving to town.

Which meant Ethan and Dare got together without him.

Now Nash knew how Ethan must have felt when he'd picked Tess up from his place only to find Nash, Dare, and Tess having breakfast without him.

Payback is a bitch, he thought, feeling more and more on edge with each passing minute.

"You're welcome here any time, Nash." Faith spoke up, obviously comfortable with her position in the house.

Nash knew he ought to thank her, but he just couldn't bring himself to be gracious to the woman whose father had destroyed the people who'd given him a home.

"What brought about the move?" he asked Kelly instead.

She shifted in her seat, hesitating and not coming up with a quick answer.

"That's easy," Ethan said, jumping in when she didn't. "I wasn't about to send Tess back to the city and Kelly saw the logic in moving here."

"I did." Kelly agreed, her expression suddenly closed.

There was obviously much more to her story.

Whether or not Ethan was in on it remained to be seen. But Kelly Moss's move to Serendipity wasn't solely about Tess. Of that Nash was certain.

But why did he care what her motivation was? What was it about her, he wondered, distracted by her mere presence.

Her mother had been involved with Nash's traveling salesman father, which made any attraction he felt for her awkward. She was Tess's half sister, which though not a problem, it didn't make the sexual attraction welcome. But there was something about her that called to him.

Given her mother's relationship with his working-class father, Nash assumed Kelly's background was more working class like his own. Which put them on similar ground, at least before his parents died. After, he'd been brought into a home more like the one his brother lived in now. Nash had never been comfortable in his adopted house, but he'd made peace with trying to please his new parents. His becoming a lawyer had accomplished that goal, but too often Nash wondered if the suit and tie really *fit*.

While Kelly appeared relaxed, at ease with herself and the world, flustered only by their inexplicable chemistry. Nash wished he had the chance to be more himself. Whoever that was. He'd long since lost track. So for those reasons and many more, he found himself drawn to Kelly Moss.

"Nash! Are you paying attention?" Tess asked, popping in front of his face. "Ethan and Faith are getting married next month!"

He'd been too lost in thoughts about Kelly and hadn't heard. "Congratulations."

"Thank you," they both said.

Ethan wrapped his arm around his fiancée. "We hope you'll all be there." His wary gaze settled on Nash.

Nash shifted in his seat but gave nothing away, needing time to think.

"And then they're going on a honeymoon," Tess said in a singsong voice. Clearly she was pleased with the upcoming plans. "And I'll be staying with Kelly while they're gone," she added happily.

"I'd have taken you, squirt, but my shifts are too crazy," Dare said.

Kelly shook her head. "I wouldn't have let you. I've been away from her for too long."

"Aww, you missed me!" Tess laughed.

Kelly's eyes warmed at Tess's pleased response.

And Nash's body heated up just watching her.

"Kelly and Tess will stay here so Tess doesn't have to uproot her routine and everyone will be comfortable."

Comfortable, Nash thought. The perfect word to describe the dynamic between them. All of them.

Except him.

They'd planned everything without him. The only good news was that with Ethan and Faith gone, he'd have the opportunity to get closer to Tess. The bad news was that to do so, he'd have to get closer to Kelly too. Not a good thing, considering she appealed to him on a visceral level he'd never experienced with any woman before.

So while Ethan enjoyed his honeymoon, Nash's life here would be equally memorable, courtesy of a female by the name of Kelly Moss.

Turn the page for a special excerpt from
Carly Phillips's next Serendipity novel . . .

Destiny

Coming Winter 2012 from Berkley!

Nash Barron might be cynical about life and more recently about love, but even he normally enjoyed a good wedding. Today's affair had been an exception. The invitation had requested the presence of "close friends and family." Nash wondered if he was the only one in the group to notice the irony.

The groom's two brothers, Nash included, were a step short of estranged, and they'd only known the flower girl, their newly discovered half sister, Tess, for six weeks. The bride's father was in jail, which left her flamboyant decorator friend to give her away, while her mother spent the afternoon downing wine and bemoaning the loss of her beloved home, which just so happened to be the site of the wedding. The landmark house on the hill in their hometown of Serendipity, New York, was now owned by the groom, Nash's brother Ethan.

Come to think of it, the irony of the situation might be the only thing Nash had enjoyed about this day.

That and Kelly Moss, the woman sipping champagne across the lush green grass of the backyard.

Tess was Nash's half sister, a product of his father and
Tess's mother's affair. Kelly, Tess's half sister on her mother's side, was a sexy woman who by turns frustrated him,
intrigued him, and turned him on. Complicated yet simple
enough to be summed up in one sentence: Kelly Moss was
a beautiful woman and they were in no way blood related.

Which didn't make his desire for her any more acceptable. A simple acquaintance-like relationship seemed the
safest route, yet Nash had been unable to find comfortable
ground with either Kelly or Tess in the time since they'd
been in Serendipity. Nash had no idea why he couldn't con-
nect with his fourteen-year-old sister, who seemed determined to freeze him out.

As for Kelly, at first Nash blamed his frustration with her
on the fact that she'd unceremoniously dumped Tess, a sister
the Barron brothers knew nothing about, on Ethan's doorstep back in August. She'd demanded he parent the
out-of-control teen. Nash hated to give Ethan credit for anything, but he had to admit his older brother had turned the
wildly rebellious kid around in a short time. But Nash still
had issues with Kelly's methods. So when she'd resurfaced
and moved to town, he'd been both understandably wary
and shockingly attracted. And she'd been getting under his
skin ever since.

Nash turned away and his gaze fell on Ethan, his brother
whose luck seemed to have done a one eighty since he'd
abandoned his siblings ten years ago. He had chosen the
perfect day for a wedding. Through early October, the temperature had hiked into the low seventies, enabling him to
have the wedding outdoors. Ethan stood with his arm around
his wife, Faith, talking to their youngest sibling, Dare. Even
he had forgiven Ethan for the past.

Nash couldn't bring himself to be so lenient.

He glanced at his watch and decided his time here was
over. The bride and groom were married, cake served, bouquet thrown. He finished what remained of his Ketel One,

placed the glass on a passing waitress's tray, and headed toward the house.

"Leaving so soon?" a familiar female voice asked.

"The festivities are over." He turned to face the woman who'd hijacked his thoughts just moments before.

Kelly, her hair pulled loosely behind her head, soft waves escaping and grazing her shoulders, stood close beside him. Her warm, inviting lemony scent enveloped him in heat.

Nash was a man who valued his personal space. Kelly was a woman who pushed past boundaries. Yet for a reason he couldn't fathom, he lacked his usual desire to find safer ground.

"The band is still playing," she pointed out.

"No one will realize I'm gone."

Or care. His leaving would probably ease any tension his presence created.

"I would." She gazed at him with perceptive brown eyes.

Intelligent eyes that seemed to see beyond the indifferent facade he presented to the world. One he thought he'd perfected in his late teens, when his life had been turned upside down by his parents' deaths followed quickly by Ethan's abandonment of both Nash and their younger brother, Dare.

"Why do you care?" he asked, even though he knew he'd be smarter to walk away.

She shrugged, a sexy lift of one shoulder that drew his attention to her soft-looking skin.

"Because you seem as out of place here as I am." She paused. "Except you're not a stranger to town or to this family."

Out of place. That one comment summed up his entire existence lately. How had she figured him out when no one else ever could?

"I need to leave," he said, immediately uncomfortable.

"What you need is to relax," she countered, and stopped him with one hand on his shoulder. "Let's dance." She playfully tugged on his tie.

He glanced over to where the rest of the family gathered next to the dance floor. "I'm not really interested in making a spectacle."

"Then we won't." She slipped her hand in his and led him to the far side of the house beneath an old weeping willow tree.

He could still hear the slow music, but he could no longer see the dance floor, and whoever was out there couldn't see them. She tightened her hold on his hand and he realized he'd better take control or she'd be leading him through this dance. He wrapped an arm around her waist, slid his other hand into hers, and swayed to the sultry sound of the music coming from the band.

A slight breeze blew through the long dripping branches of the tree. She shivered and eased her body closer to his, obviously in need of warmth.

He inched his hand up her bare back. "Cold?" he asked in a gruff voice as her body heat and scent wrapped around him.

"Not anymore."

He looked into her eyes to discover an awareness that matched his own, glanced down and caught sight of her lush lips. As they moved together to the music, warning bells rang in his head, but nothing could have stopped him from settling his mouth on hers. The first touch was electric, a heady combination of sparkling champagne and sensual, willing woman. Her lips were soft and giving and he wasn't sure how long their mouths lingered in a chaste kiss they both knew was anything but.

His entire body came alive, reminding him of what he'd been missing in the two years since his divorce. That this woman could awaken him both surprised and unnerved him. It made him want to *feel* more. He trailed his hand up the soft skin of her back and cupped her head in one hand. With a sweet sigh, she opened for him, letting him really taste her for the first time. Warmth, heat, and desire flooded through him.

"Oh, gross! Just shoot me now!" Tess exclaimed in a disgusted voice.

Nash jerked back at the unwanted interruption. "What the hell are you doing?" he asked, the annoyed words escaping before he could think it through.

"Looking for Kelly. What are *you* doing?" She perched her hands on her hips, demanding an answer.

Isn't it obvious? Nash shook his head and swallowed a groan. The kid was the biggest wiseass he'd ever come across.

"You found me," Kelly said, sounding calmer than he did.

Like that kiss hadn't affected her at all. A look at her told him that unless she was one hell of an actress, it hadn't. She appeared completely unflustered, whereas he was snapping at Tess because the hunger Kelly inspired continued to gnaw at him.

"Ethan and Faith want to talk to you," Tess muttered in a sulking tone.

Obviously she didn't like what she'd seen between him and her sister. Unlike Nash, who'd liked it a lot.

Too much, in fact.

From the pissed-off look on Tess's face, kissing Kelly and biting Tess's head off were going to result in a huge setback in trying to create any kind of relationship with his new sister. And to think, if asked, he'd have said things between them couldn't get any worse.

"Why don't you go tell them I'll be right there?" Kelly said patiently to Tess.

The teenager now folded her arms across her chest. "How about not?"

Kelly raised an eyebrow. "How about I'm the one in charge while Ethan's on his honeymoon and if you don't want to find yourself grounded and in your room for the duration, you'll start listening now."

With a roll of her eyes and a deliberate stomp of her foot, which wasn't impressive considering she was wearing a deep purple dress and mini-heels from her walk down the aisle, Tess stormed away.

"Well done," he said to Kelly, admiring how she'd gotten Tess to listen without yelling or sniping back.

"Yeah, I did a better job than you." She shot him an amused glance. "But I can't take any credit. You saw what she was like before Ethan took over. This change is due to his influence, not mine." Her expression saddened at the fact that she'd been unable to accomplish helping Tess on her own.

He knew the feeling. "Don't remind me about Saint Ethan."

She raised her eyebrow. "There's always tension between you and Ethan. Why is that?" she asked.

He definitely didn't want to talk about his brother or his past. "Is asking about my life your way of avoiding discussing the kiss?" He deliberately threw a question back at her as a distraction.

An unexpected smile caught hold of her lips. "Why would I want to avoid discussing it when it was so much fun?" she asked, and grabbed hold of his tie once more.

Her moist lips shimmered, beckoning to him, as did her renewed interest, and he shoved his hands into his pants pockets. Easier to keep them to himself that way.

"Kelly! We're waiting!" Tess called impatiently, interrupting them again and reminding him of why he had to keep his distance from Kelly from now on.

"Coming!" Kelly called over her shoulder, before meeting Nash's gaze. "Looks like you got a reprieve." A mischievous twinkle lit her gaze.

A sparkle he found infectious. She had spunk, confidence, and an independent spirit he admired. His ex-wife had been as opposite of Kelly as he could imagine, more sweet and in need of being taken care of. Kelly could obviously hold her own.

And Nash didn't plan on giving her the upper hand. "I don't know what you're talking about," he lied.

She patted his cheek. "Keep telling yourself that."

He would. For as long as it took to convince himself this woman would only cause him and his need to have a relationship with Tess boatloads of trouble.

Kelly Moss stood at the bottom of the circular stairs in the house that was nothing short of a mansion and yelled up at her sister. "Tess, let's go! If you want to have time for breakfast before school, get yourself downstairs now!" It was the third time she'd called up in the last five minutes.

"I said I'm coming!" came Tess's grumpy reply.

Ethan and Faith had left yesterday morning for their honeymoon, one week on the beautiful, secluded island of Turks and Caicos, where they had their own villa complete with private butler. Talk about living the life, Kelly thought. Hers wasn't so bad either, since she got to stay in this huge house with her own housekeeper while they were gone.

Tess's door slammed loudly, startling Kelly back to reality as her sister came storming out of her room, then stomping down the stairs.

The old days, when Kelly had been raising Tess alone and doing a god-awful job at it, came rushing back and Kelly clenched her fists. "What's wrong?" Kelly only hoped it was something easily fixable, not a problem that would lead Tess to turn back to running wild.

"This!" Tess gestured to the uniform her new private school required she wear, a navy pleated skirt, white-collared shirt, and high socks. "I hate it."

Kelly knew better than to say it was better than the all-black outfits the teenager used to wear, including the old army surplus jacket and combat boots. "You'll get used to it."

Tess passed by Kelly and headed for the kitchen. "It's been a month and I still hate it."

The clothes or the school? Kelly wondered as she followed behind her sister. "Is it the skirt? Because you didn't mind the dress you wore at the wedding." In fact, she'd looked like a beautiful young lady.

"It's the fact that I *have* to wear it. I hate being told what to do."

"Tell me something I don't know," Kelly muttered, having been Tess's primary caregiver for longer than she could remember.

"I heard that."

Kelly grinned. Tess really had come a long way thanks to Ethan Barron. Kelly shuddered to think of what might have happened if she hadn't taken drastic steps.

Both Tess and Kelly's mother, Leah Moss, had been a weak woman, too dependent on men and incapable of raising Tess. She'd been different when Kelly was young, or maybe that's how she wanted to remember her. Or maybe it had been Kelly's father's influence that had made Leah different.

Kelly would never know because her father had died of a heart attack when she was twelve. And Leah had immediately gone in search of another man to take his place. Her choice was a poor one. Leah struck up an affair with her married boss, Mark Barron. Yet despite how wrong it was, for Kelly, her mother's years as his mistress had been stable ones, including the period after Tess was born. But with Mark Barron's passing ten years ago, Leah had spiraled downward, and both Kelly and Tess had suffered as a result.

She'd immediately packed up and moved them to a seedy part of New York City, far from their home in Tomlin's Cove, the neighboring town to Serendipity. Leah said she wanted them to start over. In reality, their mother had wanted an easy place to search for another lover to take care of her. But Leah never found her next white knight, turning to alcohol and a never-ending rotation of disgusting men instead.

Since Tess had only been four years old at the time, a sixteen-year-old Kelly had become the adult, juggling high school, then part-time college with jobs and raising Tess.

Fortunately, her mother had moved them into a boarding-house with a kindly older woman who'd helped Kelly too.

But last year, their mother had run off with some guy, abandoning her youngest daughter, and something in Tess had broken. Angry and hurt, she'd turned into a belligerent, rebellious teenager, hanging out with the wrong crowd, smoking, drinking, and ultimately getting arrested. Desperate, Kelly had turned to the only person she remembered from their years in Tomlin's Cove, Richard Kane, a lawyer in Serendipity who'd put her in touch with Ethan Barron.

Kelly's heart shattered as she basically deposited her baby sister on a stranger's doorstep and ordered him to step up as her brother. But it was that, Kelly sensed, or heaven knew where Tess would end up. So here she was months later, starting her life over but still rushing Tess out for school, she thought, grateful things were finally looking up.

She and Tess ate a quick breakfast, after which Kelly dropped off Tess and headed to work. Another thing for which she owed Richard Kane, her job, working for him as a paralegal, in downtown Serendipity.

She stopped, as she did daily, at Cuppa Café, the town's coffee shop. Kelly had worked hard all her life and she'd learned early on to save, but her entire day hinged on that first cup of caffeine. It had to be strong and good.

Kelly stepped into the coffee shop and the delicious aroma surrounded her, instantly perking her up as if she were inhaling caffeine by osmosis.

She was pouring a touch of milk into her large cup of regular coffee when a familiar woman with long, curly blond hair joined her at the far counter.

"You're as regular as my grandma Emma wanted to be," Annie Kane joked.

Kelly glanced at her and grinned. "I could say the same for you."

"Good point." Annie laughed and raised her cup in a mock toast.

Small-town living offered both perks and drawbacks. Running into a familiar face fell in the latter category. Kelly and Annie frequented Cuppa Café at the same time each morning and they'd often linger to chat. If pressed, Kelly would say Annie was the closest she had to a real friend here, if she didn't count Faith Harrington, Ethan's wife.

Annie was Richard Kane's daughter, though from the pictures on Richard's desk, Kelly noticed Annie looked more like her mother than her dad. From the first day they'd met at her father's office, Kelly had liked this woman.

Kelly took a long, desperately needed sip of her drink.

"So what's your excuse for being up so early every day?"

"Routine keeps me young," Annie said.

Kelly rolled her eyes. "You *are* young." She looked Annie over, from her slip-on sneakers to her jeans and light cotton sweater. "I bet we're probably close to the same age."

"I'll be twenty-seven next month," Annie said.

"And I'll be twenty-seven in December."

Annie raised her cup to her lips and Kelly couldn't help but notice that her hand shook as she took a sip.

Kelly narrowed her gaze but didn't comment on the tremor. Instead, she dove into cementing her life here in Serendipity. "Listen, instead of quick hellos standing over coffee, how about we meet for lunch one day?" She was ready for a real friend here, someone she could trust and confide in. Kelly adored Tess, but a fourteen-year-old hardly constituted adult company.

"I'd like that!" Annie said immediately. "Let me give you my phone number." As she reached into her purse, her cell phone rang and she glanced at the number.

"Excuse me a second," she said to Kelly. "Hello?" she spoke into the receiver.

Kelly glanced away to give Annie privacy, but she couldn't help but overhear her end of the conversation.

"I'm feeling better, thanks. Yeah. No you don't need to

stop by. I called the plumber and he said he'd make it to the house by the end of the day." Annie grew quiet, then she spoke once more. "I can afford it and you don't need to come by. You weren't good with the pipes when we were married," she said, amusement in her tone.

Some more silence, and then Annie said, "If you insist, I'll see you later," she said, now sounding more annoyed than indulgent.

She hung up and put the phone back in her bag. "My ex-husband," she explained to Kelly. "He thinks because I have MS I need his constant hovering."

The admission caught Kelly off guard and she felt for Annie, being diagnosed so young. Richard liked to talk about everything and anything when he was in the office, but he'd never mentioned his daughter's disease. Kelly didn't blame him for omitting something so personal. In fact, she was surprised Annie had mentioned it at all.

"I'm sure you noticed my hand shaking earlier, and if we're going to be friends, you might as well know," Annie said as if reading Kelly's mind.

Kelly met Annie's somewhat serene gaze. Obviously she'd come to terms with her situation. "Thanks for telling me."

"Hey, if I go MIA one day, at least you'll know why." She shrugged, as if the notion were no big deal.

Kelly didn't take her new friend's confidence or situation as lightly. "Well, if you ever need anything, just let me know."

Annie smiled. "Thanks. But I think my ex will always be around to handle things," she said through lightly clenched jaw.

"That could be a good thing," Kelly mused, "having someone at your beck and call when you need something?"

"Not when you've told him you want to be independent," Annie muttered. The frustration in the other woman's voice was something Kelly understood.

Like Annie, Kelly didn't need or want a man who felt the need to take care of her. She was determined to be smart and self-sufficient, the opposite of her mother in every way. No matter how many obstacles life threw in her way. And unfortunately, there were more to come. Utter humiliation loomed in the not-so-distant future, courtesy of a man she'd once loved. The affair was long over. The fallout was not. Kelly could handle the mess. Her younger sister could not. And Kelly did not want Tess exposed to gossip and innuendo just as the teenager was doing well and making better choices. Kelly only hoped the distance between Manhattan and Serendipity would spare Tess when trouble hit.

"Men just don't get us women, do they?" Annie asked, a welcome interruption from Kelly's troubling thoughts.

Kelly shook her head and sighed. "No, they do not."

"Firsthand experience?" Annie asked.

"Unfortunately, yes." Kelly frowned, the memory of spending the last year getting over having her heart and trust betrayed still fresh.

"I'm sorry." Annie blew out a long breath. "I don't know about yours, but my ex means well. He just takes the word 'responsibility' to the extreme."

Kelly swallowed hard. "And my ex-boyfriend took the word 'commitment' way too lightly."

"Excuse me," an older man said, indicating he needed to get to the counter so he could pour milk into his coffee.

"Sorry." Kelly stepped out of the way and walked with Annie toward the exit.

"So, how about I call you at my father's office later today and we'll exchange phone numbers and make lunch plans?" Annie asked.

Kelly nodded. "Sure. That's fine."

They parted ways and Kelly headed toward Richard's office in the center of town. The buildings stretched along the road, stores on the main level, small apartments above, like hers over Joe's Bar. Coming from the overcrowded city with tall buildings and too many people, the small town appealed to her.

Using her key, Kelly walked into the office of the man she credited for helping to save her sister and her family. "Richard?" she called out.

No answer.

The small office was empty. Obviously she'd beat him here, which was unusual. Richard was an early-to-the-office, late-getting-home kind of man, though his wife had been trying to get him to work fewer hours, maybe take in a partner to lighten his load.

Kelly settled in to her desk in a small room with a window that she appreciated. She already knew which case she had to work on and what she needed to do today, but she pulled out her calendar anyway. As part of her work routine and a way to make sure she never forgot an assignment, Kelly glanced at today's date and the list she'd made on Friday before leaving work for the weekend.

Seven P.M.—parent–teacher conference for Tess.

Which she was attending with Dare since Ethan was away. Better Dare than the other Barron brother. The one she'd deliberately put out of her mind since the kiss on Saturday.

And what a kiss it had been.

Kelly prided herself on her poker face, but she still wasn't sure she'd pulled off being nonchalant after Tess interrupted them. Her sister had sulked all the way home but hadn't mentioned what she'd seen, nor had she brought it up the next day. If Tess wasn't going to discuss it, neither was Kelly.

And considering she hadn't heard a word from Nash, neither was he. Which bothered her. A lot.

Sure, she'd been a little tipsy and a lot aggressive, but she'd felt his body heat and obvious reaction firsthand. He'd obviously liked the kiss, but he'd been hard to read afterward.

She told herself she shouldn't care what Nash thought or

felt. She'd learned from her mother's choices and her own past not to rely on anyone but herself. So, though she might be attracted to Nash, his feelings on the subject didn't matter. Even if he was equally interested, a brief affair would be disastrous because it would hurt Tess. And short term was all Kelly would let herself believe in from now on.